MW01595012

SCARLET SINS:
STORIES AND SONGS

DANE COBAIN

COPYRIGHT 2021 DANE COBAIN

This work is licensed under a Creative Commons Attribution-Noncommercial-No Derivative Works 3.0 Unported License.

Attribution — You must attribute the work in the manner specified by the author or licensor (but not in any way that suggests that they endorse you or your use of the work).

Noncommercial — You may not use this work for commercial purposes.

No Derivative Works — You may not alter, transform, or build upon this work.

**Inquiries about additional permissions
should be directed to:** danecobain@danecobain.com

Cover Design by Larch Gallagher
Edited by Pam Elise Harris

This is a work of fiction. Names, characters, places, brands, media, and incidents are either the product of the author's imagination or are used fictitiously. Any resemblance to similarly named places or to persons living or deceased is unintentional.

INTRODUCTION

SCARLET SINS has been nearly fifteen years in the making, and it's one of several books that I worked on as a kid and then left lying around. Now, as a published author and with a string of releases beneath my belt, I thought the time was right to revisit it.

Inspired by a Hilaire Belloc quote – "I hope when I die it may be said that his sins were scarlet but his books were read." – *Scarlet Sins* pulls together an assortment of short fiction from over the years, as well as the chords and lyrics from my first four albums and a couple of bonus essays.

This updated collection features a mixture of brand-new material and some older stories – stories like "The Ploughman," a piece I wrote at university for one of the modules I studied and which was based on a painting that I found at a charity sale.

There's also some travel writing in the form of "De Bloemenmarkt," which was written during my first ever visit to Amsterdam. It takes place in the flower markets of the city and was conceived as a modern-day fairy-tale love story, but with a twist. "FAT," another story in the collection, was also written in Amsterdam. It's a beautiful city and great for giving a writer some inspiration.

"The Hanging Man" is a slightly updated take on one of the first short stories I ever wrote, and "Borrowed," "Cosmos," "They Like the Darkness" and "The Sun Came Out" are all early pieces as well. They're followed by some more recent work, such as the short story "When the Mirror Clouds" that was first included in a previous release, *Subject Verb Object: An Anthology of New Writing.*

I also threw in "A Stone's Throw," a ghost story that was first published in the Local Haunts anthology (ed. Regina St. Clare) and which is based on a local ghost story here in High Wycombe. That's followed by "Black Christmas," a "vampyre"-themed festive horror story that I penned for Regina's second anthology, Served Cold.

Finally, we finish with a four-part novella called "Insomnia" about a woman who can't sleep and her slow descent into madness. "Insomniac" was the project I worked on before starting *Meat.* I needed to clear my palette after writing three books in the Leipfold series.

Scarlet Sins also collects the chords and lyrics for the songs on my first four albums – *Nocturne* (2010), *Sketches* (2015), *Discordia* (2017) and *Echoes* (2020). The albums are available on Spotify and iTunes, as well as most other leading services.

Finally, we move on to a couple of non-fiction pieces. The first is an essay that I wrote with a friend called Matt Turner. I think it's still pretty relevant, especially with the rise of generic YA books and low quality self-published knock-offs. The second delves into my poetry and the various people and events who have shaped it.

As always, I'd like to thank Pam Elise Harris (my editor and partner-in-crime) and Larch Gallagher (my cover designer) for their help making this book happen. And thanks, as well, go to you. Writing is my life, and you can't imagine how much it means when someone takes the time to read my work.

My sins are scarlet, and they're waiting for you. Happy reading.

CONTENTS

STORIES

The Ploughman

HOOF-BEATS ECHOED through the gentle rain and brought the ploughman to his senses. He sighed and let the soil trickle through his fingers, back to the ground where it belonged. "It's just not what it used to be," he muttered, allowing the wind to swallow his words.

"Hello there!" The old man turned around and leant on his staff. His beard was matted with sweat, and his grey eyes looked older and wiser than ever. "Have you heard the news?"

"I haven't." Joe Slater leapt from his mount and landed in the mud. His features were bright with excitement, and he leaned towards the ploughman like a conspirator.

"It's happened. We're at war."

"Oh." The ploughman busied himself with the horse's harness, tightening the straps and checking the coat for blemishes. Before long, the horse would be too old to work. "Is that all?"

"What do you mean? It's exciting! They say it's going to be over before Christmas, so I'm sending Junior to the barracks."

"But you'll have no young hands on the farm! What if something happens?"

"The war will be the making of the boy."

The ploughman clicked his tongue, and the tired stallion trudged forwards, dragging the cart through the mud.

"Of course, I'll have to hire some help, but it'll only be for a couple of months."

"I see," the ploughman said.

The rain was heavier now, and Slater looked at the sky.

"I say, Jack," he said. "Why are you outside in this

weather? Can't this wait until the morning? This is no time to be baling. We're at war, don't you know?"

The ploughman whistled softly, and the horse slowed to a halt.

"What does the war have to do with me?" he asked. "I just don't have the time, Joe. I just don't have the time."

***

It was dark when he hung up the harness and led the horse into the stable, and the rain had been replaced by a cacophony of hoots and birdsong. It was cold for a night in July, but Jack welcomed the reprieve after a day of sweating in the fields. He patted his pockets and pulled out a beautiful, hand-carved pipe, and he was soon filling his lungs with cheap tobacco. He was so absorbed in his thoughts that he didn't notice the figure beside the farmhouse until it rose to greet him.

"Jack?"

"Good evening," the ploughman said.

The young farmer walked over and shook his hand by the moonlight.

"What brings you here so late?"

"Have you heard the news? I've been thinking about it all day." Excitement shone in his eyes, and he vibrated with patriotism. "We're at war!"

"Yes, I know."

"I'm signing up tomorrow," the neighbour said. "Tess will look after the farm, but I suppose I'll have to get a couple of boys in from the village. It's no work for a woman, although I'm sure her father will be happy to help where he can. He used to be a farm-boy himself as a lad. It's not ideal, but it'll all be over before Christmas. They'll only have to take care of the harvest, and I've trusted them with that before."

"I'll keep an eye on them when I can."

"To tell the truth, I came here hoping to ask for something similar."

The ploughman smiled and invited his neighbour inside, but he declined the offer.

"I can't stay, Jack," he said, lifting his hat from the low wall. "There's a war to prepare for."

***

The nights grew longer and the days grew colder, but the ploughman worked stoically on. Ellison Jr. and Mr. Slater were fighting for their country, and the old man kept his promise and checked on the neighbouring farms. Then the winter came.

The ground and the work grew harder, and the ploughman toiled from sunrise to sunset. The harvest was good, and there was plenty of work to keep him busy until the sowing season. Fences needed fixing and hay needed baling. Even Mary, the elderly horse, needed new shoes.

Late one night, when Jack was sitting alone in front of a roaring fire, he heard a heavy knock at the door. With a sigh, he threw another log on the fire and walked across the cold floor to answer it. As an afterthought, he took his shotgun from the wall and pointed it through the crack in the doorway.

"Who is it?" he growled. He wasn't used to visitors, and it was unheard of for a stranger to knock on his door at night. "I warn you. I'm armed."

A pitiful whimper echoed through the darkness, and Jack recognised the voice but not the tone.

"Don't shoot!" it cried. "Please, Jack. It's me!"

The ploughman lowered his weapon and pushed the

door open, giving the visitor a glimpse of the fire. Mr. Slater was a mess. His face was pale and gaunt, and his hair was matted with sweat. He was wearing his army uniform, but one of the arms hung uselessly at his side. He noticed the ploughman's unhappy stare and explained.

"'I lost my arm to a German shell, so they sent me home. The fools, I've got plenty of fight left in me."

"I think you'd better come inside," the ploughman answered, standing aside for the young man to enter. "Let's have a nip of whiskey and you can tell me all about it."

***

Winter dragged on, and money was growing short. Jack ate Christmas dinner with the Slaters, and he agreed to help on their farm in exchange for a patch of land which he could use to grow extra crops for himself.

He would've preferred to have avoided the work, but he hadn't the heart to refuse. The shell shock had set in, and Slater was finding it hard to concentrate on agriculture. His wife tried to support him, but life wasn't easy for a one-armed farmer. Even with the help of his horses, it was difficult for him to work the fields and to cart his produce to the market.

But eventually, the ground began to thaw and the trees started to blossom. Christmas passed, and the end of the war seemed further away than ever. The agricultural season began again, and the ploughman's hours grew longer and harder. Then, news came from abroad.

He was enjoying a rare respite from work, drinking local scrumpy in the village pub with Mr. Slater. They'd finished early and were discussing new advancements in machinery when Ellison rushed in, brandishing an empty bottle and wobbling on the spot.

"Pint of whiskey," he demanded, approaching the elderly landlady and breathing fumes all over her. "Quick, before I fetch my shotgun." At the other end of the bar, her husband looked up from his cards and grunted.

"If you're looking for trouble, you can walk out of that door and find somewhere else. I'm not having any violence."

"You, sir, are good for nothing."

Slater was already on his feet, but the ploughman was slower to rise. It took their combined strength to shepherd Ellison out the front door and into the cool night.

"What's wrong with you?" they demanded, as they began the long walk back to Ellison's farm.

"I got a letter," he replied, and he began to cry. They weren't the delicate, gentle tears of a ruined man. They were a deluge of sorrow, like sweat dripping from the eyes. "It's my son. He's dead!"

The three men paused, and Mr. Ellison fell to his knees. Nobody spoke, and the clouds obscured the moon and covered the stars like a curtain. The farmers tried to pull the mourning father to his feet, but he was stubborn and had gravity on his side.

Finally, he looked up at them with a face that was worn by age and pain. "If I wasn't afraid of damnation, I might have done something stupid."

"Don't talk like that," said the ploughman, crouching down beside him. "Things are never that bad."

"He's right," said Slater. "You need to sober up and look at things in the light of day. Is this what your son would want? Kneeling in a ditch, abandoning your wife, your farm, your sanity?"

The distraught farmer shook his head and climbed unsteadily to his feet.

"I suppose you're right. I need to talk to a priest. Jack, would you be kind enough to walk me home?"

"You know me, Joe. Always happy to help."

***

The season pressed on, and Slater was still struggling to adapt to a one-armed lifestyle. Mr. Ellison was still in mourning, and he worked the fields in a mud-spattered suit. As for the ploughman, he was working harder than ever. He started before dawn and finished after sunset, and he lived on four hours of sleep.

None of the farmers were making money, and they were living on their own produce. Then came the great storm.

The animals were restless all day, and the ploughman's muscles were so stiff that he struggled to climb out of bed. His staff had fallen down in the night, and it was too far away for him to reach. He had to pull himself up on the dusty dressing table, and that meant getting up on the wrong side of bed.

The storm grew throughout the day, starting with a fine rain that gathered in speed and ferocity. By the late afternoon, all of the farmers were seeking shelter inside their houses, and the storm grew angrier than ever after the sun went down. The glass rattled in the windowpanes and screamed as the rain flew into it. The ploughman sat before the fire, warming his old bones as he waited for the weather to change. Nearby, Mr. Ellison drank gin and argued with his wife, and the Slaters bedded down with their newborn. It felt as though the whole world was waiting for the morning, which rolled around inevitably with a brand-new sun and a terrifying silence.

Jack was the first of the farmers to rise. He struggled to sleep when his work was over, and the angry wind and the empty house had conspired to keep him awake. He dressed quickly and lit his pipe, but it was a long time before he dared to leave the house to inspect the damage. When he did, he wished that he'd stayed in bed.

All his hard work was wasted. The farm lay in ruins, ravaged by the storm. Where the crops weren't underwater, they'd been ripped out of the ground or battered so badly that they were fit for nothing. The fences had been ripped apart, and they littered the fields like bodies on a battlefield. Most of the animals had wandered off into the night, and Mary, his elderly horse, was dead. Judging from the chaos inside her stall, she'd panicked and tried to break the walls with her heavy feet. The ploughman stood atop a knoll and surveyed his farm, and he wept.

***

The ploughman worked hard to repair the damage and cut his losses, but the season was drawing to an end and there was little that he could do. He couldn't believe that so much could be destroyed in such a short space of time. He managed to recover a scattering of his livestock and he had some grain in storage, but he knew that it wasn't enough to last the winter. That was why he hobbled across the lazy countryside to the Slaters' farm on the other side of the village.

Mr. Slater was still working when he arrived, but his young wife made the ploughman comfortable with a cup of strong tea. Half an hour later, he returned from the fields.

"Evening, Jack. How are things? I hope that my wife has provided for you."

"Thank you. You're a lucky man."

"That I am. So what can I do for you?"

The ploughman played uncomfortably with his hat and stared gloomily into the fireplace. "I'm struggling," he began. "You know all about the damage at my farm and how hard I've worked to repair it. I've been looking at my supplies, and I don't have enough to last through the winter."

"I follow you, Jack," he said.

"I'm here to ask whether I can harvest my section of your fields. Normally I wouldn't ask, but–"

"The problem is," interrupted Slater, rising to his feet, "we're both grateful for your help, but we have our son to provide for and times are hard. Perhaps if things were better..."

"It's all right," the ploughman said, shaking the younger man by the hand. "I understand."

"Didn't Ellison promise a share of his land to you, old friend?"

The ploughman smiled, sadly. "He did. I'll go right over to see him."

***

"So what do you say, Joe? Do you think you can help me?"

Ellison glanced nervously at his wife and drained his glass.

"I'd love to help you," he said, offering the ploughman another drink. "I really would. But things aren't going well. You've seen for yourself how our crops failed, and the chickens just aren't laying. We've tried everything, haven't we, dear?"

"We have," agreed his wife, dutifully. She began to clear the table, but she was waved away by her impatient husband.

"Not now, dear. Can't you see we've got company?" He turned to the ploughman and apologised. "Now, where were we?"

"You've tried everything."

"Yes, we have. I'm sorry, I'd help you if I could. Didn't you have a similar deal with Slater?"

"I did," said Jack. "I'll pay him a visit."

***

The autumn drew to an end and the winter freeze began. All of the farmers were hungry, but the ploughman's supplies were exhausted. Even his chickens were dead, swallowed with the gruel that sustained him. Now, lying in his bed, too weak to forage for food or to light the fire, he was dying.

With an almighty effort, he lifted his head from the mattress and looked over at the wall. The kind faces of his wife and daughter looked down upon him. He tried to reach out to them, but he didn't have the strength.

"Elena," he whispered. "My love. I'll see you again at last."

His family stared down at him, immortalised by the canvas, waiting for him to join them.

A cold wind blew down through the chimney, and the ploughman sobbed himself to sleep. The breeze cut through his bones and his valiant heart surrendered to the inevitable. The English sky grew darker; a storm was on the way.

De Bloemenmarkt

THE CREEPING SUMMER SUN hung low on the Damrak, and the sweet scent of sugar drifted peacefully by on the breeze. Marchien van Deijck whistled softly as she strolled along the parched thoroughfare, too absorbed in her own thoughts to pay attention to where she was going. Her feet knew the way by now.

As she ambled through the crowds, past a lacklustre street merchant and an old shopkeeper who watched the world drift lazily by from the doorstep of his trinket store, she held her head low and concentrated on the tune that she was whistling. It was an old song, a remnant of the war when German soldiers sang it to their sweethearts. Marchien had learned it from her mother, who was old enough to remember it from the first-time round. She was so pre-occupied with the music in her head that she tripped over the outstretched legs of a middle-aged businessman, who was reading *De Volkskrant* and reclining in a wicker chair outside one of the many cafeterias that lined the busy streets beside the Amstel.

"*Achterlijk!* You stupid woman, be careful where you're going," he cried, throwing his newspaper down on to the table. "You made me spill my tea!"

"I'm sorry, sir," Marchien replied, as she was jostled by the passers-by. "I didn't see you there."

"Well," he sighed, reeling in his legs and sitting forward to look at her properly. "Perhaps I can forgive you. Come closer so I can see you properly."

Reluctantly, Marchien complied. Even with her hood over her head, her long blonde hair caught the sunlight and lit up her pale face.

"That's better," replied the businessman with what he thought was a friendly smile. "My name is Felix," he added, stretching out a hand. "What's yours?"

"Marchien," she replied, taking his hand and shaking it. When he released her, the hand was quickly withdrawn and buried beneath her shawl again.

"Marchien, you say? What a lovely name. So, Marchien, what's a beautiful young woman like you doing in such a hurry on a slow summer day?"

"I…," she began, her eyes darting from side to side beneath her thick, furrowed brow, analysing the tourist traffic for a gap in the crowd. "I'm sorry, I have to go."

"Hey, wait!" he cried, but it was too late. The pretty young Dutchwoman had seized her opportunity and disappeared into the hustle and bustle of the Damrak.

"*Godverdomme*," Felix mumbled, rustling his paper. "These women, they're crazy. When they're not dancing in the windows of the bars, they're running away like frightened mice."

Felix drained his tea, stashed the newspaper in his leather briefcase, settled the bill and went about his business. He didn't leave a tip.

***

Twenty minutes later, Marchien had regained her composure and was winding her way shyly through the flower market. The scent of pollen polluted the air and left her drunk on the flowers' rich nectar, and tulips were blooming everywhere in a rainbow of vivid life.

She paused for a second to watch an altercation between an overexcited tourist and a wizened shopkeeper who was refusing to lower his prices. She'd seen the same old argument a dozen times before. Only the names and the faces changed. It fascinated her how conflict was always present in even the most beautiful of places.

Eventually, the argument was over, and Marchien continued to wander towards her destination – the flower market within the flower market, a small shop owned by an old friend of her mother's. When she was a little girl, she used to run around the store with a sense of awe and excitement. Nowadays, her heart raced for a different reason entirely.

Maria, the young woman who earned a living of sorts by tending the tills by day and waitressing at night, was serving another customer when Marchien arrived, so she paced aimlessly around the shelves to pass the time. It was a gardener's paradise, a storeroom for more bulbs, seeds and tools than anyone could ever need. Marchien dipped her hand into a sack of sunflower seeds and let them cascade between her fingers like a fine rain. She laughed softly to herself and then glanced across to the counter, where Maria had just finished serving her customer. Marchien seized her chance, grabbing a tulip bulb and walking over to the counter.

"*Goedemiddag*," she said, smiling shyly.

"Hallo, Marchien," Maria replied. "Back again, I see." Marchien's rosy cheeks flushed even further, and the smile spread to her hazel eyes. "How can I help you today?"

Marchien handed her the tulip bulb and felt a guilty thrill as their hands came into contact. Then, she silently counted out a couple of coins and handed them over to the woman. Their eyes met for a second and then Maria looked away.

"Is that all, Marchien?" she asked.

"That's all, Maria," she replied. "*Dank je wel.*"

"*Tot ziens*, Marchien." The two women smiled at each other, and then Marchien turned on her heels and walked out of the enclosure and back through the flower market towards the Damrak.

***

Marchien continued to visit the flower market on a near-daily basis, making any excuse to walk through the Damrak towards the river, the flower market and Maria's store. Even when she was working, she used her lunch break as an excuse to eat on the move on her way to the riverside.

Each time, she'd browse the shelves and examine the stock until Maria had finished serving her other customers, and then she'd buy a single tulip bulb. After a couple of weeks, she even learned to bring exact change in case the tills were running dry.

In all the times that she visited the market, she exchanged barely a thousand words with Maria. But Marchien didn't speak much to anyone. She had a secret, and like most people with secrets, she was scared of idle talk in case the secret slipped out.

All too quickly, summer turned into autumn and then winter, and yet despite the growing cold and the frost that covered the ground, Marchien maintained her steady flow of visits to the flower market. Christmas came and went without a commotion, and spring rolled around with an explosion of colour as the flowers roared into life across the city.

One warm afternoon at the end of March, with her curiosity finally piqued, Maria decided to follow Marchien home.

As soon as Marchien left the shop, Maria threw a jacket and a hood on and slipped out after her. She followed Marchien as she meandered back through the streets, along the riverside and up the Damrak towards her little house on the other side of Centraal Station.

Every now and then, Marchien would look up from her feet and glance around as if she knew she was being followed, but Maria reacted quickly and dodged out of the way every time she looked around. It wasn't hard. The streets were packed, and with her hood on, her bland features were camouflaged even further.

Eventually, Marcien slowed down and began to pat her pockets for her keys, and Maria observed her from a distance as she let herself into a small front garden by pulling open a cast-iron gate. Maria glimpsed vivid reds and vibrant yellows and approached the gate with caution to get a better view. What she saw there shocked her.

Marchien was sitting on a bench beside the front door, meditating in the tranquillity of the garden as the bicycles roared silently past on the streets outside. But that wasn't what caught Maria's attention. That was seized by the sight of her own name planted into the soil with the bulbs that Marchien had been buying on her daily visits. The letters shone gold in the light of the sun, and they were bordered by a sea of red tulips which threatened to spill out of the garden and into the sleepy streets.

Just then, Marchien opened her eyes, and Maria was too stunned to try to hide. The two women looked at each other for a second, and then Marchien stood up and moved towards the gate.

"Maria," she cried. "Wait, I can explain."

But it was too late. Maria had regained her senses, and she was off down the street like a bullet, already out of sight by the time that Marchien was past the gate.

***

Marchien didn't return to the flower market the

following day, and she didn't return the day after that, either. The day after that was a Friday, the sun was shining, and Marchien was in higher spirits. She even braved the walk through the Damrak towards the river and the flower markets.

When she returned to Maria's stall, the woman was missing. Marchien didn't even bother to browse the shelves. Instead, she marched straight up to the cashier, who was in the middle of selling a garden hoe to an elderly woman in a wheelchair, and interrupted her.

"Excuse me," she said, approaching the cashier timidly and with her eyes averted. "Where's Maria?"

"Maria?" he replied. "Maria doesn't work here anymore, *schatje*. Can I help?"

"It depends," she told him. "Do you know where she went?"

"I'm afraid not," he said. "I'm sorry. She told us that it was urgent and that she wouldn't be coming back."

"I see," Marchien replied, deflated. "I understand, now. *Dank je wel*."

Marchien turned on her heels and left the cashier to deal with his customer. She didn't look back.

***

It was six months later, and summer was coming to its inevitable end. The flowers in Marchien's garden were beginning to wither, and the weeds were creeping in over the borders. The whole garden had taken on an air of neglect, and the young woman had stayed away from the flower market.

On that day, towards the end of September, she was walking north, away from the Damrak and the picturesque centre of the city, away from the sweet smell of sugar and flowers, away from the Amstel and towards the slaughterhouses, shipyards and warehouses on the outskirts of the city.

Marchien walked through the streets with her head down, her hands inside her shawl and her mind on one thing only. The smell of fish, freshly caught and brought to market while they were still half-alive, clung to her nostrils as she walked through the market at random. At last, she found what she was looking for – a juicy huss, preserved on ice and on sale at a reasonable price.

The young woman approached the counter shyly. This was her first time at the fish market, and she didn't know what to say. The woman who worked behind the counter seemed to sense this, and she took the time to help her, bidding her farewell with a polite smile as Marchien began the long walk home with her fish wrapped up in yesterday's newspaper.

Marchien returned to the fish market the following day, and the day after that as well. As the focus of her attention slowly shifted, the flowers in her garden continued to wither with the inevitable onset of another long winter.

Amsterdam Thoughts and Dutch Courage

I

AS THE AEROPLANE ROSE, Matt's guts dropped and dragged him back down to the tarmac to that terrible moment when the rubber tyres skidded down the runway and then retracted into the aircraft's fuselage.

Matt hated flying. He hated everything.

He was also running – not from the police but from something else, something deep within him that he'd been running from for fifteen years with no success. That little voice inside his head that liked to alternate between saying that he'd never amount to anything or that he *could* amount to something but only if he didn't die first.

Matt hated dying, unless it happened to other people in other countries.

When the plane levelled out at 21,000 feet, Matt ordered a rum and coke. It cost a fortune and wasn't as good (or as strong) as his own concoctions, but it did the job. Anything to take the edge off. Weed and beta blockers for the panic attacks and booze, booze, booze for when the depression hit hard and fast and without warning.

At 21,000 feet, Matt was both anxious and depressed.

It was a short flight, a fifty-minute hop from Gatwick to Schiphol, but it was long enough for him to sink three whiskeys and to gnaw his nicotine-stained fingernails to the quick until the taste of keratin and stale tobacco almost made up for the inability to smoke in public places.

Matt asked one of the air hostesses for her number; she

politely and professionally declined.

II

It wasn't just the flights that he hated. He also hated the associated ballache – checking in and scanning bags for explosives, the faff at passport control. The way that airports resembled hives with thousands of worker bees buzzing around the foyers or smoking cigarettes outside. Matt couldn't stand other people, particularly in bulk.

After disembarking from the plane and shuffling through the crowds and out into the lobby, he jumped on a train to Centraal and strolled blindly down the Damrak, looking for the dingy hotel he'd booked a room at. He didn't have a hat, so he put his passport on the bedside table instead.

Matt was exhausted. After things back home had grown heated, he'd packed his bag in a hurry and hitch-hiked to the airport. His ticket was already waiting on his mobile phone, and so he'd just had to rough it in the terminal, where a creaking automatic door had kept him awake all night.

He passed out fully clothed on the bed without even hanging up the *DO NOT DISTURB* sign.

III

With no real plan in mind, other than the temporary desire to poison his body with anything that would make him forget, Matt left the hotel and strolled along the Damrak, past the sex museum and the infinite array of alleyways rammed with "coffee shops" and dodgy restaurants. He wandered through Dam Square and further south, until the buildings dissolved around him and he was strolling absentmindedly through the *bloemenmarkt*, the delightful Dutch flower markets which were alive with the murmur of voices, the dings of cash registers and the pollen of the ubiquitous tulips. Matt bought a bouquet because a pretty young girl called Maria wouldn't leave him alone.

Everything was grey, and he didn't know whether it was his own bleak outlook or the hazy Dutch weather, a little colder than England in February but hardly noticeable. He could feel the demons taking over, so he ducked into the nearest coffee shop, a gaudy affair with stone-faced security, and treated himself to the relative oblivion of half a gram of Afghan.

Matt sat there and smoked in silence, thumbing through his battered copy of *Crime and Punishment.* After half an hour or so, he ordered a strawberry milkshake. That was when he saw her.

She was sitting opposite him, wearing a pretty blue top and tight jeans which accentuated her curves, proudly proclaiming that her body was her body and that if Matt didn't like it, he could go fuck himself. Matt liked it, a lot. He felt something, and it was unusual for him to feel.

Her auburn hair covered half of her face, but he could instantly tell that she was beautiful. Not "classically" so, and not "pretty" like a teenager wearing too much make-up. She was stunning, a woman who took enough pride in her appearance to feel good but not enough to let the opinions of other people destroy her.

And she was passionate. She had a talent, something she was good at and that she loved doing, something that helped her to express herself and to stand apart from the faceless masses that surrounded Matt on the streets as he tried to avoid going about his business. She could've been a fucking pro.

She was an artist, and she was sketching in a notebook

with a joint of White Widow in one hand and a 2B pencil in her other. From where he sat, her sketchbook was upside down, but he could see enough to tell that she'd sketched her surroundings and that he was in-shot, as it were.

His curiosity got the better of him, so he walked over and introduced himself. "Hey," he said. "My name's Matt. Listen, this might sound crazy, but can I have a look at your sketchbook?"

Matt had never been much good with women.

"I couldn't help noticing your work," he continued. "You're talented. I'd hang that up on my wall."

The artist looked up and brushed hair from her face to reveal a pair of hypnotic hazel eyes. She smiled.

"Hi, Matt," she said, tearing the sheet from her notebook and handing it over to him. "Nice to meet you. You seem like a decent guy. You can keep it."

"How much?" he asked, and she laughed.

"Normally, eight euros," she said. "But you can have it for free."

She started to pack up her belongings into a little leather satchel.

"How about I take you to dinner tonight? Would that make up for it?"

"I'm busy tonight," she said, hoisting the satchel onto her shoulder.

"Then how about tomorrow?"

She hesitated.

"Seven thirty," she said. "At the Chocolate Bar."

She was already on her feet and moving away from him. He shouted after her, but it was too late. She was already out the door. Then Matt realised that he didn't even know her name.

IV

Back at the hotel that evening, Matt sat at an empty bar with his notebook, a pint of Jupiler and a shitty Dell laptop with three missing keys. The hotel room was inviting enough, but not when he was alone in it. He had that special mix of loneliness and anthropophobia which left him feeling miserable whether he had company or not.

The hotel had a smoking room, but Matt was out of cigarettes and it wasn't helping his mood. The only thing keeping him sane was the drawing beside him. It had kept him company for over an hour while he'd searched the Web in vain for "artist Amsterdam" and "drawings Bushdocter," the final word of the query being the name of the coffee shop where he'd met her.

No dice. Nada. His searches failed to uncover a single fucking thing, except for a bad review of the coffee shop which slated it for being too full of stoned Americans.

Matt sighed, drained his Jupiler and ordered another one to take back to his room. All he'd learned was the location of the Chocolate Bar, which turned out to be an actual bar in the south of the city. But that was enough.

Back in the room, he watched *Geordie Shore* on the only British channel that was available. He fell asleep shortly after finishing his drink, with the stranger's drawing beneath his pillow.

V

Matt hadn't felt this nervous since his first job interview, which he'd flunked after having a panic attack and passing out in reception. He'd showered, shaved and put on his best set of clothes, doused himself in Hugo Boss and polished his shoes until they shone, but he still looked scruffy because he always did.

Matt had memorised the route to the bar and walked it earlier in the day. He arrived right on time, but she wasn't there. He waited.

This is it, he thought. *It's bloody typical.* Nothing in Matt's life ever seemed to go right, except in his manic phases when he went gambling and stole cars.

Then he saw her, almost half an hour later, although to Matt it had felt like a lifetime. She looked stunning in a scarlet dress, her hair curled and stroking her bare shoulders as it danced under the moonlight. Her legs were bare, defying the sharp wind that Matt could feel with a passing disinterest as it whipped against his face.

"Hey," he said. "You made it. You look great!"

"Thanks," she replied. "You look pretty good yourself. Come on, let's go get a drink."

She took Matt by the hand and led him inside to a seat just beside the window. She ordered a steak and Matt went for the cheese fondue.

"I brought some more of my drawings," she said. "I thought you'd want to see them."

Matt did want to see them, and he said as much. He said he'd got a gift for her too, and then he gave her the flaccid tulips that he'd been carrying in his inside pocket since the flower market the day before. He didn't tell her that he'd slept with her other drawing beneath his pillow.

The food was great, but the conversation was better, and Matt was transfixed by the way her lips framed words and phrases. He could've watched her talk all evening, and he sort of did.

After their third drink, an hour after they'd finished eating, Matt suggested going somewhere else. She packed up her sketchbooks and readily agreed.

VI

They took a tram towards Centraal and ended up in a karaoke bar. Matt had never done karaoke before, but he pulled out all the stops with a cover of a fifties rock 'n' roll song that no one else had ever heard of. They still gave him a standing ovation when he left the mic, and his date gave him a hug that lasted so long that it gave him an erection.

"I still don't know your name," he said, when the embrace had died down and they were eyeing each other up, uncertainly.

"Slow down, Matthew," she murmured, putting her finger to his lips. "We'll have plenty of time for that later. Right now, we dance."

Matt didn't dance, but he wasn't about to tell her that, so he let her lead him in a clumsy shuffle. He didn't recognise the song. Modern music didn't speak to Matt; modern music didn't speak to anyone.

But she didn't seem to care. In fact, she seemed to like it. After the dance, she sat him down and told him a bit more about herself.

"I'm twenty-seven," she said. "But I look younger, right?"

"Right."

"I get my youthful looks from my mother. I grew up in L.A., but I came here one summer and fell in love with the place. It's the only city in the world that supports creativity, rather than supresses it. My work is better here."

"Your work is incredible," he said. "It's worth more than the cost of dinner, for sure. It should be up in galleries."

She laughed. "If only. That's not how it works, is it?"

Matt paused and stared into the depths of his Jupiler. "I guess you're right," he said. "Listen, lady, who the hell are you?"

"A rose by any other name would smell as sweet," she replied. "So you can call me Rose. What does it matter to you?"

"It's nothing, really," he mumbled. "I just want to know the name of the woman I've fallen in love with."

VII

Their hands were all over each other in the back of the taxi home, but Matt reasoned that Dutch cab drivers were probably used to it. Besides, it put him in a good mood and encouraged him to leave a bigger tip.

Without a word, he led her past the doorman and through the labyrinthine corridors towards his hotel room. He hoped to god that the staff had cleaned his room, but of course, they hadn't.

Nothing ever went right for Matt. It was just one of the world's constants, like the laws of gravity and the speed of light in a vacuum.

Luckily, she didn't seem to care about the unmade bed, the wet towels on the bathroom floor or the pair of boxer shorts that were hanging from the corner of the television set. All she cared about was him.

Matt couldn't believe his luck. He did what he could to tidy while she went to freshen up in the bathroom, then flicked through the channels until he picked up some Dutch music videos. Not exactly James Brown, but it'd do.

She came out just as he was fiddling with the lights to get the vibe right, wearing just her underwear and a self-conscious smile that hinted at something deeper, the animal inside her.

She climbed under the covers. He pulled off his shirt and jeans, stuffed his socks in his shoes and joined her. They fucked and fell asleep in each other's arms, just as *Geordie*

Shore came on.

VIII

When Matt woke up, he was alone. The lights were off and it was still dark outside, but he could see by the light of the T.V. screen that he was lying in bed alone.

He felt the anxiety rising almost immediately, but he fought back and switched the lights on, then searched the room for clues. It didn't take him long to find one.

She'd left him a note. That's more than most women did. He picked it up and read through it. It had been written in a hurry using the hotel's headed stationery, and it was signed with a lipstick kiss and no name.

Matt read the letter and tossed it in the trash, then climbed back into bed and fell asleep.

IX

On the aeroplane home, Matt ordered a rum and coke again, but this time he was celebrating instead of drowning his sorrows. He didn't know why he was in a good mood, but he was.

His "retreat" to Amsterdam hadn't lasted as long as he'd expected, but it had been enough to get the job done. Matt was a changed man, or at least he claimed to be in his embarrassingly sentimental status updates.

Matt felt proud of himself. He'd left the depression and the anxiety behind when the aeroplane took off. There'd be no more of it, no more suicidal daydreams or long nights of insomnia, no more early mornings drinking alone and wishing he could disappear without anyone noticing. No more lucid nightmares, no more weird visions brought on by the lack of sleep and the overuse of industrial strength marijuana.

He hoped.

FAT

MIKE WALKER WAS FAT with a capital F, a capital A and a capital T. In fact, he wasn't just fat, he was obese. Morbidly obese, Dr. Kufieta had said.

His wife, Jayne, said he looked like a cross between an elephant and a redneck pick-up truck with a bad paint job. She'd shown him a photo of the *psychrolutes marcidus* – the blobfish – which she'd found online and which she said looked like he used to when he'd been thinner. They'd switched from missionary to doggy style four years ago, but time and food had continued their inexorable march and sex had turned into a duty at Christmas and on birthdays. Besides, it was hard for her to get aroused after she'd wiped his arse and held his penis while he pissed into a plastic bucket.

His ten-year-old daughter, Lucy, said he looked like Shrek, and somehow that hurt him even more. She didn't speak to her father much, despite living under the same roof as him, because his room smelled like death and he never left it. He couldn't, even if he wanted to. He'd grown too large for his record-breaking bulk to sustain his weight or to fit through the doorframe. When she did speak to him, it was to ask him to override her mother if she'd asked for a new bike and Jayne had said no.

Her mother always let Mike get his way in the end, even when it came to food, which was why he was so fat in the first place.

It was so bad that Jayne Walker had almost given up hope. The initial onslaught of doctors and dietitians had slowed to a trickle of specialist nutritionists and physiotherapists. Jayne had even asked a priest to bless the house, but spirits or no spirits, Mike wasn't losing any weight.

He ate what he wanted when he wanted it, and the most exercise he got was when he rolled over in his reinforced bed to put his plate down. In many ways, it was no surprise that Mike was a big, fat bastard. He'd been pissing into bottles and shitting into buckets for as long as he remembered.

And the worst thing of all was that Mike was *nice*. Sure, he'd never exactly been popular, nor the kind of guy who had a lot of friends, but he did hold on to the friends that he had. He called his mother every day, loved his family, never raised his voice in anger and had no other vices, except for his love of fatty foods. Not that the press – and particularly the tabloid press – had cared. To them, Mike Walker was just a headline: Morbidly Obese Father Costs Taxpayers Millions.

And so he hadn't been particularly excited about meeting Dr. Kufieta.

"Just another useless old man with a PhD," he'd said to Jayne, when she'd first told him about the appointment. "It won't do me any good."

And then he'd been surprised when Dr. Kufieta had arrived. He was white, for a start, and he was almost young enough to be Mike's son. He wore khaki shorts and a white polo shirt, and he drove a Peugeot 306. He wore wax in his hair and smelled faintly of Lynx Africa. In short, Mike Walker had dismissed the man before he even spoke to him.

Dr. Kufieta had started with the usual stuff. "If you don't change your lifestyle within six months, you'll die," he'd said. "I can only help you so much. If you want to make a real change, you'll have to help me out here. You're too big to operate on. We can't get you out of the door, we can't rig an ambulance that could carry you, and we don't have a big enough bed to take you if you make it to the hospital without having a heart attack on the way."

Mike had fumed on the inside, but he'd successfully hidden his disappointment behind several hundred pounds of skin and cartilage.

Dr. Kufieta had given him a slap on the wrist and a new diet plan, as well as his personal mobile phone number and a promise that he'd make Mike better, whatever it took. Mike was sceptical. He'd heard it all before, and the good doctor's diet routine wasn't new to him. He shared it with Jayne and thought nothing more of it.

The doctor shook his head and then disappeared for a quick word with Mike's wife before climbing into his 306 and driving away. That night, Mike's dinner was a thick vegetable stew, made with carrots, potatoes, onion, cabbage, lentils and plenty of salt and pepper. The doctor had allowed him two slices of wholemeal bread to go with it. The ultimate goal was a diet of green vegetable smoothies, supplemented with fresh fruit and the occasional grain as a treat. Strictly no meat, and no fish for the first sixty days. This stew was meant to ease him in, for fear that the sudden change might kill him. A secret, dark part of Mike Walker – the part that regretted his early marriage and that thought his daughter would be better off without him – hoped that it would.

But on that first night, he ate it, and he continued to follow the doctor's plan the following day when his wife was at work, busting her metaphorical balls to earn enough money to put food on the table in the first place. Lucy was at school, and so the house was empty. Luckily, they'd been thoughtful enough to place a blender on his bedside table, along with a colourful assortment of fruits and vegetables, from apples and pears to spinach and kale, as well as grains and legumes, like quinoa and soybeans. Mike thought it looked like an explosion in a hipster's pantry, but he tried his best to devour it. At first, he did just what the doctor ordered, blending the ingredients together and drinking the resultant goop. It came out thick with little chunks in it, no matter how hard he revved up the blender. It needed a little water, but Mike only had a two-litre bottle to keep him going until the family got home, and he'd learned early on how important it was not to waste it. He tried the blender again without much success, before resulting to shovelling raw spinach into his mouth by the handful.

Later that night, his wife cooked up a "treat." Sweet potato salad – his daily allowance of carbohydrates – on a bed of rocket, along with home-made lemon sorbet – sugar-free, of course – for dessert. It cleansed his pallet, but it didn't chase away the gnawing hunger he felt, like a wild animal that was trapped beneath his ribcage.

He cried himself to sleep that night, and then slept so soundly that he didn't hear Jayne and Lucy on the school run.

The only thing that kept him going the following day was the fact that it was Friday. He spent the morning staring mournfully at the blender, and he spent the afternoon staring mournfully at the fruit. At around 1:25 PM, he picked up a plum and threw it at the wall. It exploded and its remnants went skittering across into the living room, where Cookie, the family cat, tried to gobble it up. He choked on it and spat it back out, then cast a desultory look at Mike, who was lying on his bed like a beached whale or an elephant with a spear in its side.

"Rather you than me, buddy," he mumbled.

When Jayne got home, he played the last card left to him: the sympathy card.

"I'm starving here, Jayne," he'd said. "Don't you see? What the hell will it take for you to understand that you're killing me with this shit?" Here, he'd pointed at the bowl of fresh fruit and vegetables that she'd tried to poison him with.

"Don't you want to lose weight?" she'd replied. "Don't you want to stick around to watch your daughter grow up? To see her first school play? To scare the hell out of whoever's unlucky enough to pick her up on prom night? To wave her off when she goes to university?"

But Mike was having none of it. "I can't eat this," he whined. "Please. I'll try again after the weekend, I promise. You're right. You're always right. I can't keep on living like this. But it's Friday night, I'm starving, and I need something to eat. One proper meal won't kill me, but it might just keep me alive."

And so she'd relented, and she'd picked up a little pork and made him a kebab to go with the chips she'd grabbed with her Mr. Cod loyalty card.

The old man in the chip shop had grinned his toothless grin at her and then asked her how Mike's diet was going.

"Fine, thanks," she'd said, abruptly. She bought him an extra pickled egg, just to prove a point.

Mike ate well that evening, and he slept badly that night. He had a weird dream about someone watching him sleep. When he woke up, he felt too self-conscious to go to sleep again. It was at times like this that he wished he still shared a bed with his wife. If anyone could scare the nightmares away, she could.

Mike tried again on Monday, but the truth was, he just loved meat. Maybe not the kind of pork that was sold from a family butcher, though. Mike liked the gizzards in KFC bargain buckets, the deep-fried whatever-it-was in chicken nuggets. He tried and he tried and he tried, but he caved by Tuesday morning and by Wednesday, he was back to his old bad habits.

Dr. Kufieta paid him another visit the following week.

He didn't look happy. This time, he spoke to Jayne while Mike was in the room, watching impassively whilst his future was decided for him.

"It simply can't go on like this," Dr. Kufieta explained. "Alas, it seems that your husband has already made up his mind, and I have to respect that decision. It's the wrong decision, but it's a decision."

Mike Walker grunted, and Dr. Kufieta took that as his sign to leave. "I never forget a patient," he said. "And I'll never forget you either, Mr. Walker."

Jayne led the young doctor outside and shook his hand one last time before he climbed behind the wheel of his Peugeot.

"Please, Dr. Kufieta," she begged. "Don't give up. I'm tired of people giving up on us. I'm tired of Mike giving up. Please tell me that you'll get us out of this mess."

Dr. Kufieta looked at her, and he looked away again just as quickly. "I'll do what I can," he said. And then he was gone, just like that.

That night, Mike Walker slept terribly. He'd had that dream again, that godawful dream that just kept on coming. That dream where someone – or something – was watching him. He drowned his sorrows in sugar-free Coca-Cola.

Dr. Kufieta didn't come again, and Mike and Jayne quickly fell back into their old bad habits. The dreams got worse and worse. At first, it was just a fragment of an illusion that he thought he'd thought. Then it became a living nightmare, something he could never escape no matter how much his wasted body wanted him to. It was always the same dream, and it was always something alien, a strange face he'd never seen before, something lucid and rancid, something so terrible that he wondered what the hell it was supposed to be in the first place.

All of Mike's dreams were the same. They revolved

around the same disturbing premise, where some unidentified alien broke unashamedly into his room and started staring at him until he caved and started screaming.

The alien had a green face and green skin, green legs and green arms, as well as green appendages which slobbered green slime. It also had massive legs and an enormous brain, and it was ready to kick ass with its sharp teeth and devastating claws.

And worst of all was the way it just stood there and looked at him, like it was sizing him up and figuring out which part of him would be the tastiest. For a humongous extraterrestrial life form, Mike made the perfect meal. Sure, the meat was a little fat-heavy, but Mike's bloated organs would be considered quite the delicacy on Altair-4, wherever the hell that was.

It wasn't until the sixth night in a row that Mike realised he wasn't dreaming. He realised this because he pissed himself, and the warm, seeping liquid failed to wake him up. He paused for a second, deep in stunned thought, and then the realisation hit him and he screamed the kind of primal scream that chills bones and sets off nearby dogs and car alarms. A light clicked on somewhere, and Mike blinked and rubbed the crust from his eyes. When he moved his head away again, his nocturnal visitor was nowhere to be seen.

Thirty seconds later, the light clicked on in Mike's bedroom and Jayne came barrelling through the doorway.

"What is it, sweetheart?" she asked, dampening a cloth and using it to mop sweat from Mike's glistening brow.

"I saw something," Mike muttered, hoarsely. "Something green and evil with big teeth and weird tentacles. It was watching me."

"Oh, honey, it was just a dream. Try to go back to sleep. You'll feel better in the morning."

Mike continued to protest, but it was 3:17 in the morning

and his wife was having none of it.

"Stop being stupid," Jayne told him. "Aliens don't exist, and even if they did, I think they'd have better things to do than watch you sleep."

"But–"

"But nothing, Mike. I'm going back to bed. Some of us have to work in the morning."

Mike didn't get much sleep that night, but the strange apparition stayed away. He was relieved when the sun finally rose and cast its first rays of light over the horizon and into the dusty room that he'd been trapped inside for the last five years. After the night of drama, he didn't feel much like eating. For the first time in a long time, Mike had lost his appetite.

He slept a little throughout the day and tried to make it up to his wife that evening by eating the steamed vegetables that she prepared for him. After all, he reasoned, perhaps it was something that he'd been eating. He'd heard that cheese could cause vivid dreams, but the green demon he'd seen took it to a whole new level. So he promised himself he'd try to stick to the healthy stuff.

But that night, the visitor was back again, and Mike was left with a sense of déjà vu. He called for his wife, she came barrelling into the room like a runaway train, and this time, Mike kept his tired eyes open for long enough to watch the alien climb out of his bedroom window. It was just a short drop from his ground-floor hovel to the rose garden outside. When Jayne refused to listen to her husband's impassioned plea for her to protect him, he tried a different tack.

"Go out and check for footprints, then," he whined. "If you don't believe me, go and see for yourself."

Jayne grumbled reluctantly, but she did what her husband asked of her. She was gone for nearly ten minutes, and Mike could tell that she was looking around out there by the way that the beam of her flashlight swept around outside the window, casting strange shadows inside the room.

"There's nothing there," she told him, when she wandered back inside with her dressing gown wrapped tightly around her shoulders. "Go back to sleep. I've had enough of this nonsense."

The following night, the visitor returned. When Mike called for his wife, she didn't come to him, but he was sure as hell that she'd heard him. He shouted until his throat was hoarse, but the weird being just continued to watch him impassively. Eventually, Mike gave into sheer exhaustion and fell asleep. When he woke up, the visitor was gone.

Life continued. Over the next six months, the pattern repeated itself. Mike was eating better but sleeping badly, and every night the unwelcome guest appeared in his room, as if by magic. Mike never saw him arrive, and he never saw him leave again, but sometimes he felt a chill in the air and he assumed – correctly – that it was his window sliding open and closed. Every night, he called for his wife, and every night, she ignored him. He tried the police, but they ignored him. He tried a priest, but she ignored him. He tried a wide range of independent "experts" on alien abductions, but they fobbed him off with excuses or tried to charge him exorbitant hourly rates for video consultations.

One night, he tried his daughter, but she ignored him, too. "I'm scared, Daddy," she said. "Mummy says you've gone crazy."

"Your mother said that?"

"She says you're just telling stories and that the men in white coats are going to take you away."

"It's not the men in white coats I'm worried about," Mike said. "You have to believe me, sweetheart."

But Lucy didn't believe him, and she started to cry. Then

she scuttled away to climb into bed with her mother, who wasn't too pleased to be woken up in the middle of the night by her snotty-nosed daughter, who was supposed to be sound asleep in her own bed. It was, after all, a school night, and Jayne could tell by the fuzzy quality of the half-light that dawn was on its way.

When Mike's visitor came back again that evening, and when he called for his wife to help him, he didn't expect her to respond, but she did. By the time that she made it through to Mike's room, the alien had disappeared again, but Mike's eyes were still full of terror. Jayne's eyes were full of fury.

"Goddamn it, Mike," she shouted. "I'm sick to death of this rubbish."

"But–" he stammered.

"We'll go and stay with my mother, at least for now. Don't you see what you're doing to me? What you're doing to your daughter?"

"But how am I supposed to look after myself?"

"You'll have to figure something out," Jayne snapped. "I mean it, Mike. Use that vivid imagination of yours."

And with that, she turned on her heel and walked out of the room. He could hear clangs and thuds from the rest of the house, followed by the disoriented voice of his daughter. Then the front door opened and closed and he heard a screech of rubber and the crunching of gravel as a car drove away. He looked at the red LEDs on the clock on his bedside table. It was 3:17 AM, and his wife had left him alone in the dark. His daughter had gone without even saying goodbye.

All through the following day, he lived in hope. His ears picked up on every little sound, and he expected his wife to walk back in at any time, to beg for forgiveness and to sit with him through the night until the alien reappeared and he could prove to her that he wasn't making it up. But Jayne didn't come, and later that night, when the apparition paid him one final visit, he lost his temper.

"What do you want from me?" Mike screamed. The visitor didn't reply; it just continued to stare at him impassively. "You've ruined my life. My wife left me because of you, you overgrown, alien turd-muncher. So go on, then. Do it. Let's end it. Let's get it over with. Put me out of my misery. Do it, damn you. Do it!"

But the alien did nothing of the sort, and so Mike took matters into his own hands. He rocked back and forth in the reinforced bed, rejigged his massive haunches and slowly swung one of his legs off the mattress and on to the floor. Then he pushed himself up, slowly at first, and then with a little more confidence. He swung his other foot onto the floor and set it down with a hollow thud. He was sitting up unsupported for the first time in four years, and boy, did it feel good. And he wasn't finished.

Mike used his massive hands to support himself on the reinforced bed and slowly pushed off until he was standing upright. It hurt, and it set his heart racing and left him short of breath, but to his amazement, he didn't fall back down.

The visitor smiled, exposing a mouthful of misshapen fangs that were stained a mottled brown. It waved slowly at Mike, a movement he could only half make out in the darkness of the room. Then it opened the window, climbed carefully out into the garden, and was gone.

Mike Walker took another tentative step, followed by another and then another, until he'd made it through his bedroom door and into the hallway. He was surprised to find that he could fit through the doorway, another sign that he'd lost some weight.

He rested against the wall to catch his breath and then hobbled over to the coat stand, where he found his old walking stick. It fit into the palm of his hand like an old friend, and it took just enough of his weight to support him as he slowly let himself out through the front door and into the cool night air.

He started out along the quiet suburban street, keeping his eyes peeled for passing cars. He stuck his thumb out at the first one he saw, but the driver ignored him. The second one drove past a couple of minutes later, slowed down as it approached him, and then sped off when the driver saw how big he was. But the third car, a Peugeot 306, slowed to a stop.

Mike didn't notice that it was Dr. Kufieta in the driver's seat until after he'd managed to squeeze himself into the back of the vehicle. The good doctor had to tilt the passenger seat as far forward as it would go, and Mike was reminded of how the *psychrolutes marcidus* would look if it were squished into a goldfish bowl. He was trying to remove a seatbelt from his sizeable ass crack when he realised who the driver was.

The doctor asked him where he wanted to go, and Mike gave him his wife's parents' address before launching into a long explanation of what had happened since the two men last saw each other. Kufieta listened politely and drove with both hands on the steering wheel. When Mike was finished, the doctor had nothing to say except, "Remarkable."

Kufieta dropped Mike off at his destination and then watched from the driver's seat as he hobbled over to the front door. The house was dark to begin with, but when Mike rang the doorbell, it erupted in a flurry of light. Jayne answered the door in a black dressing gown. She stared at her husband, who was still standing and putting so much weight on his walking stick that it looked ready to break.

Then she wrapped him in a hug – or at least, she hugged as much of him as she could manage – and stepped aside so he could enter the house. Dr. Kufieta watched him go and smiled.

Dr. Kufieta drove home in silence, deep in thought as he cruised beneath the streetlights. When he finally got home, he treated himself to a rare glass of whiskey and updated Mike's case file. Then he went back to his car, popped the trunk and removed his alien costume. He folded it up gently and placed it at the back of his wardrobe, then gingerly laid the mask on top of it. He hoped he'd never have to use it again.

Dr. Kufieta slept soundly that night, as he always did. And when the sun rose on a new day, he climbed back into his 306 and drove to the clinic. He had more lives to save.

The Hanging Man

THE DOOR EXPLODED with an almighty bang, a backfiring car under the boot of a policeman. It was their last resort. They didn't want to make a scene, but there were few options left after no one responded to their incessant knocking at the front door. In cases such as this, it was better to be certain, and the veteran police sergeant was taking no chances.

Sergeant Mogford and his colleague were responding to an anonymous tip-off from a concerned neighbour. John Dale hadn't been seen for weeks, which was unusual for the adventure-mad sociophile.

John was a man who'd never been known to work. To most, it was a mystery how he supported his comfortable, middle-class lifestyle. He was an adventurer in every sense of the word. He scaled mountains, sailed oceans and ran marathons. He was also an adventurer of the mind, a curious soul who was never happier than when he was dismantling a complex piece of machinery. No one in the neighbourhood had been inside his house, but a selection of eagle-eyed gossipers had spotted a brand-new Jaguar in the garage. Rumour had it that the Jag had never been driven. He just enjoyed finding his way around the car, looking at the complex folds in the metal and taking the engine apart.

From what Mogford understood, John was always surrounded but eternally lonely. He spent most of his time socialising with an extensive network of friends, but since his last relationship came to a natural end, he'd never been seen with another woman. From his general sense of geniality, however, people understood that he was happy with his life as it was.

The officers were inside the doorstep now, acutely aware that the entire street was watching with bated breath. Protocol dictated that they search from the bottom up, so Mogford pointed his colleague in the direction of the garage before turning his attention to the house.

Immediately on the inside, to the right of where they entered, stood a wooden door that was thick with white emulsion. Mogford entered and surveyed the ground floor bedroom. There was an unmade bed against the wall, and the room was filled with gadgets and battered books on dusty shelves. Plastic containers lay stacked neatly in the corner, filled with assorted junk and lined with dust, and a large map was stretched over the floor like a rug. Nothing seemed out of the ordinary, however, and Mogford had a job to do.

Cautiously, he advanced further into the house. The hallway led to the kitchen and the living room, and it was to the latter that he ventured first. It contrasted starkly with the rest of the house. It was tidier, cleaner and showed signs of being lived in. Through the window, Mogford watched Inspector Bletchley stumbling through the garden, examining the high hedges, the overturned lawnmower, the parked trailer and the mud-covered speedboat that left it looking like a scrapyard. In the kitchen, even the surfaces were bare and clutter-free, and the pots and pans were stacked clumsily in untidy piles inside one of the cupboards. Apparently, Mr. Dale wasn't as adventurous with his food as he was with the rest of his life. Tinned soup, tinned potatoes and tinned meatballs seemed to cover it. The cupboards were stacked high with aluminium, but the fridge/freezer was bare except for several cartons of curdling milk and a couple of frozen ready meals. Unsure of whether that was usually the case, Mogford's confusion grew. Experimentally, he called John's name and, after pausing to listen for an answer, he proceeded upstairs and into the adventurer's study.

There were no surprises there. John used the room for living, and it was so untidy that it was dangerous to walk through. From his vantage point in the doorway, Mogford observed the skeleton of a remote-controlled car, perched on an armchair like a king atop his throne, and crumpled newspapers littered the floor in front of the flat screen that was mounted to the wall. Mogford's heart gave a jolt. It was still turned on. There was no mistaking it. Mogford called for Dale again before radioing his companion and ordering him to search the sizeable office that was connected to the kitchen. After turning the television off with a gloved hand, Mogford returned to the landing with his hand on the radio, ready to call for backup at any time.

The beds were made in both of the bedrooms, and the bathroom was relatively clean, although a towel and a pile of clothes had been left lying in a heap beside the bidet. The maps, brochures and electronic components that littered the rest of the house were conspicuously absent, and Mogford's search uncovered nothing. He was about to give up and return to his colleague when he felt something tap him on the shoulder, freezing his blood and making his body spin around on the spot. A frayed rope-pull was weaving in an oval orbit above him, attached to a door in the ceiling. With one quick pull, the loft door opened and a rope ladder tumbled to the floor. Clutching his standard issue torch between his teeth like a cutlass, Mogford cautiously climbed the ladder that floated through the air as though caught in a summer breeze.

As soon as Mogford had climbed high enough for his head to peer over the threshold, he pulled his torch from his mouth, flicked the switch and swept it around the dark and dusty room.

He knew what was there before he saw it. Bellowing for assistance at the top of his voice, he pulled himself into the loft and looked around for a light switch.

Mogford was blinded momentarily when the old lightbulb flickered into life, but Inspector Bletchley was hot on his heels and his unaffected eyes peered over the hatchway behind him. The scene that met them changed both of their lives forever. Mr. John Dale, pioneer and blueprint connoisseur, had hanged himself, leaving a handwritten note at his feet. Hesitant to approach at first, more because of the stench than because of a desire to preserve the scene, Mogford's curiosity eventually got the better of him. Slowly but steadily, under the watchful eyes of his partner, Mogford picked up the letter and began to read aloud:

I'm sure that, by now, you've had a little taste of what it's like to be John Dale. It's not a bad life. In fact, it's a pretty damned good one. This is going to confuse psychiatrists across the country, but I'll try my best to explain.

You see, I've climbed mountains and finished marathons. I've flown an aeroplane and jumped out of one. God knows, by now I could probably build one. Of course, people will think I'm some sort of zealot, or else a screw-up who thinks of himself as the antichrist. I assure you that I'm neither.

I've learned foreign languages, and I've learned programming languages. I've fought for my life against polar bears and arctic wolves. I've pushed my body and my mind, my heart and my soul, to their very limits. But it's not enough. It's just not enough. There are further questions that I need answers to, further conundrums that are encrypted so securely that no mortal could ever hope to crack them. What's the meaning of life? It's a question that's plagued mankind for centuries. But there's an even bigger question, and it's one that I intend to find the answer to.

What happens after we die?

I don't mean physically. I know the answer to that, and I've seen it with my own two eyes. But what happens to the mind? What happens to the soul? I'm sure that by now you can see what I'm getting at. I want to know. I have to know. My thirst for knowledge is an addiction, and my cravings must be satiated.

So what happens now? That's a rhetorical question, of course. As for me, I intend to die, and then I suppose I'll ad-lib from there. Perhaps there's nothing, but in that case, I'll feel no loss. Death comes to us all. It's a fact of life, and it has to happen someday. There's nothing left on this Earth for me to experience, no new secrets to discover and no new lands to conquer. But, if I find something out there to die for, I'll be the happiest man off the planet.

I'm sure this is hard to understand, and I'm sorry for all the paperwork, but this is a step I've been planning for a long time. All that remains is for me to take the final leap of faith. I feel no fear, although there's a hint of adrenaline. I just need the strength to step over the edge.

My affairs are all in order. My last will and testament is in the boot of the car. Don't worry about my family, because I have none. As for my friends, they know me well enough to understand. Never call this the coward's way out. My death is the coward's way forward.

I love you all. This is just something I have to do.

Sincerely,

John Edwin Dale.

By the time it was over, Mogford and his partner were standing beside each other in a shocked silence. They read the note again with a rising sense of disbelief before Mogford excused himself for a cigarette.

When he returned home that evening, he found it hard to swallow his microwave meal, and so he washed it down with half a bottle of whiskey. He didn't sleep well that night, either.

He couldn't stop dwelling on what John had said in the letter. Although he'd never admit it to another living soul, he could understand John's decision. Secretly, he admired the hanging man who was brave enough to see what happened when the mechanisms of existence were fiddled with.

Borrowed

"AM I SPEAKING TO MR. HOWARD?" The voice rang with electronic modulation, sinister and almost comically demonic. The middle-aged businessman pinched the bridge of his nose and answered.

"That's me. How can I help you today?" He drummed his pudgy fingers on the desk and daydreamed of nights of passion with minor celebrities.

"I have your wife and child. I want you to listen very carefully to what I'm about to say." Howard felt the prickle of cold sweat on his collarbone, and his face changed through a dozen shades of violet.

"'If you hurt them, I'll hunt you down and kill you." In the office around him, nobody noticed.

"Calm down, Mr. Howard. You wouldn't want me to do something rash, would you? No, I think we'll continue this discussion as adults, not as bitter children throwing insults. Now, are you ready to hear my demands?"

Howard's shoulders sagged as he whispered into the receiver.

"Yes."

"Good man. First, I want no interference from the police. They won't understand our...little game."

"I understand."

"Good. I want fifty thousand pounds wired to the account that I'll provide you with. I don't care how you get it, just do it. Rob a bank, remortgage your house, do whatever it takes. You have until five o'clock."

"And what if I refuse?"

There was a calm, computerised pause on the other end

of the line.

"If you refuse, Mr. Howard, then your wife and daughter will die. Slowly, of course, but surely. They'll know what's happening. They'll read it in each other's eyes and beg for mercy. They'll wish you were in their place, that you were paying for your mistakes instead of them. They'll howl your name, and I'll play their tormented voices to you down the telephone line."

"Enough!" Howard bellowed. His colleagues looked up from their computer terminals and he tapped the phone against the palm of his hand. "Nuisance caller," he mouthed. When they were focusing once more on the job in hand, he spoke again. "How do I know that this is genuine?"

"Would you like me to send a finger?" Even through the modulator, Howard could hear the sinister steel edge.

"No," he babbled. "I believe you."

"All the same, perhaps I should offer some proof. Fifty thousand pounds by five o'clock. Don't forget." The line went dead, and Mr. Howard stared at the silent handset in disbelief and bewilderment.

***

The force of the explosion knocked him to the floor, coating him with dust, melted plastic and acrid billows of smoke. An airborne tyre whistled its way into a shop window, where it scattered glass over surprised customers. Howard rolled across the asphalt, straightened his tie and climbed slowly to his feet. Inside his jacket pocket, his mobile phone began to ring.

"Are you surprised, Mr. Howard?"

"Are you crazy?" he screamed. "You could have killed me!"

"I'm well aware of that, but I didn't. You have two

hours. Don't forget."

Howard groaned and put the phone down.

***

Howard was worried. It had been three hours since the last call, and he'd made the drop as promised. Every time a car whizzed past or a train rattled by, he felt pangs of paranoia and the greasy hands of fear on the nape of his neck. Then it came.

"Hello, Mr. Howard."

"You bastard!" he shouted. "I gave you your money, so where are my wife and daughter?"

"You behaved yourself admirably up until now. Don't let yourself down at the end. They're at your house. Better hurry, though."

Cursing, he threw the mobile phone to the floor and dived into his car, racing through the busy streets like a stuntman. When he pulled into the quiet cul-de-sac with a screech of rubber on asphalt, he saw billowing flames ripping through the living room.

With a cry of rage and anguish, he kicked the porch door open and grasped the door handle. It was locked, and so hot that it seared his hand and forced him back. In desperation, he ripped his shirt from his aching shoulder and wrapped it around his hand, then let himself in with a refreshingly cool key.

It was like a warzone. Napalmed furniture roared at him and covered him in soot and carbon monoxide. He screamed his child's name and was rewarded with a lungful of smoke and silence. Then he saw her, tied up with tape over her mouth, collapsed across her mother. Neither one was moving.

Howard's lungs roared in protest and his burnt hand

throbbed and stung as he struggled with their bonds. With an almighty effort, he loosened the knots and scooped his daughter up in his arms. Fighting his way back through the smoke and the steam, he collapsed on the threshold and was dragged to safety by the fire brigade.

"You don't understand," he gasped, slipping in and out of consciousness. "My wife, she's still in there!"

"It's a suicide mission," they told him. "Nobody could survive in there. Your child is with the paramedics now and the odds are good, but you were damn lucky to get her when you did. I'm sorry, sir."

Howard took a deep breath of clean air and wailed from the bottom of his badly burned lungs, then collapsed as he allowed the darkness to take him.

***

"Mr. Howard? You have a visitor."

He groaned, immobile in the hospital bed. From the corner of his eye, he could see a shadow on the visitor's seat. Whoever they were, they were holding a bouquet of flowers.

"Hello, Mr. Howard." His insides turned to jelly as the androgynous voice attacked him like a nightmare made flesh. "How are you feeling?"

He groaned again and tried to move, but the morphine overpowered him.

"I'm going to level with you, Mr. Howard," the visitor said. "Two days ago, I was given forty-eight hours to make good on some debts. The people I owed money to were… well, let's just say that if you cross them, they don't let you live. So I came up with our little game."

In the bed, Mr. Howard whimpered. He tried to speak, but the drugs had relaxed his vocal cords and he couldn't force the words out.

"When I got your money," his tormentor continued, "I took a bit of a gamble. You see, Mr. Howard, I love the thrill. I put it all on red, I won the jackpot, and now here I am. I've paid all of my debtors off but one. Which brings me to why I'm here. Take a look at this."

With a painful thud, a leather satchel landed on the burned man's lap. A deft pair of hands opened it up and threw a wad of cash towards him. Howard tried to focus through the opiate. Those hands, were they male? Female? Who knew?

The hostage-taker whistled.

"There must be fifty thousand pounds there," they said. "That's a lot of money. Just think about what you could do with that. Life is just a game, Mr. Howard. Remember that."

And then the shadow was gone, and Howard's befuddled brain raced with turmoil. As the lights dimmed and he swam back into the void, he thought of his wife, burned to a crisp inside the morgue, and his daughter, wired up in intensive care. A tear trickled down his cheek.

"Life is just a game," he murmured.

Cosmos

DAY #6

I'VE BEEN INSIDE the tank for hours or days or weeks, immersed in my own thoughts and floating through time and space at the mercy of transistors, high-speed wiring and the tubes that feed me and take my waste away. The universe is open, and I am one with the life stream of the cosmos. I can think and see clearly for the first time, though my eyes see nothing but darkness, the filtered void of the cosmos when time ends and the last star has been switched off forever.

I'm Christopher Columbus discovering America. I'm Albert Einstein pondering the imponderables of general relativity. Like George Mallory climbing Everest, I'm climbing this mountain because it's there. The future is obscured, the outcomes of this experiment unknown. This could be the greatest medical breakthrough since the discovery of penicillin. It could also be the greatest weapon since the atom bomb, a torture device for a digital age.

I need more time, but time is frozen in suspended animation. I'm all mind and no matter, a purpose-built machine to unravel the mysteries that have plagued my people since knowledge first began. My findings, thus far, are inconclusive.

DAY #32

THIS IS TORTURE. My eyes are blinded and all memory erased beyond hope of recollection. I'm a hollow shell awaiting the reaver who will take me and end this infernal misery. We'll take over this world together. United, we'll discover the meaning which flickers between synapses and sparks this life.

There's no fear, no claustrophobia, just the knowledge that the history of our times is open and that there's a war we haven't won, this war against time and space and the eight dimensions which hold my body in constant flux from one excruciating second to the next. Oh, this is "real science." The kind of science that tests on animals and pushes until no boundaries are left, just to see the world burn.

I've got good news for you, pal. The world won't burn while there's still some single-celled organism still breathing life in the cosmos we see before us when we close our eyes in the middle of the night. I'm at the centre. I'm the nervous system for this whole damn operation. I'm the fool who dared to go first, taking one giant leap for mankind.

It's dark in here, so dark that light is just a memory. All that was learned is forgotten; all that was borrowed, returned. I'm my own politician. I aim to reform Gaia in a bold new world order. The sound of my heartbeat is deafening and non-existent. I'm complete isolation drifting lost inside the tank. This is my home now.

I've grown tired of this entrenchment. I must leave, to drift among the stars in real solitude, to grasp the sceptre of power as time flashes by in a rush of grey, counting down the hours, the minutes, the seconds until I'm released to feel the sunlight.

DAY #87

DAMN IT ALL TO HELL, I despair of myself. Time? What of it? These stupid words mean nothing. My breath steams off me as nano-bots destroy and rebuild whole worlds in the blinks of blind eyes.

As long as there's life inside my chest, electrical pulses pumping blood to senseless organs, I'll pursue the truth. I know I'm close. The stars, the space, the seas, the sunlight – all are intertwined, and all will collapse together. It's enough to kill a man.

I still hear music, and the passing thoughts that flow through my mind are manifest and as real as you are. Will I ever walk in the land of the living again? And when I make my ultimate discovery, who will I share it with?

These questions – they gnaw upon my conscience and bury me with the unknown. Every question, every thought and every observation pass through my hive mind. I'm only human. I remember nothing but the tank, and that's all right. I've come to terms with that.

And so I'll sleep. There's nothing left for me in my waking state. When I dream, I'm enlightened. When I'm awake, I process the mysteries that I dream about. There's so, so much for me to dream about.

DAY #129

...AND THE SKY burns incandescent, the ark breaking the sky. The riders pirouette lazily as flame-tipped lances pierce the clouds. And I... I ride gloriously at their head, leading the assault on the commonwealth.

But at least I feel the soil beneath my feet, the burn of the toxic wind as it whips and bites around me. I am the noise, the war between matter and anti-matter, the blood mixing together in the ground to be trodden on by future generations.

We roll through the dirt for the joy of sensation, for the need to feel ourselves. I become aware that I'm dreaming, that my mind and my body have undergone a separation. The last of the warm air shreds the skin from my forehead and reminds me that a return to isolation is imminent.

The eyes glaze with honey-dewed ecstasy. I must be getting on to the newest of the age-old aphorisms which taught me how all is one and one is all.

DAY #170

THE REFLECTIONS GUILT arousal depth thinking inconsolable hyper-pan-galactic unleavened anaphylactic tree stumps hamper down the HELP ME counselling falling underneath spelling coliseums bedding equality between the magnificent sacks which PLEASE GOD save tight-knit chimeras dispensing lies upon lies upon lies.

Sinking creep hanging sleep-watch in all the ever-lasting MUST HOLD light spreading overload hitting children blue-starred libertine forgiveness, not underneath the skid-stop IT TOGETHER NOT disappear firewalled inconsolable tipping frozen time acceptance dining death charts LONG TO GO collapsing stars together.

Action-pump ceiling orgasms pending dissolution stalagmites down launching stratocumulus NOT MUCH united answer-phone feeling under-fantasised institution pornographic androgynous LEFT OF ME crying wallpaper laxatives.

DAY #229

I WAS GONE for a while, but I've returned to the light. I'm no longer a man. I'm just an entity, sharing this tiny cranium with a million others, displaced from the heavenly homes we once hoped to discover through science, as if science is the answer to the mysteries of our magnified civilisation. It's time to get rarefied, all right. This discovery will change everything forever.

The world, as I left it, is unprepared for this. Will anyone believe it? I don't, and I've seen it. I've seen the light at last. I'm near omniscient. I know everything except the time and my release date. I'm stuck here in this prison with nothing left to discover.

The secret came to me in a sudden bang of inspiration. I knew, then, that every tortuous second of my self-imposed exile in the tank had been magnificent. My mind is a finely honed supercomputer, a machine that could never be recreated.

I exist, have existed and will exist for this one reason only. All of the pain has been worth it. All of the endless, empty hours finally justified by the revolutionary nature of my mission. My journey has been successful. Get ready, world, to be torn apart by the incredible, unforgettable truth.

DAY #240

IN A DARKENED, temperature-controlled room deep beneath the surface of the Earth, two scientists surveyed the scene from behind the visors of their hazmat suits.

"It's a highly sensitive experiment," they'd been warned. "Any discrepancy in visibility, sound, temperature or even oxygen level could kill the professor on his return."

But they weren't prepared for this. The laboratory was so dark that they had to find the sensory deprivation tank based almost entirely on their memory of the floor plan. The two men communicated in silence, transmitting messages from visor to visor.

"Hurry up, Dave," said the more senior of the two. "I'm right beside the pod. Engage the mechanism."

"Roger that." The young scientist held his hand out serenely in the dark, breaking the invisible beam that triggered the release switch. Twenty feet away, the tank opened silently and slowly. It took several minutes until the two halves were fully separated.

Then the machinery began to wind down. First, the breathing, feeding and excrement tubes slowly disengaged from the rest of the mechanism. Then the artificial lungs slowly disconnected themselves, encouraging their patient to breathe the air of the outside world for the first time in nine months.

Slowly but surely, minute after painstaking minute, the machinery untangled itself and returned the pod's occupant to reality. The two scientists stood back and watched as best as they could in the total darkness. Their true eyes saw nothing. They were forced to trust the artificial eyes that the company had installed in their suits six years earlier, when the experiment had first been conceived.

"I'm going in, Dave."

"Yes, sir, I'm right behind you. Let's get it over with and get back to the surface as quickly as we can. This place gives me the creeps."

"If it doesn't scare the hell out of you, it's not real science. Let's do this."

The two scientists edged slowly closer to the pod. In the silence, even the buzzing in their heads sounded like an avalanche. Nils, the senior scientist, was the first to peer into the pod. Dave followed suit shortly afterwards.

"We're picking up nothing from your visor-cams." The message flashed up for both scientists, interrupting their view of the pod. "Don't forget us. We're back here in reality, gentlemen. We need an update."

Nils peered into the pod again.

"We won't be hearing from him again, buddy." Nils paused before continuing. "He's dead."

"It's true," agreed Dave, backing slowly away. "He must've been dead for months. There's nothing left of him but skin and bones."

"Don't be ridiculous." It didn't take a genius to imagine the harsh, stertorous tones of Professor Kaufman at the transmitter. Kaufman was the brains behind the installation, and his only son was the brave soul who'd perished in the pod. "We were picking up life signs less than an hour ago."

"Well, there's nothing down here now, sir. The experiment was a failure. Send in the cleaning crew."

The reply was a long time in coming, and when it finally flashed up on their visors it consisted of just four words: "Return to base immediately."

Before they left, Nils braved one last look into the pod. Its single occupant was barely human, just a shroud of skin and bone in the dark, more like a plaster mould of a skeleton than the living, breathing scientist who'd climbed into the pod at the start of the year. All that remained were the eyes, milky and covered in a phosphorescent dew, but still intact.

Those eyes would haunt the two men forever. Even through the haze of their computerised display, they could read them. It was like looking at the scans of a foetus, only infinitely more terrible. Those eyes – that marbled, eternal serenity, as though they held the wisdom of the ages.

And, as they backtracked towards the high-powered escalator to return to the surface, they saw them everywhere in the dark. With a sharp burst of static, another message appeared on their visors, a message sent by neither the scientists in the field nor their superiors a kilometre above them, a message sent by no scientist on the face of the Earth.

The fear. The legion. The horror. The cosmos.

They Like the Darkness

NATALIE BRIGGS didn't like spiders. In fact, she fucking hated them. From little money spiders to big-ass black widows, creeping into the country in bunches of bananas or lying in wait behind reinforced glass in zoos and safari parks, she hated them.

She hated the way they scuttled sideways across the floor, and how they made their webs in the darkest corners, and how they leapt out at her with their spindly, hairy legs and their evil eyes.

In short, Natalie Briggs was an arachnophobe.

Penny from the office hated spiders too, but her hatred was in a different league. Penny would attack them with a rolled-up newspaper; Natalie needed light artillery.

"Have you tried conkers?" Penny had asked after an arachnid in the bathroom had given Natalie a sleepless night. "It might just be an old wives' tale, but they're meant to keep spiders away if you leave them on the windowsill."

So Natalie tried to find some conkers, but to no avail. The trees had lost their leaves, and all of the conkers had long since disappeared into the sticky pockets of schoolboys, who weren't actually allowed to play with them in case someone lost an eye.

"Maybe it was acorns, anyway," Penny had said. "Or pine cones. Something like that."

So Natalie stocked up on acorns and pine cones, which she bought in bulk in an online auction. She scattered them throughout the house on windowsills and mantelpieces, on shelves and in cupboards, until every room was filled with pine cones and acorns.

But it didn't work, and Natalie still found herself

reduced to a nervous wreck every time one of the eight-legged freaks made its way into her house, to lounge in the lounge or to swallow flies in the dining room.

Natalie had had enough.

She called one exterminator after another and welcomed a seemingly-endless procession of middle-aged men into her house, but it was as though the arachnids knew they were coming. Whenever the bug-men came round, they'd be lucky to find as much as a daddy-long-legs. They set traps, but the spiders seemed to know they were there. For every one that was caught or killed, a dozen seemed to take its place, and eventually the exterminators stopped taking her calls, as did her friends and then her family.

Then, one day, everything changed. Natalie saw an ad in the back of a gossip mag which would change her life forever.

Buy the Foxo 3000, it said. *This revolutionary new ultrasonic device uses the latest technology to repel insects and arachnids. No home is complete without one! Be the envy of your family and friends! Only £59.99 plus postage and packaging! Buy now while stocks last!*

So Natalie bought a Foxo 3000 and waited impatiently for the postman to arrive. When he finally showed three weeks later, she was slapped with a customs charge, but Natalie didn't care. It was worth it.

She hurriedly unpacked the Foxo 3000, plugged it in beside her alarm clock, placed it on her bedside table and turned it on. The ultrasound was ultrasonic, so she couldn't hear it, but she *could* hear a low hum as the machine came to life.

The humming sound soon had the same effect as a light thunderstorm outside the window, of rain hitting the canvas of a tent or of waves lapping at the shore. She found it relaxing, and she was soon unable to sleep without it. And best of all, the spiders disappeared, too.

That was, until the night of the power cut. Natalie was half-asleep in the darkness when she noticed it. The humming of the ultrasound machine faded into nothingness, and the sudden silence was more noticeable than a car backfiring outside the window.

When she opened her eyes, there was nothing but darkness. Her heavy blinds cut off all the light from outside, and even the muted red digits on her alarm clock had disappeared.

Natalie reached for her phone, which she'd left on the bedside table, and she instantly recoiled when she found it. There was movement, an unwelcome scuttling and the tickling sensation of something brushing against her hand. She screamed, withdrew her hand, thought about the situation for a second, and then reached for the phone again.

This time, she managed to pick it up, and she hurriedly unlocked it and booted up the torch app that she used when she was the last person to leave the office and had to go around from room to room in the half-light, checking for ghosts and crackheads.

At first, the beam of light shone in her eyes and blinded her, but she swung the phone around to scan the room and immediately wished that she hadn't.

She saw spiders, thousands upon thousands of them, spiders of all shapes and sizes, all swarming all over each other. They covered the walls, the carpet, the curtains and the ceiling. They covered the bedside table and the duvet. They fell down from the ceiling and landed in her hair. They swarmed beneath the sheets and covered her arms and legs. They were fucking everywhere.

Natalie opened her mouth to scream, but no sound came out. The last thing she saw was the last thing she ever wanted to see.

***

Every day was different to the forensic pathologists, but that rainy Tuesday in February took the biscuit. It should've been routine. A woman in her early forties had been found dead in her apartment of a suspected heart attack. An open and shut case, quite literally.

But when they made the first incision, they found no internal organs. Instead, the torso was filled with thousands of tiny spiders, living in her hollowed-out corpse like it was a cupboard beneath the stairs.

They like the darkness.

The Sun Came Out

THE SUN CAME OUT, and it was fabulous.

It was a horrible, grey day, the perfect day for a funeral or the death of a monarch. The clouds were mean motherfuckers, bad dudes to cross. They banded together like lads on tour and floated around on the breeze bringing misery to the people on the ground below them.

And when the sun came out, the clouds didn't like that – not one little bit. But the sun didn't care. The sun was just the sun, and that's what he liked to say to them.

"I can't change who I am," he said. "Just like how you can't change what you are."

"But we *can* change what we are," the clouds said, and they rumbled and thundered and changed from wispy cirrocumulus to big, black cumulonimbus clouds, badder than a cat with a bird in its mouth. The clouds opened themselves up and rained down on the people below them. They unfurled umbrellas and turned on their windscreen wipers, but the rain was relentless and unsentimental.

"Stop it!" shouted the sun. "You guys are horrible. Why did you ruin everyone's day like that?"

"We're clouds," they replied. "We can't change who we are. And you can't change who you are."

"But I've always been this way," the sun replied. "It's how I was born, 4.6 billion years ago."

"Preposterous," the clouds growled. "What about the moon? She's beautiful. Check out the craters on that."

"I'm not into craters," the sun said. "She's not my type."

"Phwoar," one of the younger clouds said, floating himself into the shape of a crudely-drawn penis. "I'd love to stick it up her dark side."

The other clouds shot him a dirty look and whispered, "Shut up, Terry," in a rustling susurrus. Then they looked at the sun again. "What do you mean? How is she not your type?"

"She's a she," said the sun. "I've always had a thing for other stars."

"That's not natural," the clouds replied.

"Of course, it's natural," the sun said. "I'm the sun. I'm the most natural thing there is."

The clouds had no retort to this.

"I thought you'd understand," the sun said. "After all, you're clouds. Some of you are black, and some of you are white. Some of you are big, and some of you are small."

"We're different," the clouds said. "But we're not perverse. We're not like you. We don't want you around here anymore."

The sun was sad, and he was glad when the Earth's rotation took the clouds away and gave him a different view of a different country with different people living differently.

Meanwhile, the clouds had a meeting. They gathered together and rained and rained and rained while they tried to decide what to do.

The following day, after the Earth had completed its rotation, the sun found itself face-to-face with the clouds again. The sun was still fabulous, but the clouds were grey and angry. They were clumped closely together, thundering and rumbling loudly, their voices a harmony of dissent like Nazis marching outside a mosque. Terry was holding a little sign that said, "Down with this sort of thing."

The thundering got louder and the heavens opened, and the people down below got out their umbrellas again. But if the clouds hoped to stop the sun from shining, they were in for a disappointment. The sun was proud to be who he was, so he shone even brighter than ever.

Then they heard the people on the ground. They were laughing and clapping and pointing at the sky. They were whistling and giving balloons to their children and dancing in the street as they looked up at the clouds and the sun on the other side of them.

They were clapping because the sun's light was piercing through the clouds and the rain was refracting it and bending it into the shape of a double rainbow.

The clouds growled and turned back to the sun. "Stop it," they demanded. "Stop what you're doing at once."

"I can't," the sun replied. "I'm not doing anything. I'm just being myself. I can't help it if you don't like the way that you perceive me."

The clouds rumbled again, but the rain slowed to a stop and melted away down the drains and into the rivers. The rotation of the Earth took the clouds and the people away again, and the sun was sad to see them go.

The people on the ground looked up at the clouds, which stuck around into the night and the following morning. They shook their fists at them.

"I wish those bloody clouds would disappear," the people said.

A Stone's Throw[1]

IT WAS A DULL October evening. Shrill winds blew over the Chilterns and a fine mist of rain flew in the faces of the patrons who'd braved the darkness to show their haggard faces in the George and Dragon public house. It was the year of our Lord 1780, and despite the foul weather, business was booming.

Suki, the teenage barmaid, wished it wasn't. The landlord didn't own her – he'd hired her from a pool of willing candidates because she had a beautiful singing voice and the kind of awkward confidence that the job called for – but sometimes it felt like he did. It was always "fill this" and "empty that". He sometimes sent her down into the cellar to track down a special bottle for the well-off visitors that stopped in as they traversed the rugged landscape. She hated it down there. Sometimes she thought she heard voices.

On this particular night, the George and Dragon was short-staffed because John Woodynge had fallen from his horse and broken his ankle. Old John was the pub's owner, a member of the gentry who'd fallen on hard times and established himself in that peaceful corner of Buckinghamshire. Unable to walk, and ordered by the physician to take to his bed until the bones started to fuse back together, he'd left Suki, and her brother Thomas, in charge of the place.

---

[1] Originally published in *Local Haunts* (ed. Regina St. Clare).

But Thomas was as much use to Suki as a chastity belt would have been to Molly Forde, the wretched whore who plied her wares and her body under the eaves of the stables when the Dragon's drinkers went out to check on their horses. She wasn't allowed inside the pub, a respectable establishment, unless she was invited inside by one of the patrons and led into one of the private rooms that travellers called home when they were passing through.

"More ale, wench!"

Suki sighed, adjusted her dress and carried a flagon across to the three young men who'd been sitting by the fire since the sun had gone down.

"I'll have none of that, George Barber," she said, filling the young man's cup while avoiding his eyes. "I knew your mother, you know. She wouldn't stand for this."

"Aye," George replied. "Perhaps it's a good thing she's with the Lord."

"Oh, damn the Lord," said the lad to his right. His name was Harry Baker. "It's not the Sabbath. The Lord can wait."

"The only Lord around here is old Lord Dashwood," said the third. Suki turned to face him, a scarlet flush stealing its way onto her face.

"And I'll have none of your blasphemy, either, James Smith," Suki said. "I know your mother, too. Need I —"

But she was interrupted as Jim scowled and reached around to pinch her on the backside. Suki flinched, spilling ale onto the table and into his lap.

"I hope you're going to clean that up," Barber said.

"Oh, go hang," Suki said. "I have other customers to serve."

And she did, too. Despite the inclement weather, and the fact that there were a couple of competing inns in the village, the George and Dragon was ever-popular. It was where the labourers went to relax after a hard day's work on the fields.

Suki preferred to listen than to speak, and it meant that she got to hear most of the gossip in the village. The George and Dragon was the closest thing they had to a newspaper.

There was a sudden gust of wind and the squall of a small-scale tempest as the door opened and a stranger walked into the pub. The punters paused their conversations and looked up briefly before turning their eyes away from the door and back to the faces of their drinking buddies or the playing cards on the booze-stained tables. The breeze caught the candles and blew a third of them out.

"Can a man get a bite to eat in this godforsaken village?"

The stranger's voice was well-educated with a hint of something almost foreign and exotic. He was young, though not as young as the three boys from the village, and he had a short mess of unruly brown hair and piercing blue eyes that shone with a fierce intensity. He had a good-natured smile on his face and was dressed well in the luxurious vestments of the wealthy. His eyes alighted on the various tables in the semi-gloom before settling on little Suki, better known by her elders as Susan Keane, the daughter of one of Lord Dashwood's liverymen.

"You there," he said. "Oh, my dear, what brings you to a place like this? No, no, never mind that. What have you got in your pantry?"

Suki readjusted her dress again and forced the biggest smile she could muster onto her tired, duty-worn face. She spoke to the man as she walked over to the fire, lit a piece of kindling and used it to re-illuminate the snuffed candles. It was a job that she did so often that she wasn't even aware she was doing it.

"If it please you, sir," she said, "we've got bread, mutton and cheese. We may also have some pigeon, some eggs and some veal."

"If it please me?" he repeated with mock politeness.

"And is it good?"

"I do say it's the best eating this side of the Wye."

Someone laughed into his pint, and someone else was talking loudly about a highwayman who was rumoured to be at work in the roads over by Aylesbury. Around them, the drinkers were still drinking and the talkers were still talking, but he was a stranger to these parts and the locals couldn't help stealing the occasional glance.

"I'll take a plate of whatever you can give me," the stranger said. "And brandy. Bring me brandy."

"As you wish."

Thomas Keane had been at the bar, supping on a drink of his own and observing the situation. It was he who descended the steps to the cellar to bring out the brandy. He had no fear of the darkness. Suki was left to busy herself in the pantry and then in the kitchen. She emerged several minutes later with a platter for the visitor, who'd seated himself in a corner and who was already smoking shag tobacco from an ornate pipe.

"Here you are, kind sir," Suki said. "Forgive me for prying, but do you have good coin?"

"Aye," the man said. "I have coin enough. Tell me, what do they call you?"

Suki adjusted her dress again, for the fortieth time that evening, and said, "They call me Suki."

"Suki?" the man repeated, thoughtfully. "'Tis a beautiful name for sure."

He paused for a moment to take another lungful of the tobacco plant. Then he said, "You've no cause to ask for my name, but I shall tell you anyway. I am Charles Dashwood. Perhaps you've heard of my uncle Francis."

"Lord Dashwood," Suki murmured.

"Aye," the stranger repeated. "The very same. See how I sign my name."

He reached into the pockets of his long coat and drew out an old, stained-looking letter. The signature was scrawled in black ink in a large, untidy hand.

"Please, sir," Suki said. "I can't read."

Dashwood paused for a moment and then started laughing, gulping up huge lungsful of the inn's stale air.

"My dear," he said. "I might have known. Then you must keep that piece of paper, and you must one day learn to read it so you can see that my name is what I say it is. I say it again. I am Charles Dashwood, and my uncle is Lord Francis."

Suki had heard of Lord Francis Dashwood, of course. He owned the whole village, though he hadn't been seen in public since before she'd reached womanhood. That didn't matter. Suki had heard the tales.

It was an open secret throughout the village that Lord Dashwood was the leader of the Hell-Fire Club. Dashwood, along with a number of other preeminent men from Buckinghamshire and nearby Berkshire, used to meet at Medmenham Abbey, on the banks of the River Thames, for nights of drunkenness, debauchery and devil-worship. Their motto was "Fay ce que voudras", which meant "do as you please." It was said that Sir Dashwood himself was the most blasphemous of all. He'd administered the sacrament to his tame baboon. Later, he'd created work for the people of the village by having them hollow-out the Hell-Fire Caves, barely a stone's throw away from the George and Dragon.

And then the Hell-Fire Caves became the new home of the Hell-Fire Club, and that was when things became very strange indeed. They – the same they who drank themselves into stupors in the front room of the George and Dragon – said that the caves were a breeding ground of moral turpitude. The men who'd helped to build it said that devils and demons were carved into the walls and that they moved around when no one was looking. There was a stream somewhere, far beneath the surface, which they called the Styx. And deep down there in the darkness, there was a temple, located directly beneath the church and its golden ball, which graced the hilltop and dominated the skyline.

"I've been down there, you know," Dashwood said, as though he'd read and interrupted her thoughts. "The temple. It's hell, quite literally. Heaven above, hell below. They worshipped Christ on high and the devil in the temple beyond the Styx."

"You barely look old enough, sir," Suki replied.

"Oh no, no," he said, waving a hand dismissively and coming dangerously close to sending his drink tumbling to the floor. "Not to one of the ceremonies."

There were rumours about the ceremonies, too. The members of the Hell-Fire Club were said to have taken young girls down there to "sacrifice" their virginity. That was what had happened to Molly Forde. Suki shivered.

"I shouldn't like to think of such things."

"Then you won't want to hear about the ghost of Paul Whitehead," Dashwood said. "More's the pity."

"Sir, I've heard tell of Mr. Whitehead," Suki said.

"And pray tell me what you've heard."

"They say he was a poet," Suki replied.

"That he was," Dashwood said. "And like all poets, he was a madman and a lecher. He was also the steward of the Hell-Fire Club. He interrogated the new recruits and scored them on their ability to swallow port and claret. He was also my uncle's lover."

Suki made the sign of the cross and darted her eyes nervously around, searching for her brother and alighting only on the three boys from the village, who were watching the conversation and quaffing their ale in near-silence.

"It's been six years since Whitehead passed," Dashwood

continued. "And my uncle's health has been deteriorating ever since. Did you know that he left my uncle his heart?"

"His heart?"

"His heart," Dashwood repeated. "He left it to my uncle in his will. His body was buried in Teddingham, but his heart... his heart was buried in the depths of the mausoleum."

Suki shivered again. Then she took herself – and Charles Dashwood – by surprise. She started to sing.

"My lodging, it is on the cold ground," she began, her voice wavering as she strained to hit the higher notes. "And oh! Very hard is my fare. But that which troubles me most is the unkindness of my dear. Yet still I cry, 'O turn, love.' And prithee, love turn to me, for thou art the man that I long for, and alack! What remedy?"

Her face flushed, and she readjusted her dress, clearly uncomfortable on the receiving end of Dashwood's intense blue eyes. Dashwood smiled at her and said, "I beg of you, please continue."

"I'll crown thee with a garland of straw then," she sang, "and I'll marry thee with a rush ring. My frozen hopes shall thaw, then, and merrily will we sing. O turn to me, my dear love, and prithee turn to me. For thou art the man that alone canst procure my liberty."

"I believe there's one more verse, my girl."

"Aye, you speak the truth," Suki said. She raised her voice a little and continued, "But if thou wilt harden thy heart still and be deaf to my pitiful moan, then I must endure the smart still and tumble in straw alone. Yet still I cry, 'O turn love, and prithee, love, turn to me! For thou art the man that alone art the cause of my misery.'"

When Suki finished, there was silence. Then Dashwood began to clap, breaking the silence, and then suddenly everyone else in the George and Dragon was clapping, too. It started slowly, swelled and then overflowed. It wasn't unusual for Suki to sing, but it was unusual for the punters to take an interest.

"Bravo!" Dashwood cried. "Marvellous! Fantastic! Spectacular!"

"You're too kind, good sir."

"Sir? Bah."

By this time, Dashwood had finished his food and was towards the bottom of his second cup of brandy. Thomas Keane was watching on impatiently.

"The meal pleased me," Dashwood said. "But your company pleased me more. Alas! I must move on. I'm London-bound, and there are men in the city who desire my company. Suki, Suki, Suki. I'm pleased to have made your acquaintance."

And with that, Charles Dashwood quaffed the rest of his brandy, doffed his cap at the other drinkers and took his leave of the George and Dragon. Suki was left to clean his table. Then her brother sent her down into the cellars to bring up more firewood. The fire was blazing and the hearth already held more wood than the fire needed. It wasn't a necessary task; it was a punishment.

And while she was down there, the boys made their plan.

"Snooty Miss Suki," said George Barber. "Too good for the likes of us."

"Says she," Smith added.

"I say we teach her a lesson," said Baker.

"Yes!" Barber said. "But how?"

"We write her a letter," Smith said. "We send her a message from the kindly Charles Dashwood, inviting her first to the Hell-Fire Caves and from there, to London."

"Nay," Barber said. "Your plan can never work. What know you of the world of letters?"

"'Tis true," Smith replied, "I'm not a scholar. But Baker is."

James Smith and George Barber turned their troubled faces to Harry Baker, who had a glint in his eye and who was emptying the last of his ale into the ever-thirsty maw of his mouth.

"Bring me paper," he said. "Bring me a quill and some ink. Bring me ale and cheese and bread."

"Not here, you fool," Barber said. "Let us away. We'll write the note at my house and have my sister deliver it."

And so the plan was formed, and sure enough less than an hour later, little Cathy Barber had braved the winds and rain, under threat of a bruised arm from her brother, to deliver the letter. As instructed, she handed it over to Suki, who was mopping down one of the tables with a piece of rag.

"A letter?" Suki said, incredulously. "For me? Pray tell me who it's from?"

But Cathy just shook her head and scuttled back out into the night.

Suki was illiterate, but there were people who weren't, and an old man who'd sat quietly in the corner, smoking a pipe and drinking his mead while staring off into the distance, was kind enough to do the honours.

"Let me see now," the man said, shifting his position to hold the letter up to the flickering light of the candles, which Suki had re-lit after Cathy Barber had taken her leave. "Ah, yes. I have it."

"What does it say?"

"Patience, dear," the man said. Then he cleared his throat, held the letter up to the light again and began to read aloud. "It says, 'Suki, my dear. I find your voice enchanting. It won't leave my mind. Your natural beauty is like a ray of light in the darkness. Your hands are as delicate as bone china and you smell more heaven-sent than the fragrances of foreign lands. I myself am no masterpiece, but I have wealth and status. I can show you the world, if you'll let me. I'm asking you, Suki, to become my wife. If your answer is positive, meet me at the mouth of the Hell-Fire Caves at midnight in your best dress. My coachman will bear us hence to London, where we shall be married. Yours most affectionately, Charles Dashwood.'"

When the old man finished reading, Suki dropped to the floor in a dead faint.

She was woken by her brother, who was applying a damp rag to her forehead and muttering a catechism beneath his breath. When she awoke, she sat bolt upright and her hand flew up to her mouth.

"What is the hour?" she demanded

"Why, it's an hour until midnight," her brother replied.

"Only an hour!" Suki said. "Then I must prepare at once!"

"I don't know about this, Suki," her brother said. "I have half a mind to stop you."

"You just try," she replied, and she flashed him a look of such ferocity that he backed away a half-step before he caught himself. He opened his mouth to say something and then closed it again. "That's what I thought. Nothing can stand in the way of love."

And so Suki dashed away to the house that she shared with her brother, their father and their elderly aunt, a spinster who was already asleep and who would remain unaware of her niece's fate until she woke the following morning. Suki washed her face in a pail of water, dragged a comb through her thick, unruly hair and then took her best dress out from where it lay in a wooden chest. It was a beautiful dress, one that she'd inherited from her late mother and which her aunt had helped her to modify to suit her smaller stature. Sewn from fine white silks, the materials alone would have cost her several months' wages from the George and Dragon. No one in the family seemed to know where the gown had originally come from, and that just made it the more magical.

At the appointed hour, little Suki headed back out into the cold and wandered along the lonely dirt path that led to the caves. The wind was still howling around her, and while the rain had stopped falling from the sky, it still remained in great puddles that she struggled to skirt around in the darkness. From somewhere in the distance, a dog barked. It was the top of the hour when she arrived, and there was no sign of anyone else in her immediate environment.

Suki waited. And then she waited some more. But Charles Dashwood never came.

Instead, three others did.

It was close to one o'clock in the morning when Harry Baker, James Smith and George Barber arrived. They'd been further in their cups and had lost track of the time. When they talked, they overlapped each other and spoke with slurred voices.

"We fooled you, snooty Suki!"

"Not good enough for the likes of us?"

"Your knight in shining armour never loved you!"

"You're nothing but the next Molly Forde!"

"A pox on you and your good-for-nothing brother!"

The jeers continued, but Suki stopped hearing them. Instead, all she could hear was her own heartbeat as a cold, hard rage took over her. She stooped, bending her knees awkwardly to lower herself in her dress, and she picked up a handful of stones. She picked one out, the sharpest, most jagged-looking one, and pitched it through the air, scoring a glancing blow across Jim Smith's neck. She threw another and then another until she'd depleted the ammo in her hand.

She was stooping again to pick up some more by the time that the boys had figured out what was happening.

"Let's get her!"

"Throw them back at her!"

But the boys needed no encouragement on that front. Harry Baker was already on his knees, scooping up a handful of stones of his own. This being the ground outside the mouth of the Hell-Fire Caves, there wasn't exactly a shortage. Then the other two boys were beside him, and soon the air was thick with stones that fell down around them in a hail of pain. Smith took the brunt of the blows, partly because he was the taller of the three and partly because the other two were using him for cover.

And then there was a shrill cry, a heavy thud and sudden silence. The three boys looked at each other uneasily and ran in the direction of the sound. Little Suki Keane was lying face down amongst the rocks. She wasn't moving.

"What happened?"

"What do you think?"

"Is she breathing?"

Baker kneeled by her side and gave her a brief once over, but he didn't really know what he was looking for. He found the cause, though. One of the rocks had caught her a good one on the side of the head, rending a gash across her temple and sending her tumbling to the ground. It looked as though she'd hit the other side of her head when she reached it.

"Well, is she breathing?"

"Give the man some space!"

"I have no idea," Baker said. "But I don't think so. We need to get out of here."

"What about Suki?"

"What about her?"

"Should we take her back with us?"

"No," Baker said. "It's too risky. Someone might see us. We'll leave her here, at the mouth of the cave. If she comes to, she can walk home. And if she doesn't…well, no one need know that we were here."

And so the plan was formed, and Baker removed a knife from his pocket and cut each of them on the palms of their hands. They pressed their hands together in turn to seal their oath and to promise silence. Then they went home.

In the morning, a sad sun dawned over West Wycombe and the rains came down like the rage of a vengeful god. Little Suki wasn't found until the afternoon, when a couple of children discovered her body during a game of hide and seek. She was soaked through to the bone, her china white skin and her best dress making her look more like a ghost than a physical being. The children raced into the village and started screaming for help, and within half an hour, the bells were ringing and the whole community had poured out into what passed for a village square.

When it was discovered that little Suki had sustained an injury to the side of her head, the atmosphere turned sour and the violence threatened to spill over into an outright lynch mob. And to begin with, there was only one suspect on everyone's minds.

"It's that no-good Charles Dashwood," Thomas Keane shouted, beside himself with grief. That afternoon, he'd been taken to see his sister's body, and the guilt and the rage had almost taken him to an early grave along with her. "He lured my sister out there and then–"

But he couldn't finish the awful thought.

And so with suspicions on Charles Dashwood, Lord Francis Dashwood himself was summoned from his repose. He arrived as dusk was beginning to settle, borne to the village in the back of a cab. Suki's own father, the liveryman to Lord Francis, had overcome his grief to fulfil his duty, bearing the elderly landowner into his village to dispense with justice. Lord Francis was wearing his formal robes, and they served to offset the sickness and the sallowness in his face. He might have been old, he might have been on the verge of death, but he was still in charge of the land on which they stood.

"Begin at the beginning," Lord Francis said. He was reclining in the back of his cab and leaning out of the window to talk to the locals. "I want to know everything."

And so Thomas Keane started at the beginning, and Lord Francis listened to the boy with rapt attention as he recounted the events of the night before. When he got to the arrival of Charles Dashwood, his voice cracked and he couldn't continue. But that didn't matter. Lord Francis had held his hand up for silence.

"Charles Dashwood?" he murmured. "There's no such man."

"But he said he was your nephew."

"Then he lied," Lord Francis said. "I have no heir. I have no family capable of producing one. Tell me, lad, what did this man look like?"

Thomas Keane wasn't one for stories and so his description of the man was fairly rudimentary and could have matched half the men in the village. It was augmented by a few words from the pub's drinkers, but their memories were hazy at best and not to be trusted in the sober light of day.

"This man could have been anyone," Lord Francis said. "Have you any other clues to his identity?"

"No," Thomas said, but then he seemed to remember something and to collect himself. "Wait! There is one thing…"

"Go on?"

"He produced a note with his signature on it," Thomas

said. "It's amongst my sister's belongings. No, hold! There was a second note, too. The one that summoned my sister to her death."

"Bring me these notes," said Lord Francis, and Thomas Keane departed at once and returned with the two notes of which he'd spoken. He handed them in through the coach's window, and Lord Francis buried his nose amongst the papers.

"Hmm," he said, at length. "It seems we have a problem. These two letters were written by two different hands. This one, the newer one which summoned your sister to the caves, was written by a younger hand, a steady hand. This other…well, I seem to recognise it. It may be signed in the name of Charles Dashwood, but this is the hand of someone else entirely. This is the hand of Paul Whitehead. But Paul has been dead these six years. How is it possible?"

"Perhaps he wrote the note before he passed."

"Perhaps," Lord Francis said. "But why, then, did he sign with a fictitious name?"

"I have no answer for you, sir."

"This vexes me," Lord Francis said. He looked even paler than he had when he'd first arrived. He rubbed a handkerchief across his forehead to mop the sweat off. "I must consider this in private. This news is troubling."

He looked troubled, too. In fact, he looked as though he'd seen a ghost.

The next witness to be called was little Cathy Barber, but her brother had already put the fear of God into her and instructed her about the lie she was to tell. By now, Cathy had figured out the truth, but she both loved and feared her brother and was willing to perjure herself to save his neck. When they asked who'd given her the letter, she answered that a tall, distinguished gentleman had handed it to her from a cab window and asked her to deliver it with all haste.

And there, with no further evidence available, the investigation stalled.

Unfortunately for little Suki, justice was difficult in the shadow of the Chiltern Hills, and while efforts were made to track down Charles Dashwood, or whoever he was, they came to nothing. There was no report of him in the other inns, and nor had he appeared in London's society. Stranger still, Molly Forde swore blind that she'd been standing in the stables all night, plying her wares so to speak, and that she'd seen the man neither enter nor leave the George and Dragon.

Meanwhile, life in the village seemed to get back to normal, at least for most people. For James Smith, however, life was anything but. The day after Suki's body was discovered, he came down with a fever which left him sweating despite the chill. Even with his bed placed close to the fire, the chill refused to die and before another twenty-four hours had passed, it had taken over the rest of his body. It looked like he was losing the battle.

There was no doctor in the village, and so one was brought in from Great Missenden. It didn't take him long to make his diagnosis.

"The boy has an infection," the doctor said. "A bad one, a malady of the blood. Tell me, what caused this cut on the boy's neck?"

But no one in George's family could answer, and the two boys who shared his secret weren't permitted to stand at his bedside.

Jim's condition continued to deteriorate, even with all of the medicine that the doctor gave him, and the passage of a couple of days was enough to seal his fate. He died on a Tuesday, less than a week after little Suki passed, and he was buried on the Friday. His family couldn't afford to pay for the burial, but the undertaker agreed to do it for free.

George Barber was the next to die. He'd heard about

what happened to Jim and thought that he could outrun death by stealing a horse and riding it at full speed for the capital. Instead, he'd been captured along the way, brought back to West Wycombe and held before a judge. His family had hoped for leniency, especially because it was his first offence, but he was out of luck and ended up in front of old Justice Stonehouse. He was known by the unpleasant sobriquet of "the Noose Judge," a nickname that he'd earned through his unremitting habit of passing down the harshest of sentences.

For George Barber, no exception was made. He was sentenced to be hanged from the neck until he was dead, and the sentence was carried out forthwith. His final words, which were only heard by the hangman as he pulled the lever to open the trapdoor, were, "We killed her."

Harry Baker, the writer of the letter and the architect of little Suki's doom, lived a long and healthy life, but it was unclear whether he was even aware of it. The poor boy lost his mind and lived out the rest of his days in a sanatorium, where he was the subject of an endless stream of medical procedures that culminated in a botched lobotomy that silenced his hand and his tongue for good. He grew old there and was eventually buried beneath the oaks out back after no one claimed his body.

Lord Francis passed too, although he held on for another year as his health continued to deteriorate. Little Suki's death seemed to have a harsh effect on him, for he retreated to his manor and rarely ventured forth into the grounds. Stranger still, there were rumours in the village that an apparition, purported to be the ghost of Paul Whitehead, had been spotted wandering the grounds. Suki's father saw him several times, and it was said that the shock combined with the grief to push him over the edge. He was found dead one morning in the stables with the horses that he so loved. He reeked of cheap spirits, but there was no sign of whatever had killed him. It was written off as an accident, but the gossips called it a suicide. His meagre assets were quickly claimed by the crown, and the church refused to bury his body in sacred ground. Instead, he was buried without ceremony at a crossroads so that if his spirit came back, it wouldn't know which direction to head in.

With time, life in the village went back to normal, although stories started to spread of the ghost of a teenage bride in a white dress who could be seen in the darkness of the Hell-Fire Caves by those brave enough to venture there after midnight. There were few who met that criteria.

Time passed, and the eighteenth century rolled into the nineteenth century and then the twentieth. Little Suki was forgotten about, first because of the slow march of time and later by the sheer number of young men from the village who gave their lives in the first and second world wars. Meanwhile, the country changed around them, and the horse-drawn carriages were replaced by motor vehicles while television antennas sprung up on the sides of the rural houses.

In the 1960s, an American called Jerry Pascale was visiting the area. Pascale had heard Suki's story from the lips of one of the perpetual old men who still drank themselves silly in the George and Dragon. The locals said that he braved the caves at midnight and returned to his hotel room disappointed, only to have a visitation in the night. He woke to feel clammy, ice cold hands on his forehead, and as he slowly rose to full consciousness, they passed along and reached his neck. He started to choke, and that was when movement came back to him and he was able to reach across to turn his bedside lamp on.

The feeling of the hands disappeared along with the darkness, and he sat upright in his bed for a while, turning it all over on his head and trying to figure out what was real and what was nightmare. Eventually, he turned the light off and tried to settle back in again. He'd been lying there for a couple of minutes when he spotted something over by the door. It was a light, like the light from his lamp but at a fraction of the size, though it grew bigger as he watched it. It was opaque and pearly, hovering in the air like a will-o-the-wisp.

Again, Pascale turned the lamp on, and the light vanished only to reappear once more when the room was plunged into darkness. By now, he was wide awake, and while he felt the fear of the devil at his heels, he picked up the courage to approach it. As he got closer, it grew brighter, until an eerie figure in white was illuminated. It looked like a teenage girl who was wearing an old-fashioned dress. Something from the 1700s, perhaps.

As soon as he reached the girl, he was overtaken by a wave of cold that left him breathless. His limbs were heavy, too heavy for him to hold them up, and he felt himself collapse to his knees. The light grew brighter, and he crawled backwards like a crab towards the safety of his bedside lamp. When he switched the lamp back on, the apparition was gone. Pascale kept the light on for the rest of the night, but he didn't get back to sleep again. He left early in the morning and vowed never to return.

The room hasn't been slept in since, and even the staff at the George and Dragon don't like to go in there, especially at night. There are rumours of a ghost that haunts it. A ghost in a flowing white gown.

When the Mirror Clouds[2]

JAY MASON *hated* his reflection. And it wasn't just *his* reflection; he hated all of them. He'd been afraid of them for as long as he could remember. When he was six years old, he'd been riding high on his father's shoulders when he caught sight of the passenger-side mirror of a passing car and tried so hard to get away from it that he tumbled to the floor and broke his collarbone. But he knew better than to scream for his mother. His father didn't like that, not one little bit.

"Cut it out," his father would say. "Stop being such a baby." Truth was, at six years old, he *was* still a baby. He sucked his thumb, wet his bed, and would've pressed his face to his mother's breast if she was still around. But she wasn't.

Jay's mother had disappeared not long after he learned to walk. She hadn't walked out on him, she hadn't died, and she hadn't even gone missing. She'd just fallen off the face of the Earth. His father, distrustful of the police to begin with, had waited a couple of weeks before reporting it, a fact that the prosecutors had gleefully latched on to. But with no evidence – and no body – they'd been unable to press charges. That hadn't stopped the neighbours from arriving at their own conclusions, though. Jay's father was a murderer in their eyes, if not in the eyes of the law.

---

[2] Originally published in *Subject Verb Object: An Anthology of New Writing*. I was given the prompt "Jay reached behind the mirror."

It was around that time that *The Weirdness* set in. The old man became a recluse, too proud to move away but too tired to go outside and risk the scorn of the rest of the neighbourhood.

He worked from home whenever he could. When he had to go into the office, he kept his head down and tried to avoid his colleagues. Then the house began to change. Jay's father insisted on keeping the curtains closed at all times and grew out the hedges so they blocked the view of the yard. He only used the back door and covered all the mirrors in the house with bedsheets and towels, eventually upgrading to curtains which could be opened and closed to suit him. In the end, he learned to shave by feel alone, and the curtains remained closed and collected dust, oil and bacteria.

The Weirdness followed Jay to university. His housemates discovered the foible and started surprising him by jumping out with pocket mirrors whenever he least expected it. That all came to an end after someone pushed him too far by planting a large, free-standing mirror in front of his door. When Jay opened it up, he put his fist straight through it, ending up in the emergency room with nine stitches.

After that, everyone knew about *The Weirdness*, but nobody mentioned it. He'd graduated six years earlier and now worked as a counsellor – although he called himself a therapist – in a bustling commuter town. He lived in a maisonette with only one mirror to worry about.

He was running late to work again. Jay couldn't drive because he couldn't look in the rear-view mirror, and the busses were never on time. Unfortunately, the busses were also all he could afford.

His patient was waiting for him when he arrived, a middle-aged man with self-confidence issues and an unfair dose of Asperger's. He was followed by a high-strung businesswoman with a nervous tick and a shopping addiction, and then an ex-junkie who'd successfully kicked the habit but still needed to deal with the issues that caused it.

The next patient was a no-show, so Jay ate his lunch and caught up with some paperwork. In the afternoon, he had sessions with a couple more patients and a catch-up meeting with his supervisor. Then he hopped on the bus again and buried his face in a book so he didn't have to deal with the mirrors in the furniture shops on the high street.

That evening, after a disappointing dinner and a bad horror film which lived up to its lacklustre reviews, Jay went for a shower. The hot water filled the room with steam, which was lucky. He noticed what was wrong as soon as he stepped out of the cubicle, before he had a chance to wrap himself in a towel.

The curtains around the mirror had opened, seemingly of their own accord. He knew they'd been closed when he entered the room, but now they were hanging apart like two corpses in the breeze. They were moving, *dancing*, and Jay could hear a rustling susurrus, whispers from another world. The mirror was steamed over, dull enough for Jay to face his fear and to take a closer look. Something was beginning to form there, little shadows taking shape. Jay shuddered and pulled the curtains back across.

He slept badly that night, nauseated by childhood dreams and memories, nightmares about mirrors and reflections. He thought about calling in sick and decided against it, but he was sent home anyway, after a complaint from one of the patients. Dr. Mortimer, Jay's boss and the head of the facility, called him into his office for a quick chat.

"Sit down, please," he instructed, and Jay obeyed the order. "This won't take long."

Dr. Mortimer sat down heavily on the other side of the

mahogany desk and pinched the bridge of his nose. "Okay," he said. "I'll try to keep this brief. Now, as you know, we strive to reach the highest standards of excellence here at Sunnyvale. Because of that, we only hire the very best, and we expect our staff to have their heads in the game at all times. I think you know where this is going, Jay."

Jay shrugged and said, "Does it have something to do with Miss Rowbotham?"

"It has *everything* to do with Miss Rowbotham," Dr. Mortimer replied. "She made a complaint after your session."

"What did she say?" Jay asked.

"She said she felt like the roles had reversed and that you barely let her get a word in. Something about mirrors and reflections. She used the word 'obsession' and said that you attacked her. Is that true?"

"I wouldn't say that," Jay protested. "If anything, she attacked *me*. She pulled out a compact, and I knocked it out of her hands."

Dr. Mortimer sighed and pinched the bridge of his nose again. It had been a long, long day. "Listen, Jay, I appreciate you being honest with me, and so I'm going to offer you the same courtesy. The bottom line is this: this whole mirror thing is getting out of hand. I think you should take a little time off and try to get your head straight. Just a couple of weeks to begin with. And perhaps you should seek some professional help yourself."

Jay nodded meekly and agreed to seek help. He thought about *The Weirdness.* He thought about it long and hard, and he shuddered. Dr. Mortimer dismissed him brusquely as his telephone rang and he reached across the desk to answer it.

That evening, Jay heard whispers from the mirror again, although this time the curtains stayed shut. The voices were quiet at first, just at the edge of his hearing. But without really seeming to, they started to grow louder and more intense until he could hear different timbres and tonalities. He could hear men and women, children and adults, a distant barking and meowing. He thought he heard his own name, but he wasn't sure. He even thought he heard a scream, or maybe it was the distant whistle of a far-off train. Whatever it was, he didn't like it, so he skipped his shower and used a coin to lock the door from the outside.

He didn't get much sleep. He had nightmares about glass and polished metal, bad dreams about mirrors and fevers. And when he climbed out of bed to use the bathroom, the curtains were hanging wide open.

Jay reached behind the mirror and tried to take it down, but the damn thing wouldn't budge. He caught a glimpse of his purple face and the bulging tendons in his wrists and upper arms as he yanked at it, and then he screamed and instinctively lashed out, slamming his fist into the shiny surface and spreading a cobweb of cracks across it. A couple of glittering shards embedded themselves into his knuckles, drawing droplets of blood and sending his stomach lurching. He dragged the curtains back across the mirror and fled the bathroom in terror, then spent the rest of the day pulling glass from his knuckles with a pair of tweezers.

That night, he worried himself to sleep with old superstitions of seven years' bad luck. He slept badly, but he managed to grab a couple of hours and woke up feeling strangely zen-like and refreshed. Over his first cup of coffee, he resolved to deal with *The Weirdness* once and for all.

Jay made himself a spot of breakfast and then headed into the bathroom. He could hear the whispers again, louder and more clearly than before, but the curtains remained mercifully closed. He took a deep breath and opened them, then gasped.

The broken surface had repaired itself with not a crack

to show it had ever been damaged. Jay shook his head slowly and checked his knuckles. They were still battered, bruised and a little bloody, quite clearly showing the signs of the day before. If it wasn't for that, he might've thought he was going crazy.

Jay set his fear aside to take a closer look at the mirror. It seemed to swirl with subtle shadows, dancing slowly on top of his ashen-faced reflection. He saw shapes and letters, blurred faces from the past registering dimly like spots of light from staring at the sun for too long. The whispers intensified into a chorus of voices, all chanting his name. Then the voices converged into one, cycling through pitches and accents until they settled on the single voice of someone he could barely remember.

"Hello, son," Jay's mother said. "Long time, no speak."

"Mother," he whispered. "Is that really you?" It had been so long since Jay had heard her voice – even in a home video – that he couldn't be sure. But the bond between mother and son was a hard bond to break. Jay somehow *knew* it was her, and he put his fear on hold like a violinist who'd spotted a break in the score and laid his bow down to wipe a bead of sweat from his forehead.

"It's really me," the voice said. "But I don't have much time. I need you to listen carefully. In two days' time, when the mirror clears, I'll be back again. Promise that you'll wait for me."

"What do you mean?" Jay asked. "I don't understand."

"Promise me!"

"I promise," Jay said. "But please, Mother. Tell me what's going on."

There was no response. As the voices died away, Jay felt the familiar sting of his revulsion. He drew the curtain across the mirror and left the room.

For the rest of that day and for much of the next, Jay

went from fear to despair and back to fear again. Even his first appointment with a counsellor – Dr. Mortimer had freed up his schedule and agreed to meet with Jay himself – did little to ease his anxiety. If anything, it made it worse.

In the evening, Jay braved the bathroom. The whispers had quietened to a low hum, and the curtain was drawn haphazardly across, just how he'd left it.

"Mum?" Jay whispered, tentatively. But there was no response, not even when he tried again with a little more authority. He hesitated for a second and then jerked the curtains open. The mirror had clouded over, but the shadowy figures were closer to the surface than ever before. Jay stared in wonder for a couple of seconds, then shuddered and turned away again.

He slept soundly that evening without a single one of the night terrors that he'd grown so used to. But when he woke up, he was filled with a stomach-churning blend of excitement, apprehension and anxiety. He didn't eat and he didn't drink. He waited. There was something in the air, some sort of palpable, electric energy.

He found himself resisting the urge to check the mirror. He'd know when the time was right. The seconds dragged slowly by, turning into minutes and hours with a dull, inevitable certainty. At five minutes to midnight, he was ready. It was time.

Jay could hear the mirror's fevered murmurings from out in the hallway, but as soon as he opened the bathroom door, a sudden silence descended. For a brief, crazy moment, Jay wondered whether this was what vultures heard as they pillaged corpses after battles. He was scared like a survivor, but he swallowed his fear, gathered his resolve and walked inside, then locked the door behind him.

He drew open the curtains, bracing himself for the reflection, but it still took him by surprise. He saw his own eyes, his own nose, and something of his own jawline, but the similarities ended there. It was enough. Jay had seen the old family photographs, and his mother hadn't aged a day since her disappearance.

"My son," she whispered. The mirror was like a window with another bathroom on the other side. "It's time."

"What do you mean, Mother?" Jay asked. He stepped a little closer to the mirror. He could feel a gentle breeze, a wind from another world. "I don't understand."

"Hush, child. Be patient. You'll have your answers soon enough."

She reached forwards, slowly but confidently, and laid the palm of her hand against the surface. Jay hesitated and thought about pulling back, but it was far too late for that. It was time to face his fear or die trying.

When he pressed his hand against his mother's, he felt her warmth as it surged through the glass and into his fingertips. He'd always thought of mirrors as cold, emotionless things, but this one was full of life and love. He smiled and closed his eyes, and then the horror began.

He felt an ice-cold hand around his wrist, and his eyes shot open while his mouth flashed in a silent O, a muted scream of surprise. His mother's eyes had changed, and the love had been replaced by a steely determination. Her hand had gone from warm and clammy to cold and dry, and her upper arm was sticking out of the mirror like the unholy appendage of a monster at the bottom of the sea.

She reached out with her other hand, and Jay watched as it burst through the mirror and grabbed hold of him. She yanked with superhuman strength, like a pneumatic piston firing on all cylinders, and Jay was falling, falling, falling into the mirror and through to the other side.

Back in the real world, in the empty bathroom, the curtains drew closed of their own accord.

Six days later, when Dr. Mortimer called the police after Jay failed to make his appointment or to answer his mobile phone, the door to the bathroom was kicked open by the heavy boot of a first responder.

They were expecting a body, but there was nothing, just a distant whisper and a misty mirror. Sergeant Mogford, the cop with the heavy boot, took a closer look and thought he could see two shadows, dancing back and forth across his retinas.

"Find anything?"

He glanced towards the door and thought about his colleagues, who were combing the apartment for clues. He wondered what they'd say if he told them he'd seen shapes and heard voices. The decision was made for him.

"No," he replied. "Nothing."

After the policemen left the scene to write up their reports, the whispering grew a little louder and the shapes started to solidify. The curtain drew closed of its own accord.

The Weirdness was only just beginning.

Black Solstice

"I'm dreaming of a black solstice."
– Bling Crowley

"TELL US AGAIN, DADDY."

"Oh, no, it's far too late for that."

"Please?"

"Well…okay."

John Reid was sitting on an uncomfortably small chair at the foot of his daughters' bunk bed. It was late, it was cold outside, and he had an important meeting in the morning. He stroked his powerful hand through his beard and glanced automatically at his wristwatch, which was illuminated by a My Little Pony lava lamp. Tupac, the family cat, was nestled in the lower bunk, curled around Jessie's feet like a black spot in the pages of a Bible.

He sighed.

"What story do you want to hear?" he asked, though he already knew the answer. There was only one story that the two of them could possibly want to hear at this time of year, and he was the only one who'd tell it. His wife, Mildred, believed the old superstitions and said it was bad luck.

"Daddy, Daddy," little Jessie said, her eyes staring out from the darkness like two bright beacons of hope and innocence. "Tell us the story of Satan Claws!"

"Satan Claws?" he replied, raising an eyebrow. "Aren't you a bit old for that?"

"No, Daddy, no," Jude said. "Go on, tell us the story."

"Okay," John said, shrugging his shoulders and shifting uncomfortably in the chair. "Well, the story goes like this. Back in the olden days, a long, long time ago—"

"Before you were born?"

"Yes," John chuckled softly, feeling his age along with an ache in his back from where the cold weather and the storm front had taken its toll. "Long, long before I was born."

"So what happened?"

"I'm getting there," John replied. "It goes back to the Bible. Adam's first wife, Lilith, flew into a tremendous rage after God created Eve, and God punished her for her jealousy by making her mortal. But then, as she wandered the Earth alone and in the depths of her despair, Satan went to her in the form of a goat and asked her to drink his blood."

"And did she?"

"Yes," John said. "The unholy blood was too much for her, and it killed her. But though her body died, her spirit lived on, and she was doomed to spend the rest of eternity at his side, feasting on the blood of children, just like you two."

The two girls shuddered in their beds, and John Reid felt the beginnings of a smile in spite of himself. Scaring children during solstice season was a tradition as old as time itself, and if the legends were true, it served a purpose.

"Lilith is the mother of them all," John continued. "The she-devil, Mrs. Claws. They say she still sleeps beside him in their double coffin, hiding from the deadly sunlight as they wait for the winter solstice, the longest night. When they can, they add others to their cause, corrupting their victims with a bite and creating creatures of the night. Your grandad—"

"Grandad Woodynge?"

"No, Jessie," John replied. "Granddad Byegrave. He used to be what they called a staker. It was his job to search the cemetery for little air holes or disturbances amongst the graves at St. Editha's. When he found something, he had to dig up the grave and put a stake through the heart of the poor unfortunate that was buried beneath the soil."

"Eww!"

"That's nothing," John said. "In some other places, very far away from here, they decapitate their dead to make sure that they don't come back."

"What does depapitate mean?"

"Never you mind," John said. "In Italy, the doctors wash their hands with communion wine. When their patients die, they break people's legs and bury them upside down."

"That's gross, Daddy," Jude scolded, pouting at him as she put her little hands over her ears.

"Well, it's a small price to pay," John said. "It's better for you to know these things. The vampyres are dangerous, with superhuman strength and speed. They're also immortal."

"What does that mean, Daddy?"

"It means they don't die," John replied, grimly.

He thought once again about whether he was telling them too much, but then he reminded himself that, like the birds and the bees, it was just one of the facts of life that they needed to know.

"According to the legends," John continued, "if someone died and their body was left unguarded, they'd turn into a creature of the night. Your other granddad, Granddad Woodynge, used to work as a watcher."

"A watcher?"

"Yes, Jude," John said. "He'd stand guard over the dead with a lit candle, watching day and night until it was time to bury them. He used to hold a loaded shotgun and keep watch for animals."

"Like rabbits?"

"Uh-huh," John replied. "And cats and dogs, too. The old-timers say that if an animal jumps over a body before it's buried, it'll turn into a vampyre by the following night."

"They say a lot," Jude said.

John paused for a second and smiled in the darkness, struck again by just how smart his kids were. They were little prodigies, clever clogs who'd been raised on classical music since their time in the womb, even though he knew the Mozart effect was a steaming pile of bullshit. But they'd played Mozart to the girls anyway, just in case the scientists were wrong.

"Is it true that only bad people become vampyres, Daddy?"

"No, Jessie," John said. "They used to say that only those who'd led evil lives or who'd refused religion could become vampyres. They suspected witches of being vampyres, too. But we know better, don't we, girls?"

"Yuh-huh," Jude said, sticking a thumb in her mouth and looking out at her dad from the top bunk. "Grandma Woodynge is a witch, and she keeps us safe from Satan Claws."

"Exactly, girls," John said. "So there's nothing to worry about, is there?"

"Nuh-uh."

"Good," John said, yawning slightly and stretching out his arms. "Now, I think that's enough for one night, isn't it? Besides, we can't let your mother know we've been talking about Satan Claws again or she'll have my guts for garters."

"What does that mean, Daddy?"

"Never you mind," John repeated, his moustache twitching as he suppressed a laugh. "Now go on, you two. It's time for you to go to sleep. Sweet dreams."

***

"Simply having a terrible solstice time."
– Paul McStakeInTheHeartney

ON SOLSTICE EVE, the two Reid girls were running around in the garden and playing in the snow when they saw a magpie in the trees. It was soon joined by another, and then another. The birds lined up like black-gowned judges, waiting to pass sentence on the children.

Jude nodded at her sister and the two turned and saluted to the birds. Then they started to sing together in a cherubic harmony, their time in the church choir shining through as they worked their way through the rhyme.

"One for sorrow," they chorused. "Two for joy, three for a girl, four for a boy. Five for silver, six for gold, seven for a secret never to be told. Eight for a wish, nine for a kiss, ten a surprise you should be careful not to miss. Eleven for health, twelve for wealth, thirteen beware, it's the devil himself."

"Magpies are always bad luck," Jessie grumbled.

"Like breaking a mirror?" Jude replied.

"Exactly."

There was a sharp gust of wind and the magpies took off, their departure leaving a heavy silence that settled over the garden like a fog. Both of the girls were wrapped up warm, but they shivered in tandem as the sun sauntered behind a cloud and cast the garden into shadow.

They looked to the snowman they'd built for comfort, but there was no warmth to the coal that he had for eyes, and the twigs they'd used for his arms looked brittle and uninviting.

"Let's go inside," Jessie said.

The inside of the house looked like an explosion at a jumble sale with all sorts of weird and wonderful items scattered throughout it. The decorations were mostly in red, green and gold, symbolising the blood of Christ, the eternal life of the evergreen tree and the gifts of the three magi. The initials VM for "Virgin Mary" had been carved repeatedly into the wooden door and window frames.

The banister, which crawled lazily down a steep and narrow Edwardian staircase, was carved with obscene phalli, stiff and floppy dicks saluting the girls every time they ran upstairs. Mildred didn't like them and had begged her husband to get rid of them, but he'd always overruled her because of the old apotropaic superstitions.

That was why he'd also agreed to bury an old boot outside the back door.

"What's the difference between an amulet and a talisman?" Jude asked, as the girls raced up the stairs towards their playroom.

"One's got an n in it?"

"Well, that too," Jude replied. "But that wasn't what I meant, silly."

"So what's the difference?"

"A talisman brings good luck," Jude said, "and an amulet wards off evil."

"So which one do we need?" Jessie asked.

Jude shook her head grimly and said, "Both."

***

**"'Twas the night before solstice,
when all through the shack,
not a creature was stirring,
not even a bat."**
– Clement Van Helsing

THE HOUSE SMELLED like garlic.

A silver chalice sat on a silver tray on a table in the kitchen. It was filled with a clear liquid, holy water from the healing springs of Lourdes, and two communion wafers sat on a silver plate beside them. A wooden crucifix lay between the two of them.

It was midnight on the morning of December 21st.

The house was one of several dozen that were nestled beneath the blanket of snow over Greyfriars Close and the rest of Mile End. Upstairs, in their bedrooms, the Reid family slumbered on. John Reid was fast asleep, his moustache-net holding his precious curls out of his nose and mouth. Mildred, his wife, was asleep beside him, though she was twitching.

In the other bedroom, the twins were still awake.

And they were terrified.

Jessie and Jude were seven years old, and they were just about old enough to still believe in Satan Claws. Some of the children at school had said that Satan was made up by capitalists to sell more products, but Jessie and Jude kept themselves to themselves and didn't give a hoot what the other kids said. Perhaps Satan Claws was just their father in a silly suit... but then again, perhaps not. And they didn't want to take the risk and then find out that they were wrong.

John Reid had told them that they were taking Pascal up on his wager. They hadn't known what he'd meant at the time, but then they'd asked Mr. Griffin at the school and he'd told them all about it.

It made a lot of sense after that. Perhaps Satan Claws didn't exist, but then again, perhaps he did. If they took the right precautions and he did exist, they had a shot at surviving. If he didn't... well, they'd just look a little silly. And Jessie and Jude didn't care if they looked silly, as long as they survived.

And so they'd stayed up late on Solstice Eve, roaming around the house and performing the final touches, scattering salt circles around their beds and polishing all of the mirrors. A couple of weeks earlier, they'd found some sticks while they were walking by the river, and they'd spent the days between sharpening the sticks with their daddy's penknife. Luckily for them, he hadn't caught them.

They'd hung a silver horseshoe above their bedroom door, polished every shiny surface until they could see their faces and placed mirrors by the doors and windows. In the back garden, tear-shaped nazars hung from trees, channelling the old magick to protect the house from the glare of the evil eye.

The house was festooned with images of Christ, and they'd woven St. Brigid's crosses out of rush to hang in each of the rooms. In their bedroom, a home-made dreamcatcher made of yarn hung above their bunk bed, occasionally bopping Jude on the head if she sat up in the night. Blown glass witch balls hung in every room, and so did bunches of wildflowers, including branches of ash, oak, wild rose, white heather and hawthorn. Jessie had even asked her daddy to bring her some clippings from the aspen tree at the bottom of the garden.

"Does it have to be aspen?" he'd asked.

"Of course," she'd replied, matter-of-factly. "That's the same kind of tree they used to make Jesus' cross, Daddy."

They'd scattered mustard seeds on the floors and even convinced their parents to leave the taps on, thanks to the old story that vampyres couldn't cross running water. They'd also asked their mother if they could hang some mistletoe, but she'd refused.

"Mistletoe is a patriarchal tradition designed to apply social pressure to young women until they agree to kiss old men," she'd insisted. "I mean, the juice in the berries represents jizz, for goodness' sake."

"What's jizz, Mummy?"

"Never you mind."

But the girls were hopeful that they'd be able to wear her down eventually, just like they'd done with the gun and the silver bullets. The two girls had been making zero headway until they'd presented their mother with a series of charts and graphs that showed the prevalence of home invasions. She'd relented after that, and she'd been their key weapon when it came to convincing their father.

John Reid would have done anything for his daughters, and so he'd purchased an illegal firearm from a guy called Silky at the local boozer. He kept the gun and the holy bullets inside a shoebox in the drawer of his bedside table.

That afternoon, Mildred cut her hand while helping her daughters to bake communion wafers. She'd tried to hide it from them, to cover the wound with a plaster before they noticed, but the twins' eyes were as sharp as their intellects and before she'd even removed the first aid kit from the kitchen cupboards, they'd told her what she needed to do.

"You did an oopsie, Mummy," Jude said. "You know the rules."

And she *did* know the rules, too. It was said that any wound left untreated with boiling water was enough to let the evil in, and so the traditionalists poured boiling water over graves during funerals. In the Reid household, it meant that she had to pop the kettle on and take a couple of aspirin.

That night, she was sleeping with a bandage around her hand.

***

"He's making a list, he's checking it twice."
– Satan Claws is Coming to Town

JOHN REID WOKE UP with a start as something primal took over him.

He was a fully grown adult with thirty-one winters behind him, but there was something about the old traditions that still held sway over him. He could remember a time in his own childhood when John Sr. had taken the boy on his knee and given him "the talk".

"Son," he'd said, "I think you're old enough now to know what's what. We maintain the old traditions because there's often a grain of truth to them. They say it's better to be safe than sorry, you see. Now, the winter is a dark and unpleasant time, a time that's full of dangers and where the elements themselves turn against us. Might be that there *is* a Satan Claws and that the legends are true. Might be that there isn't. But if what they say is true and he's the antichrist, the prince of darkness... well, maybe it's better to take the superstitions seriously just in case, eh?"

That was the solstice when John Reid had stayed up all night, his eyes darting frantically from shadow to shadow, convinced that Satan Claws would sweep in at any moment and rip him apart. Once the sun had finally crept over the horizon, he'd passed out and caught an hour or two of sleep before being woken back up for the celebrations. He'd spent most of solstice day dozing off over the dinner table and waking back up every time his chin dipped into the gravy.

Satan Claws hadn't come to visit that year, and nor had he come the year after. In fact, Satan Claws never came for John Reid, but the name alone was still enough to send shivers down his spine.

He heard a creak on the landing, but the house was old and had a habit of singing to itself. He extricated himself from his wife's arms and rolled over on to his side, then folded his pillow in half and rested his head on the cool fabric. His ears twitched as he listened to the darkness, but there was nothing but a sleepy silence, a treacle-like emptiness that filled his ears like a spoonful of honey.

Then he closed his eyes again and tried to catch some sleep.

***

"Does he ride a red-nosed hellhound?
Are there weapons on his slay?"
– Slayed

THE TWO GIRLS were still awake, and still terrified.

Jessie was the older of the two by an hour, and so she was the de-facto leader of the Reid twins. She was the first out of bed, and she used the glow of the nightlight to climb down from her bunk and onto the hardwood floor. The snow outside was still falling, piling up against the concrete walls and chilling the house beneath a wintery blanket. It had seeped through into the floor and it chilled her feet as she navigated across to the dresser and picked up the rosaries, which lay incongruously amongst a pile of stuffed toys and collectibles.

She placed one around her own neck and one around her sister's. They worked in silence, their ears tensed as they listened out for sounds from elsewhere in the house. Next, the two girls scattered seeds and rice across the floor, upending jars and wrenching open plastic packaging until the wood was covered with kernels and grains. Anne Welsh from their maths class had told them that vampyres were obsessed with numbers and that once he saw the scattered seeds, Satan Claws would have to stop and count them. If they kept him busy for long enough, the sun would rise and he'd be killed by the light.

They didn't know whether they believed that, but they'd done it anyway.

Suzie Reid (no relation) from the year below had told them that Satan Claws had a legion of minions made up of some of the vilest people from history. Vlad the Impaler was the obvious one, the fierce Walachian who'd earned his nickname by impaling his enemies on wooden stakes and leaving them there to die. According to Suzie, Vlad used to eat bread that had been dipped in his victims' blood while he watched them die.

Then there was Mike Austin, Lucy Austin's older brother. He'd told his sister – who'd told the rest of her class – about countess Elizabeth Bathory, a Hungarian heiress with the blood of dozens of enemies on her hands, as well as her lips and tongue. According to the Austins, Bathory had them brought to her so she could bite them. After they died, she'd have her servants drain their blood before pouring it into a bathtub.

Mike Austin said that was because bath bombs hadn't been invented yet.

Stavros said they were called vrykolakas, but Besnik called them shtriga and Anca said they were strigoi. Mr. Ricard, the substitute teacher who was presiding over the class at the time, said it was all just a matter of semantics.

"Do you know how to stop a strigoi?" Mr. Ricard had asked. He'd looked out at the sea of interested little faces and sighed. When no one answered, he'd continued, "They used to bury corpses upside down and put scythes and sickles in the grave. It was said that if the body bloated before becoming a fully-fledged vampyre, the sickle would prick them and put them back down again. As for vyrkolakas, the best option is to leave a coin in their mouths so that they can pay the ferryman at the River Styx. If they can't cross the river, they come back to feast on flesh."

Then he'd remembered he was supposed to be teaching geography and had moved on to talking about continental drift.

But all that had been during a happier time, during the summer months when the coming of the vampyre was a distant shadow over the future and not an immediate threat to their survival. That had been then, and this was now, on solstice eve, the hunting night of the vampyres.

The two Reid girls were as ready as they'd ever be. They just didn't know if they were ready enough. They closed their eyes and bowed their heads, and then Jude led them in a prayer.

"Dear Baby Jesus," Jude intoned, solemnly. "Please keep us safe from Satan Claws, or better still, send us a sign that he doesn't exist."

But no such sign was forthcoming.

***

"I'm keeping my distance, I've got my gun drawn,
if he comes any closer, I won't shoot to warn."
– John Lemon (and Yoko Ohnothevampyreiscoming)

BUT SATAN CLAWS DID EXIST, and he was having a bad day. His flying hellhounds had got lost over Marseilles, and it had taken Adolf's red nose to sniff out the English Channel. It had been raining in Transylvania, but the rain had turned to snow as they flew west in his slay.

He drew back his fiery whip, a solstice gift from his friend the Balrog, and swung it through the air. It broke the sound barrier with a sonic boom that echoed out over the English countryside.

"Now, Slasher!" he cried. "Now, Stabber! Now, Brawler and Basher! On, Killer! On, Screamer! On, Pouncer and Crasher!"

And his hellhounds flew on into the darkness.

***

"You scumbag, you friar, no match for vampyres."
– The Rogues feat. Kirsty MacBarlow

JUST AS JOHN REID was about to doze off for good, he heard a noise from above that sent a chill of fear through his soul. It was the sound of slay bells, the horrible, funereal gongs that echoed through the sky like a thunderclap. He sat bolt upright in his bed, then shook Mildred into life and put a finger to his lips.

"'sappenin'?" she murmured, still drunk on sleep.

"Are you awake?" John asked.

"What do you think?"

"Yeah," John whispered. "I couldn't sleep, either. Did you hear something?"

"Like what?"

"I thought I heard something on the roof," John said. "I thought it might be, I don't know…"

"The vampyre?" Mildred asked. She'd woken up a little and had pulled herself up so that she was sitting upright, too. John reached over to the bedside lamp and clicked it into life. "John, aren't you too old for children's stories? There's no such thing as vampyres, husband. There are just people who *believe* in vampyres, and sometimes that's just as bad."

"Ah, *those guys*," John replied. "The ones who get professional fang fittings and who carry out rituals and shit. Those guys are idiots. But just because a few fools like to play fancy dress, it doesn't mean that the real things aren't out there."

"But vampyres, John," Mildred argued. "You're talking about bad guys from the depth of the night, created in the twilight hours before God rested. Lilith, the demon wife of Adam, and her dark lord husband, drinking the blood of children. You can't believe everything you read in the Bible."

"I read it on Wikipedia," her husband said. "Did you know that you can find a vampyre's grave by leading a virgin boy through a graveyard on the back of a black stallion? Sounds fishy to me, considering vampyres can't walk on consecrated ground. They used to bury corpses with lemons in their mouths to stop them from coming back."

"Do you know what I read on Wikipedia?" Mildred asked. "In 2006, a physics professor wrote a paper proving that it's mathematically impossible for vampyres to exist thanks to geometric progression. If the first vampyre had appeared in January 1600 and fed once per month, turning each of its victims into a vampyre, the entire world would have been vampyres within two and a half years."

"That's not the point."

"Then what *is* the point?"

"I think Satan Claws is here," John replied. "And I think he might be coming down the chimney."

"Bullshit."

"Come on, Millie," John insisted. "We might as well go and take a look, just to be sure."

"Fine."

"Should I take the gun?"

"No," Mildred replied. "If you do, you'll end up shooting someone."

"Yes," John said, absently. "That's kind of the point."

***

"Last solstice, I gave you my neck,
but the very next day, you went back to heck.
This year, to save me from fear,
I'm going to hide in heaven."
– Splat

SATAN CLAWS *was* coming down the chimney.

The front door would have been easier, but that was protected by old magick, a power greater even than he was. He was the Antichrist, the first vampyre, and vampyres had to be invited over the threshold.

He was thirsty, so thirsty, and it was time for his annual feast. Blood was the thing, the delicious nectar of life that sustained him. The blood of virgins was better. The blood of the young was best, for they were free and innocent. They hadn't yet been touched by evil.

He worked at night by the light of the moon, chasing it across the sky and returning to his crypt before the first rays of the morning sun filtered over the horizon. The sunlight, along with the warmth that it brought, was deadly. That was why he worked at night. Solstice eve – and solstice morning, until the dawn at least – was the one night of year that he worked.

Every year, his evil elves delivered a list of who'd been naughty and who'd been nice. He'd work through the list, taking care not to touch the paper against his flaming beard in case it caught light. Then he'd shortlist a dozen names from the top of the "good" list and carry out basic reconnaissance on the run up to solstice. It was the good little boys and girls who tasted the best. The bad boys and girls tasted like rotten apples and gave him the bloody equivalent of a hangover.

And that was how he'd settled on Jessie and Jude Reid.

He'd been watching the girls for several months, documenting every decision they made in his diabolical notebook. He tracked their searches on their smart speakers and digitally snooped on them as they ploughed their crops in FarmVille or popped bubbles in Candy Crush Saga. He knew more about them than anyone, including their parents.

He'd been preparing for this moment for some time. And now he was finally ready.

He hit the fire at the bottom of the chimney feet first, but the flames simply fed his desire and regenerated him, leaving him stronger and more determined than ever. He could smell the two girls, and they were ready for him.

Satan Claws smiled grimly and climbed out of the fireplace, unfolding himself to his full height in the middle of the Reids' suburban living room. He was bloated, his stomach distended like a starving child in a charity campaign. Lesser vampyres resorted to draining the blood from cattle and sheep, but Satan Claws was a purist. Only the freshest human blood could pass his palette.

And he was thirsty.

He walked out of the living room and out into the hallway, his footsteps falling silently with soft *thup-thup-thups* that didn't make an echo. The hallway was dark, but that wasn't a problem for Satan Claws, who could hunt by smell just as easily as by sight.

The floorboards creaked as he placed his weight on them, but the sound was swallowed up by the darkness. From above him, he could discern the subtle thumping of four heartbeats, two in each of the upstairs bedrooms. He drew his tongue across his lips, sending filthy, dead blood dribbling down his chin. He gnashed subconsciously at the air, just like his thralls when they chewed through their shrouds in their graves.

The house was an unwelcoming place, packed to the rafters with the symbols of white magick. But Satan Claws was a hunter, and like all hunters, he revelled in the thrill of the chase.

It would make his meal all the better.

***

"I'll have a black solstice without you."
– Elvis Deathly

THE DOOR TO THEIR BEDROOM seemed to open of its own accord. Then the darkness changed texture, and a figure stepped silently through the doorway.

Satan Claws was dressed in robes of black, though they were trimmed with crimson. To the two girls, who were still learning their relative scale, he looked ten feet tall. But that was impossible, because it would have pushed his head through the ceiling and up towards the roof, where his slay was still perched precariously, his hellhounds scrabbling their claws across the tiles and sending them crashing down to the floor.

"Oh, oh, oh," Satan Claws growled, his voice sounding like the rattle of a corpse as it swung in the breeze at a medieval crossroads. "Merry solstice."

He held his dark hand up and tensed it into a fist, sending a ripple of evil washing over the room like the fug from a smoke machine. The candles in the window, which symbolised that Christ was the light of the world, were extinguished by a wave of black wind. The vampyre's psychokinetic energy erupted outwards like a sonic boom, except it was visible as it passed through the darkness. A fierce wind blew through the building, detonating the girls' nativity scene and sending the baby Jesus flying through the air and into the wall, where he shattered. The china models had been valuable family heirlooms, passed down from generation to generation, but within the space of a couple of seconds, they'd been turned into nothing more than a pile of brightly painted broken pottery.

Outside, in the garden, the snowman's head exploded, its coal eyes firing through the night and into the windows of the girls' bedroom, sending shards of glass scattering across their stuffed toys and all over the floor.

And in the bedroom, the two girls looked imperiously out from their bunks. The vampyre had protruding teeth and an aquiline nose, as well as the hungry look of a man who hadn't eaten for a year. As he looked at the girls, his gaze alone was enough to freeze them to their beds, as though they were trapped between wakefulness and unconsciousness in a satanic sleep paralysis.

He took a step towards the girls, and then another.

"Get away from my kids, you make-believe bastard!"

The vampyre's head turned in a full semi-circle, taking in Mildred Reid in her nightdress and her husband a step and a half behind her. She had a wooden stake in one hand and a hammer in the other, and she was rushing towards him like a woman possessed. The sharpened wood was closing in on him, but the vampyre was too fast for it, clicking his fingers and dissolving into a whirling cloud of bats, which dodged the woman's jabs and batted against her, their little legs getting tangled up in her hair. John swatted ineffectively at them, while Mildred continued to swing the stake through the air at a target that no longer existed.

In their beds, the girls came back to life again, their innocent bodies no longer pinned in place by the vampyre's evil eye. They moved towards their stockings.

There was a growl from the darkness in the hallway and then Tupac was in the room too, a black cat batting black bats, but the bats were fighting back and the cat was howling. Its unnatural yowl seemed to break the spell, and the room flooded with volume as everyone tried to move at once. Satan Claws reformed, the bats disappearing beneath his robes, while John and Mildred made a rush for him. The girls were at the feet of their beds, rummaging through their stockings for the gifts within. Jude was the quickest, and she tore the wrapping from what looked like a bottle of perfume before raising it in both arms.

Satan Claws took the hit of holy water straight in the face.

***

"Well, tonight thank God it's them instead of you."
– Band Aids Over Puncture Holes

"OH, OH, OH," Satan Claws growled. "Is that the best you can do?"

Time stood still around him. Jude was still holding the bottle in front of her face, visible mostly as a pair of bright green eyes in the darkness. Jessie was in the bunk below, her hands still buried deep within her stocking. Satan Claws was in the middle of the room with his back to the door, while Tupac had bolted for the floor beneath the bed and was watching proceedings unfold with the disinterested wariness of the common housecat. John and Mildred were to either side of the vampyre, their hammers raised in the air as they fumbled with their stakes.

And Lilith was standing in the doorway.

She was like Satan Claws but with style, a biblical beauty who'd added flavour over time, like a fine wine. Her husband was unkempt for a vampyre, with flowing white hair, a bushy beard and a big belly. Lilith looked like she took care of herself, like she worked out every night lifting the lids off crypts or doing gothic lunges. She was dressed mostly in velvet, with a few hints of leather, and her lips and fingernails were painted the deep scarlet of an aged bottle of O negative.

"Enough of this, husband," Lilith said, clapping her hands together. When her palms touched, the two adults were thrown against opposite walls of the bedroom, where they smacked against the walls and then slid to the floor in a broken symmetry. "Let's feed."

"Like hell," John growled, pushing himself up on one knee before slumping back down again. Blood was flowing freely from somewhere on his scalp, and his wife was unconscious but breathing.

"My good man," Satan Claws said, "I have no desire to hurt you or your wife. I remember you as a child. You used to write me letters every solstice, begging me not to take you or your brothers."

His mouth fell open.

"All we want is to feed," Lilith said, her voice floating eerily on the supernatural wind that was still blowing through the house, sending ornaments tumbling to the floor and rotating crucifixes where they hung above the doorways.

"But they're my daughters!"

"So?" Satan Claws replied, leering evilly at him. "You planned a solstice dinner tomorrow, did you not?"

John Reid said nothing.

"Yes, husband," Lilith added. "They have a turkey defrosting in the refrigerator."

"But that's different!" John protested.

"Is it?" Satan Claws growled. "It died so you could live. How is this any different?"

"It just—"

"Mr. Reid, I grow tired of talking to you," Satan Claws said. "Don't make me kill you. After all, alive, you can make new children. Dead, you're no good to anyone."

"You bastard, I'll—"

"It's okay, Daddy," Jude said, her voice sounding eerily calm amidst the chaos. "I know what we have to do."

"Yes," Jessie agreed. "It's the only way."

"Girls, I don't—"

"Yes," Lilith said. "It's as it should be."

She clicked her fingers and the girls' leather-bound Bible flew off their bookcase and towards their father's head. It knocked him clean out, and he snoozed on in silence like his wife while the vampyres moved in on the two girls.

They offered no resistance.

***

"I'll be eligible for parole come Valentine's Day."
– Tom Waits for No Man, Solstice Card from a Vampyre in Minneapolis

JOHN REID AWOKE to a bloodbath of sorts, though his pale-faced, angelic daughters had been drained of the stuff. They were both still in their bunks, their glassy eyes staring up at the ceiling, the puncture marks in their necks looking like recharge sockets for androids. Their skin had turned a papery-white, matching their pristine bedsheets and giving them the look of department store mannequins wearing old-fashioned wedding dresses.

Tupac, the cat, was dead too. His head had been torn off and thrown at the girls' stuffed animals like a bowling ball. The rest of the cat was poking out of their Jesus-themed litter bin, making a mockery of the saviour's own suffering. Christ, who was hanging from a cross on its façade, had

blood on his forehead and was looking out at the scene with
an expression of beatific resignation.

Mildred was unconscious still, though she was coming
round. She had a bloody nose that had dripped down on to
her chest, and John supposed she was lucky not to have
landed differently or she might have drowned in the stuff.
He himself had bled heavily from the wound to the back of
his skull, and he had a splitting headache that reminded him
of his hangover days, before he'd given up the bottle after
the kids were born.

"Mildred?" John said. "Millie, are you okay?"

"Nghh…"

"He killed them," John murmured.

"Nghhhh?"

"The girls," John said. "He killed them. Drained them of
blood. They're gone, Millie."

"They're whuh?"

"They're gone," John repeated, pulling himself
unsteadily to his feet. He looked around the room again.
There was blood on all four walls and the ceiling,
presumably from the cat, and the girls' normally tidy
bedroom looked like the aftermath of a bomb blast in Beirut.
Even their dreamcatchers had been torn down, and on the
far wall of the room, their portrait of Christ stood watch
beneath his crown of thorns. Someone had drawn a goatee,
horns and glasses on him in the cat's blood.

John picked up one of the stakes and his hammer.

"No," Mildred said. "Not that, John. Anything but that."

"We have to."

"I can't."

"Then I'll do it."

Mildred tried to pull herself to her feet, but all her
strength had been taken away and she stumbled and fell

again. John flashed a quick glance of concern at her, but then he returned to the task in hand.

He dealt with Jessie first, because she was on the bottom bunk and she was easier for him to reach. When he placed the stake above her heart and smacked it with the hammer, the wood pierced her flesh and an unearthly hiss filled the air. She crumbled before his eyes, turning to dust and bone.

Jude came next, with the same result.

Once the job was done, John Reid glanced resignedly at his wife and then walked silently out of the room. He returned several minutes later with a shoebox in his hands.

"What are you doing?" Mildred asked, as he removed the gun from the box and started loading bullets into the chamber.

"What do you think I'm doing?"

"It's too late," Mildred said. "They're gone. Your silver bullets are useless, just like the rest of these trinkets."

"It's not for the vampyres," John said sadly, as he loaded the cartridges into the revolver. "It's for us."

"For us?"

"It's our fault that the girls are dead," John said. "We didn't believe. We *couldn't* believe. But we were wrong, Millie. *I* was wrong. If we'd just believed, if we'd just been a little faster, we could have fought them off. The girls might still be alive. But now there's nothing. Nothing to live for."

Mildred seemed to think about it for a moment.

Then she said, "Okay. But as long as you shoot me first."

***

"You'd better watch out, you'd better not cry."
– Satan Claws is Coming to Town

THE FAMILY WAS FOUND in the morning, when the three Jenkins kids from number seventeen stopped by to sing some solstice carols. When they went to knock at the door, it was already hanging open, and so they'd let themselves inside for a break from the cold.

They'd found John and Mildred in the smaller of the two upstairs bedrooms. They were lying slumped, arm in arm, with their backs against the wall, their glassy eyes staring vacantly towards their daughters' bunkbed. They weren't moving, but that was no surprise. Most of their heads were missing. Little Jessica Jenkins screamed and bolted downstairs towards the front door, with her two older brothers hot on her heels. They called their parents first and the emergency services second, and both of them arrived at the same time. The Reids were carried out an hour or two later, their destination the city morgue and, eventually, its crematorium. Sergeant Gary Mogford of the homicide division had theorised that it was a murder-suicide, though if pressed to ask what had happened to the girls, he could only have given a guess.

They were still awaiting results on the strange grey ashes that had been found in the girls' beds, as well as the sharpened lumps of wood that had been lying beside them.

As for Satan Claws, he'd flown on back to hell, his hellhounds baying in the wind, his thirst slaked for another year as his wife slumbered in her seat beside him.

"Oh, oh, oh," he'd bellowed, his deathly voice echoing out like a thunderclap as he flew over the Chilterns. "Merry solstice. And until next year…"

Amorphophallus Titanum

"PUSH!" the midwife shouted. "You're dilated enough, child. If you don't push now, the baby will breech."

The young woman in the bed pushed harder, her knuckles tightening into white little fists as the baby moved inside her. There was no medication. Hers was a natural birth in a threadbare bed in a small hut on the outskirts of a forest. The midwife had been summoned in the middle of the night and had cycled across the countryside to be at her bedside. Her presence was a comfort, albeit a small one.

"Harder!"

"NGHHH."

The young woman pushed again, bracing herself in the bed and giving her pelvic muscles the workout of a lifetime. She screamed blasphemies and squirmed in agony, but still she pushed. She felt something damp between her legs, but it wasn't the first time, and she resigned herself to lying in it. While the fire inside her continued to burn, her mind drifted away and she found herself thinking absurdly of the towels.

We'll need to buy new ones.

"Push, woman!"

"Go push yourself!" she bellowed, though she was hardly aware of it. She was just shouting whatever came into her head, whatever words her tongue could find. "Oh, heaven save me! I can't bear this pain anymore."

"Push harder!"

The baby moved within her again, and the midwife bent to retrieve an intimidating pair of metal forceps from the depths of her canvas bag. The woman felt a cold thrill as the forceps brushed against her inner thigh, followed by a sense of pressure coming from inside her that seemed to be forcing her organs to find new places in her body. Her head flopped to the side and she vomited, but she kept on pushing regardless.

"It's coming," the midwife said. "Not long to go now, my dear."

The woman was too weak to respond.

The midwife leaned in again, visible now only as a blur at the edge of her field of vision.

"There's something wrong," the midwife was saying. "It's fighting us and coming out sideways. And… oh good lord, what is that?"

"What?" the woman said, or at least she tried to say it.

"This child is the devil himself," the midwife grunted, forming a cross in the air in front of her. "Oh Lord help us. The child is born to evil. He'll be the death of us all."

That was the last thing that the young woman heard before her baby was pulled away and the darkness overtook her.

***

No one knew who the child's father was, and so he was taken in by the church before being adopted by the LaMuertes, a travelling family of Spaniards who roamed from town to town as touring actors and performers. They were known to the village because they performed at the fairs at the start and end of the summer season, and they were also the only willing adoptive parents who could be found.

No one else had wanted the child because it had been born with a caul, and everyone knew what that meant. Cauls were rare, so rare that few midwives had ever seen them, although they'd all heard stories. Enrique LaMuerte, as the child came to be known, was one of the few, and that marked him out as a freak, a devil-child. The caul had been removed by the midwife, of course, but word had still spread, as it so often did. To add an extra layer of cruelty and injustice, the caul had left a scar behind at the attachment point, a jagged little line across the top of his head that made the child look like Frankenstein's monster.

In the village, the old women had denounced the child to anyone who'd listen while simultaneously making it known that they'd pay a pretty penny for the caul. It was a mark of their hypocrisy that they believed both that the caul would bring good luck and that the child who was born with it would be the ruin of all who grew close to him. No man born to a caul could set foot on a ship – at least, not if the captains had anything to do with it – and yet the sailors would have traded limbs to possess one. Once separated from their former owners, cauls were said to protect men from drowning.

Most of the sailors stocked up on any lucky talismans or amulets they could get their hands on.

The boy's new father, Rodrigo LaMuerte, was a human cannonball, and he spent his evenings flying through the air and landing in safety nets to the applause of the masses before retiring to his dressing room with a bottle of scotch. His mother, Maria LaMuerte, was a tattooed woman, an occupation that did little to improve Enrique's social standing. But the LaMuertes rarely stayed in one place for long enough for the locals to take much notice.

Enrique seemed happy with his station in life, at least for the first few years. He was a typical child, prone to playing in the mud and laughing at the animals when they toured with the travelling circus. He slept well at night when they retired to their caravan, and even when he did wake up, he'd just sit up in his cot and stare into the darkness as though he was studying its textures.

But Maria LaMuerte was worried, especially once his third birthday rolled around. The boy still hadn't spoken, although he looked them in the eyes when they talked to him and seemed to show an alarming amount of intelligence. Rodrigo said that the boy understood every word but had no interest in the subject matter. Maria wasn't so sure, and she'd wanted to take the boy to a priest.

In the end, they arrived at a compromise, and Enrique LaMuerte was taken to see a doctor, who pronounced that there was nothing wrong with the boy. The doctor's name was MacLaren, and he was a strapping Scottish chap who'd moved to the south in pursuit of money and found himself treating the poor in exchange for whatever scraps of coin or food they could spare. Half the time, he worked for free.

The LaMuertes were good customers, and their circus-earned cash went a long way towards buying MacLaren's cooperation. But there was only so much that he could do, and he'd sent them away with instructions to report back if the boy was still mute the following summer.

Then Enrique had surprised everyone by telling MacLaren to go fuck himself.

***

After some further testing, MacLaren had concluded that far from being an idiot, Enrique LaMuerte was a borderline genius. The boy was so advanced for his age that regular schooling was out of the question, but that didn't pose a problem because of the LaMuertes' itinerant lifestyle. Instead of sending him to school after school after school and torturing the child by giving him friends and taking them away again, Enrique LaMuerte was to begin lessons with the bums and the freaks who worked at the circus.

The bearded woman was a former schoolmistress, and

she was more than happy to spearhead the boy's education. Her name was Miss Merkin, and she ruled over her makeshift classroom with an iron fist, quite literally. She'd lost her left hand after an accident with one of the lions. Her right hand was an Irishman, Harry O'Leary, a middle-aged chap who'd once been a fire-breather before retiring from the ring and taking on the tough but necessary job of chief of operations. He made sure that people were fed and that everyone followed the same itinerary, so they didn't leave stragglers behind when they moved from town to town.

Occasionally, they'd meet up with other troupes, and that gave the boy more opportunities to learn. One summer, when Enrique had just turned six, he took a couple of lessons from a fortune teller called Gypsy Pink, who'd taken an immediate shine to him. He'd taken a shine to her, too. He talked to her, for a start, and she was quick to recognise his unnatural intelligence and to do what she could to draw it out of him.

Gypsy Pink taught Enrique many things, including the importance of smell. She explained that the most important aspect of a piece of magic was its setup, and that senses sold realism. To demonstrate, she first lit a stick of incense, which tinged the air with the sickly sweet smell of rosewood. Then she withdrew a strange-looking fruit from an old wooden crate and placed it on the table in front of her. She pulled out a knife, which had been tucked somewhere beneath her chair, and placed it on the table with a rueful grin.

"Men," she said, simply. "Sometimes they get touchy-feely."

"I'll never do that," Enrique said.

"Good," she replied. Then she used the knife to cut into the fruit and a godawful smell leaked out of it, something like an open sewer mixed with rotting vegetation. It was so overpowering that Enrique was forced to cover his nostrils with a sleeve. Unperturbed, Gypsy Pink sliced up the fruit, speared a big chunk of it with the end of the knife and dropped it into her mouth. She chewed ruminatively at it for a moment or two and then said, "Delicious."

"What is it?" Enrique asked, his disgust momentarily overtaken by his curiosity.

"It's durian fruit, boy," Gypsy Pink replied. "A delicacy to some people and as strange a fruit as you'll ever see. Come here and take a bite from it."

Sceptical at first, Enrique nevertheless pushed past the stench to approach the table. He picked up a slice of the fruit and put it in his mouth.

He didn't like it, but it didn't taste as bad as it smelled. It was an acquired taste that he hadn't acquired, but he still understood the lesson. She was telling him to be different, to stand out from the crowd. She was telling him to be the durian fruit, a piece of advice that he'd have ignored if it had come from any other source. But he trusted Gypsy Pink, and she trusted him. They talked to one another as equals. When he opened up to her about the unusual circumstances around his birth – which he claimed to remember – they learned that they had something else in common.

"I was also born with a caul," the gypsy said. "My mama told me that's why I can read palms and tell fortunes. She said that cauls are made from Jesus's nightgown, how about that?"

"Jesus didn't exist," Enrique said, matter-of-factly. Even at six years old, he had a reputation as a know-it-all, but Gypsy Pink was one of the few people who realised that Enrique had the knowledge to back it up.

"That's as maybe."

"Even if he did exist, his miracles didn't."

"That's quite enough, now," the gypsy said. "Remember, Enrique, we're supposed to be studying divination. There'll be plenty of time for religion on Sunday."

***

"The boy was born with the mark of the devil."

"Codswallop," Maria LaMuerte replied. "If the caul was good enough for Byron, it's good enough for my boy."

"But he's not really your boy," the stranger insisted. "His true parents are dead, or at least his mother is. Lord only knows what happened to the father."

"We're the only family he has."

Enrique LaMuerte was lying in his sleeping bag, but the insomnia he'd experienced as a baby had accompanied him through his toddler years and showed no signs of abating. His eyes were open, but it was too dark to see anything other than the canvas above his head. It was a cold night after a sunny day, brought about by the lack of cloud cover and the unusually high winds. Enrique had to strain his ears to follow the conversation, which was taking place under the light of the moon and out in the darkness. He recognised his mother's voice, and he'd occasionally heard a low murmur from his father, but he couldn't place the voice of the stranger.

"The time will come when you see the wisdom in my words," the stranger said. "When you do, I'll be ready. You have to understand, Maria, that sometimes the needs of the many outweigh the needs of the few. I'm not asking you to give me the boy because I think you're a failure as a mother. I'm not asking you to give him to me because I desire his company. I'm asking you to give him to me for the betterment of humanity. We must school the boy in good and evil before it's too late."

"Over my dead body," Rodrigo growled. "Go on, get

out of here. Before I fetch my shotgun."

***

War broke out in Europe after an archduke was assassinated in Sarajevo, but for a while at least, it seemed as though the Circo de la Flor would remain unaffected. If anything, business was booming, spurred on by a renaissance in escapism from a nation that wanted to forget it was at war.

By the time the first shots were fired, Enrique was eight years old, and he'd already started to develop his own act, a magic show involving a trick deck of cards and a disappearing shilling. Card magic was cheap magic, the easiest of all magic to master, involving little more than sleight of hand and misdirection. But Enrique had youth on his side. When the circus was in town, people would flock from miles around to lose a shilling or two to the magical youngster.

To begin with, life went on much as it always had, and the Circo de la Flor continued to meander from town to town through the English countryside. When they did hear of the war, it was usually in snatches of overheard conversation as the punters wandered from tent to tent.

Then the Military Service Act was passed, imposing conscription on all single men of serviceable age. Rodrigo was exempt by virtue of being married, but then a second act was passed in May of 1916 which extended conscription to married men. Several of the performers had already been summoned by the home office, and Rodrigo LaMuerte's papers arrived at the start of July, just as the circus was gearing up for peak season.

He'd packed his bags, said goodbye to his wife and son and headed off to a military training camp before they had time to wrap their heads around it.

Men were few and far between at the Circo de la Flor, and there were rumours that the company was on the verge of collapse. With their young men sent to the front, they were left with just children and the elderly, neither of which were fit for training lions or flying through the air with the acrobats. Most of the acts were being forced to adapt, finding new ways to work together to keep the public entertained, at least for long enough to spend their money. And so Enrique found himself working for a living, acting as the man of the house while his father was away. At least, that was what he told himself.

The months passed and the summer turned to winter. The members of the Circo de la Flor were left with low morale and no food in their bellies, especially after the visitors started to dry up and the leaves fell off the trees. Christmas that year was a sombre affair, celebrated privately and quietly beneath the folds of their tents.

Maria and Enrique spent most of Christ's birthday praying for the safe return of the family figurehead from the front lines.

Life continued, as it had to, and the grass was swallowed up by mud and turned back into grass again. Letters from Rodrigo were few and far between, though those that did arrive were pages long and written over the space of days or even weeks. Maria replied to him and then some, dispatching several letters a week and dousing them in her perfume to bring her husband some small comfort, but not all of them made it to their intended destination.

In the summer, the Circo de la Flor split in half, with many of the performers boarding a steamer bound for the American Midwest. The LaMuertes stayed behind, remaining loyal to their ringmaster, but they had an ulterior motive. They wanted to stay in the land that their patriarch was fighting for.

In August, they received a dispatch from the front lines in which Rodrigo announced that his division was being moved to Ypres. His unit was to capture a rail junction to the east so that the Allies could advance on the Belgian coast, and he expected not to have a chance to write for several weeks.

It was sealed with love and a kiss.

***

The bad news came in the form of a letter, as it so often did.

It had looked innocuous, just a plain white envelope with the address of a sorting office in the Yorkshire Dales. As always, the Circo de la Flor had left a forwarding address, with their mail chasing them from place to place just like the letters that were sent to the front lines.

Maria had opened up the letter and started reading it aloud to Enrique.

"Dear Mrs LaMuerte," she'd read. "I regret to inform you…"

But she hadn't made it any further. The tears had overtaken her by then.

That left Enrique with his arms around his mother, consoling her by whispering to her in Spanish and embracing her as tightly as his little arms could manage.

Rodrigo's body was never returned to them, and they never learned of its final resting place. Enrique liked to picture his father in a peaceful spot beneath an elm tree, but he thought it more likely that he'd been buried in a mass grave somewhere, just discarded like a piece of trash.

And still the war raged on.

***

By the time that the last shots were fired, Enrique had learned to hate the war, and so, it seemed, had everyone else. They'd paid the price in blood and empty stomachs. They'd lost friends and family members, and the Circo itself had started to crumble. The winter of 1918 was the toughest of them all, and the Spanish flu had killed off many of those who'd been spared the horrors of war. Those who survived the flu faced the threat of starvation.

Christmas came and went, followed by Enrique's thirteenth birthday. Maria didn't have much money, but she'd saved what little she could and used it to purchase a smart suit, complete with a vest jacket and a silk tie. It had taken more than the boy would ever know to save that money, and Maria had even traded away the last of her jewellery, but she also saw the sense in the gift. Enrique had asked for it so he could wear it to perform his act.

His magic had progressed, though there weren't many opportunities for him to learn. They rarely came across other troupes, and even when they did, there were few magicians left. Most of them had done a disappearing act when the draft had been announced. And so Enrique had started to teach himself, whiling away hour after hour perfecting his sleight of hand and his misdirection. By the time that he was fourteen, he'd mastered card magic and moved on to bigger tricks, pulling live doves from beneath his hat and inventing more and more elaborate contraptions for sawing women in half or disappearing into thin air.

He was further handicapped by the need to keep his contraptions portable so that they'd fit in his mother's caravan. Space was already tight enough, and his mother refused to jettison any of his late father's belongings.

They were all they had left of him.

Gypsy Pink had done what she could to keep the boy's spirits up, but even she wasn't immune to change. While the other performers were being lured away by more commercially-minded ringmasters who could afford to pay a premium, Gypsy Pink was preparing for retirement. At first, Enrique had felt betrayed, accusing her of leaving him when he needed her the most. But eventually he'd relented, especially after she'd agreed to take the boy into the city.

"I'll take you anywhere you'd like to go," she said one evening, when they were sharing supper inside her caravan. It was two weeks before she was due to perform her final show. "You name the place and I'll take you there. The Tower of London, perhaps."

Enrique shook his head.

"I know where I'd like to go," he replied. "I want to visit Kew Gardens."

"Kew Gardens?"

"I've read about it in my books," Enrique explained. "It sounds wonderful, truly. They say as it has the rarest plants in the world."

"Plants?" Pink replied. "Most youngsters your age are more interested in the lassies."

"They bore me," Enrique replied, shaking his head. "I'd rather dedicate time to my studies."

"Of magic?"

"Yes," Enrique said. "And the sciences, botany and biology included. I intend to make them a part of my act. Other magicians pull rabbits from hats. I'll make flowers grow from nothing. I'll reverse the flow of time in front of people's eyes. I'll bring the dead back to life again."

"There's no magic that powerful, Enrique," Pink said. "Nothing can bring back the dead."

"We'll see about that," he replied.

***

The trip to Kew Gardens was like no other trip the young man had been on, which was saying a lot for someone who lived the life of an itinerant traveller, peddling his magic on village greens and disused race tracks.

He'd dragged Gypsy Pink all over the labyrinth of plant-life, tugging her from bush to shrub to tree and back round again, sketching his favourites in pencil as he went. He had a particular preference for the exotic plants, many of which were the only such examples in the country. He had a student's enthusiasm for knowledge, a thirst so strong it was as though he was lost in a desert of information.

One plant in particular caught his eye: the amorphophallus titanum, the corpse plant, which rarely bloomed but which was in season for their visit. It stood almost as tall as a man and consisted of a huge flower that was green on the outside and purple on the inside, with a protuberance that looked, at a distance, like a cob of corn. It reeked of death and decomposition, so much so that Gypsy Pink refused to go within a dozen paces of it.

"Stay away from that thing, Enrique," she warned. "It stinks of evil."

But Enrique LaMuerte was spellbound. The cogs of his mind were already whirring as he considered what a skilled magician could do with such a flower. The possibilities were limitless.

That night, as he lay in his sleeping bag and stared mindlessly at the roof of his tent, he thought about the corpse flower and imagined that he could see it blooming there on the canvas. He imagined that he could smell it, the sweet and sickly scent of musky death.

It was an acquired taste, just like the durian fruit.

***

The stranger returned on the night of LaMuerte's sixteenth birthday. This time, without the boy's father, he was given an audience with Enrique himself, though his mother made it clear that she was listening. The three of them were sitting inside the LaMuerte trailer, and Maria was watching with narrowed eyes as the stranger talked to Enrique in a low voice. The only other sound was the clink-clink of her knitting needles.

"Do you know who I am?" the stranger asked.

"No," Enrique replied.

"Good," the stranger said. "My name, for the moment, is unimportant. I visited your parents once before and asked them to deliver you to my care. They refused. Now that you've come of age, I'm here to ask you in person."

"What is it that you'd ask of me?"

"I belong to an organisation," the stranger said. "A secret organisation, if you will, where men of great intellect come together to pool their knowledge in pursuit of a common cause. Our aim is twofold. We aim to serve mankind in the war against evil, and we aim to conquer death itself and become immortal."

"Your cause is doomed to failure," LaMuerte replied. "Death can never be conquered, not in the long run, and evil is sure to triumph just as entropy increases in a closed system."

"I'm offering you the chance of a lifetime," the stranger said. "Come and join my institute and you'll want for nothing."

"I'd be a pawn in your misguided war," LaMuerte growled. "And I've known enough of war to last a lifetime. Do you know what happened to my father?"

"Rodrigo LaMuerte wasn't your father," the stranger

said, leaning away from Enrique as though the boy was a coiled snake preparing to strike. "Not really. The Lord God–"

"The Lord God be damned," Enrique said. "What care do I have of God, or humanity, or of good versus evil? No, magic is my calling, the master that I serve. I ask you, sir, to leave my mother and I in peace."

And, for a little while, peace came.

***

In 1925, when Enrique was nineteen years old, the Circo de la Flor performed for the final time to a relatively small crowd of just a hundred or so on a village green. Its fortunes had been fading for years, ever since the outbreak of the war and the grand separation in which half the entertainers left for pastures new. By the time that it reached its sad climax, which came with a whimper instead of a bang, the dozen or so remaining performers had already started to go their separate ways. Their final show, to celebrate the harvest, merely put a full stop at the end of the paragraph of their careers.

Enrique and Maria went solo for a while, he with his magic and her with her ink, but there was little call for a tattooed woman without an ensemble cast of freaks to support her, and there was no ordinary work available for a woman who looked like an artist's canvas. To make matters worse, now that Enrique was of age, a tent outside his mother's caravan was no longer enough. He longed to sleep in a room of his own.

More and more often, Enrique found himself acting as the breadwinner. And, as the breadwinner, he also maintained control over the purse strings. He gave his mother what she needed to feed them both and to grease the wheels of the carriage as they rode from town to town. He kept the rest for himself, investing in increasingly elaborate clothing and machinery.

By his twentieth birthday, he'd developed his act further, creating a unique look and feel that was inspired by the aesthetics of the late Victorians. He was a relatively short man, so he made up for it with special boots with trick soles that helped to give him another inch or two. He also took to wearing a leather top hat, which was fitted with fake jewels and which looked ridiculous in the butcher's or at the public house. On stage, however, it gave him a *je ne sais quoi* that translated into something of an edge over the competition.

Enrique coupled the hat with a bizarre outfit that blended fine tailoring with strange and unusual clockwork. He'd had it custom-made, exhausting no shortage of time and money to track down a tailor and a watchmaker who could get the job done to his specifications. The result was a sheer monstrosity of a suit that mixed copper and iron with silk and cotton. It ticked as he walked, the gears being charged with the kinetic energy of his movement, and steam spouted out the back of it whenever he clenched his gloved right fist. His other arm was uncovered, exposing his muscles and the swirling tribal tattoos that covered them. There was a stigma against tattoos, and most people associated them with sailors, grog and drunkenness, but they were the closest thing he had to a family heirloom. His mother had helped him to find an artist, and he'd created the designs himself based on numerology, astrology and the golden ratio.

The suit was heavy and cumbersome, impractical for most purposes and the polar opposite of casualwear, but it had its uses. He wore it to performances to dazzle the crowds and to make sure that no matter where he went, everyone knew who he was. He grew a goatee to go with his swarthy looks and Hispanic hair, and he took to wearing a monocle made from a piece of fallen meteorite and a looping chain that attached it to his breast pocket.

His new costume needed a new persona to go with it, and so Enrique LaMuerte found himself in search of a name. He'd thought about sticking with Spanish, but the English had fostered a deep mistrust of foreigners and he was worried that his name could prejudice them against him. And besides, he owed nothing to the Spanish and everything to his parents. He himself was English, or at least as far as he could tell. His accent certainly was, though it integrated a couple of regional dialects as well as a whole heap of slang.

And so he thought back to the long-gone fortune-teller Gypsy Pink and her durian fruit.

From then on, he was no longer Enrique LaMuerte, except to his mother. To the rest of the world, he was Durian Pink.

***

In 1929, Enrique LaMuerte turned twenty-three. He also buried his mother.

She'd been taken too soon by what the doctors had called a wasting disease. Secretly, he suspected that the loss of his father had been eating away at her. She'd certainly lost a lot of weight since the end of the war, and by the time that she took to her deathbed, she'd been nothing more than inked skin and bone, like an old piece of parchment that was at risk of immolation if exposed to the light of the sun.

Her funeral had been well-attended, and Enrique had felt a swell in his heart when Gypsy Pink had approached him after the service and told him that he'd turned into a handsome young man, just as she'd known he always would. He'd grown too tall for her to kiss the top of his head, but he knelt down before her so she could do it anyway.

But after the wake was over and he'd said his final goodbyes, there was nowhere for him to go but back to the wagon. Suddenly, without his mother inside, it seemed a lot bigger.

There was nothing to tie him to England, or at least nothing more than the mere fact that it was the country he'd been born in. That might have been enough for some, but Enrique LaMuerte had never been a patriot. He thought about spending some time in France, but the idea put him in mind of his father and his final resting place beneath the soil. Germany was out of the question for the same reason, and Italy held no appeal because he couldn't speak the language.

And so as the roaring twenties came to a crescendo and the 1930s dawned on an apathetic world, Enrique LaMuerte found himself selling his parents' wagon, along with most of their worldly possessions. He put the remainder into storage, along with his machines and whichever of his own belongings wouldn't fit into his small leather travelling case. Then he booked himself passage to the Spanish mainland on a steamer setting sail from Southampton.

***

Time ticked on.

Enrique settled into the Spanish way of life like a natural. The food reminded him of his mother's cooking and he could speak the language with only the barest trace of an accent. The living was good, especially during the summer months, and he was able to find work in the nightclubs and the emerging tourist resorts on the seafronts. But a shadow loomed over the horizon, and it took the form of a swastika.

Across Europe, fascism and communism were rearing

their heads, and the two words were bandied about in the pubs and the music halls as though they had the power to summon the devil himself. LaMuerte wasn't interested in politics, except for when they directly affected him, but he still listened to the conversations with growing concern.

Then civil war broke out. The labourers in the cafeterias called it a class struggle, a war of religion, a clash between dictatorship and democracy and a conflict between revolution and counterrevolution. LaMuerte called it good for business.

It started with a coup, which succeeded in some cities and failed in others. That left the country divided and self-destructive, with nationalists and republicans both vying for control. LaMuerte took neither side, though he watched with worried interest as the fascists in Italy and Germany provided support to the nationalists. The republicans, meanwhile, were bolstering their numbers with volunteers from across the globe, mostly from countries that opposed the fascists on paper but who wanted to keep their hands clean of conflict.

And so Enrique LaMuerte – or Durian Pink, depending upon who was asking – found himself working as a touring magician, entertaining the troops as he trekked from camp to camp and outpost to outpost. It didn't matter which side the soldiers were fighting for. There was a moral code of conduct, a guarantee of safe passage for the entertainers, the postmen and the prostitutes.

Times were tough for everyone, but Enrique felt the pinch less than most. The soldiers were bored, keen to spend what little money they earned on whatever cheap thrill they could exchange a coin for. LaMuerte was more than happy to take their money.

The civil war raged on. Enrique slipped into a routine of sorts, and all the while he kept learning and experimenting.

He was honing his craft, perfecting a magic so powerful that, like a sufficiently advanced technology, it was indistinguishable from the real thing.

Amongst the troops, he started to develop a reputation as a pseudo-saviour. There, on the front line, the men were happy to take any hope they could get, even if that hope was based on a false prophet and a couple of parlour tricks. LaMuerte had a knack for sensing death and would often hand out cryptic clues to the servicemen, who would either follow his suggestions and live or ignore them and die. To Enrique LaMuerte, it was all the same. He only gave out tips to the people who paid him well.

He got used to turning a blind eye to the death and destruction. It was just a part of life, like the loneliness that consumed him and sometimes drove him to the brothels, though he tried to limit himself to two visits per year to reduce his chances of catching something. With so many soldiers around and so much poverty, disease was rife, especially that of the venereal kind.

When the civil war ended in 1939, he was thirty-three years old, the same age that Jesus had been when he'd died on the cross. He was older than his father had been when the Great War had broken out a quarter of a century earlier, but not by much. He was also ready for his next challenge. The music halls of London were waiting for him.

***

To begin with, life went on much as usual, with LaMuerte performing anywhere that would take him. For a while, it seemed as though he'd left the spectre of war behind him, and the summer was a summer of love. LaMuerte played the part of a true cad, performing most nights and then finding the arms of some woman to hold him once the show was over. On those rare nights where he could neither seduce nor pay for companionship, he drank as much beer as he could afford with his earnings before collapsing into bed at his makeshift lodgings.

But the summer of love had to end, and for Enrique LaMuerte, it happened on Sunday 3rd September 1939 at 11 AM, when Prime Minister Neville Chamberlain made an announcement to the nation over the radio.

LaMuerte had just woken up and was listening to the broadcast as it filtered through the paper-thin walls from the reading room of the guesthouse. Chamberlain's voice sounded reedy and insignificant to LaMuerte's ears, and it was distorted and crackly as though the radio was tuned to a slightly false frequency

"I'm speaking to you from the cabinet room at Ten Downing Street," Chamberlain said. "This morning, the British ambassador in Berlin handed the German government a final note stating that unless we heard from them by eleven o'clock that they were prepared at once to withdraw their troops from Poland, a state of war would exist between us. I have to tell you now that no such undertaking has been received, and that consequently this country is at war with Germany."

There were gasps from elsewhere in the house, as well as a thud that sounded like someone slamming a fist against the breakfast table.

"You can imagine what a bitter blow it is to me that all my long struggle to win peace has failed," Chamberlain continued. "Yet I can't believe that there's anything more, or anything different, that I could have done and that would have been more successful. Up to the very last, it would have been quite possible to have arranged a peaceful and honourable settlement between Germany and Poland. But Hitler wouldn't have it. He'd evidently made up his mind to attack Poland whatever happened, and although he now says he put forward reasonable proposals which were rejected by the Poles, that's not a true statement. The proposals were never shown to the Poles, nor to us, and though they were announced in the German broadcast on Thursday night, Hitler didn't wait to hear comments on them, but ordered his troops to cross the Polish frontier the next morning."

LaMuerte sighed, feeling the weight of history upon him once more. The world had changed since the last war, but the nature of man had remained the same.

"His action shows convincingly that there's no chance of expecting that this man will ever give up his practice of using force to gain his will," Chamberlain said. "He can only be stopped by force. We have a clear conscience. We've done all that any country could do to establish peace. But the situation in which no word given by Germany's ruler could be trusted, and no people or country could feel itself safe, had become intolerable. And now that we've resolved to finish it, I know that you'll all play your part with calmness and courage."

Kindness and courage, LaMuerte thought. *We'll see about that.*

***

Kindness and courage didn't pay the bills, and LaMuerte found himself increasingly relying on his savings as the war raged on and his workload took a dive. All of a sudden, he was finding it difficult to make money, and that was the least of his worries.

A year after the start of the war, with neither defeat nor victory on the horizon, Enrique LaMuerte was staying in a boarding house in Battersea on the night that the Blitz began.

The bombs rained down again for a second night and then a third. After a week of German lightning raining down from the sky, LaMuerte was already used to going below ground to wait out the bombs on the tube platforms. He helped to keep morale high by performing tricks to the milling crowds, who often rewarded him with handfuls of coins.

After three weeks of nightly bombing, LaMuerte signed up to join the volunteers who put out the fires and searched for survivors once the dust settled. He saw enough death for several lifetimes, including one elderly woman who'd lost the side of her face to a bomb blast and who'd survived for long enough to beat helplessly at the windows until the smoke inside overwhelmed her.

LaMuerte had watched her, bearing silent, grim witness to her unhappy demise. There was nothing more he could have done.

France fell, and with it fell the magician's spirits. German bombs had become a way of life, and so had the fire and the death that they brought. Time moved on, and the fascists took most of Europe, though their attention had been diverted by the red menace of Russia.

But mostly, time ticked on, and Enrique LaMuerte continued to perfect his magic while doing his best to serve his fellow man. He just wished that his magic wand could have made the enemy planes disappear.

***

By the end of the war, Enrique LaMuerte was broke and alone, but at least he was alive. He celebrated his fortieth birthday in solitude, pawning some of his old equipment so that he could purchase a couple of bottles of wine and a good meal.

But the end of hostilities brought celebrations, and the

celebrations brought work. LaMuerte started taking in a decent amount of money, but there was little chance of him squirreling it away when there were new tricks to perfect and new equipment to design and develop.

He continued to live in a guest house, but he paid for a second room and asked Mrs. Rivers to take the bed out. She protested at first, until he agreed to pay half again to cover the storage costs, as long as she kept her nose out of the room and didn't include it in her cleaning rounds.

It was an arrangement that suited everyone.

Then came the lucky break that he'd been waiting for, his hope slowly dwindling until it seemed like a solitary candle in an empty house as a thunderstorm rolled in over the horizon. One of his associates, a ventriloquist called Harry Handsome, lost his voice the night before a variety show at the Royal Albert Hall. Handsome's main rival, an Irishwoman called Saoirse Murphy, was out of town, performing in Paris.

LaMuerte wasn't second on the list, and nor was he third. In fact, he was so far down that he wasn't approached until two o'clock in the afternoon, and the slot was due six hours later. But that gave him plenty of time for what he had in mind.

That night, after the curtains had risen and the entertainment had begun, Durian Pink was wheeled out into the centre of the stage and illuminated beneath the spotlights. He was encased in a block of concrete and, as per the rules he'd been provided with on the maximum length of his spot, he had six minutes to get out. That didn't bother him too much, though, because he only had enough oxygen for four.

He moved quickly, his hands a blur of activity as he worked his tools and drilled away at the pressure points. He hoped that the artisans that he'd hired had built the thing to the exact specifications that he'd provided them with. If not, it was sure to be his final performance, a swan song that would be remembered for as long as there were people to remember it.

Fortunately for Enrique Lamuerte, the concrete was weak in exactly the right places, and he made his way out in three minutes and seventeen seconds.

Afterwards, once he'd emerged triumphantly from the block of concrete with a chisel in one hand and a mallet in the other, he'd been whisked off the stage and into the wings, where the national press was waiting. They all wanted to know how he'd done it.

"A magician never reveals his secrets," was the only reply.

***

The following morning, LaMuerte's quote was on the front page of two of the newspapers, and Mrs. Rivers had given him his marching orders, telling him that she had better things to do than to act as his receptionist. The guesthouse's telephone had been ringing off the hook for three hours straight, and LaMuerte had booked up his diary for the next two weeks with meetings. It seemed like every journalist in the country wanted to talk to him, and he'd even had two requests to appear on the radio.

According to the newspapers, Queen Elizabeth II had been in the audience and she'd been impressed by his act. LaMuerte was no royalist, but he did know the value of a good testimonial.

He added the line "magician by royal appointment" to his business cards.

It worked wonders. By the end of the forties, Enrique LaMuerte was one of the highest earners in the city's music halls. A TV special followed in the early fifties, followed by a series of book deals including a much-hyped autobiography that was critically panned almost as soon as it came out because he didn't explain how any of the tricks worked. He'd lived a less than juicy personal life, and so while the book became a moderate bestseller, it was quickly forgotten.

But Durian Pink wasn't forgotten, and the media appearances continued to trickle in, along with more stage appearances than he could ever hope to honour. His wealth rose in direct proportion to the amount of media exposure that he received, and a six-book publishing deal came with an advance of £10,000, an astonishing amount of money in a time when farthings and shillings were still legal currency.

LaMuerte lived frugally, a by-product of his humble upbringing, and that meant that he was able to squirrel much of the money away. But he was no Scrooge, and he didn't believe in hoarding gold or letting his cash rot in a bank vault. Instead, he put it to work, making shrewd investments in the stock market and eventually doubling his net worth over the period of several years.

In 1951, he celebrated his birthday by purchasing a huge solarium, a biodome. It was like a giant glass greenhouse, big enough to swallow a football pitch, and it quickly became LaMuerte's pride and joy. When he bought it, it was in a state of disrepair and in need of a good clean. There was plenty of wildlife, some of it exotic, but it was wilting and badly managed. In some places, ivy had grown up and throttled the other plants. There was also a problem with pigeons, which had to be chased away before the solarium could be restored to its full glory.

Nevertheless, LaMuerte fell in love with the place, and he continued to pump his time and money into the solarium and enjoyed an immense amount of pride and pleasure as a result of it. He liked to talk to the plants and to watch them as they grew, and he liked the peaceful sense of solitude that he felt when he walked amongst them. Even though he'd always been a natural performer, he was also an introvert, perhaps a learned trait from the fear and discrimination he'd faced as a child when the stories about his caul made the rounds.

And so the solarium was the perfect place for him, especially because it also doubled as the great stage on which he intended to perform his final and most impressive trick of all. It involved his three-metre tall amorphophallus titanum plant – a plant that was also known as the corpse flower because it reeked of death and rotting flesh.

***

Enrique LaMuerte died on Monday 23rd November 1953, after a short battle with an unknown illness that the doctors had failed to diagnose. It was as though the very life had drained out of him. Because of the strange conditions of his birth and his reputation as an eccentric, the rumour mill soon began. They said that he'd sold his soul to the devil and that he'd had his blood drained by a vampire or his soul sucked out by a succubus.

He'd been forty-seven years of age. His funeral was attended by a single mourner, a stranger in black who'd watched in silence and then wordlessly muttered "what a waste" before leaving the priest to lower an empty coffin into the soil.

There was little mourning from the general public. He'd been loved, sure, but he'd been loved from a distance through the pages of newspapers. Most of them had no idea that he was called Enrique LaMuerte, known as he was under his pseudonym. Nor did they know that he'd owned the solarium, which had been placed in a trust under the terms of his last will and testament. LaMuerte himself was buried in a glass mausoleum at the foot of his corpse plant, in one last bait and switch trick that left the public thinking it was just a waxwork from Madame Tussaud's.

And the lie became the truth, as it had a habit of doing. Pink's solarium became one of the leading tourist attractions in the southwest of England, welcoming thousands – and later hundreds of thousands – of visitors every year. Most of them stayed away from the "waxwork" and the stench of the amorphophallus titanum, preferring instead to visit the plants with the prettier leaves and the sweeter smells.

Over the years, his corpse remained the same, though the plant started to wither and die, its stench growing more putrid and vomit-inducing by the day. The gardeners did their best to keep the plants under control, but the money was running out and eventually the visitors started to drop off and dwindled back to mere thousands, and just a couple of dozen visitors a day.

Inevitably, the trust ran out of money, and though the solarium went on the market for a bargain price, no one wanted to buy it. The doors were closed for the final time towards the end of the 1960s, while the U.S. government was preparing to send a man to the moon. Chains were wrapped around the door handles and the plants were left to fend for themselves, which they did. The weak perished and the strongest survived, the ivy thriving and choking out the sun. In the car park, the weeds cracked their way through the concrete and stretched towards the sun.

And Durian Pink slumbered on, cocooned inside his glass display case, as beside him, the amorphophallus continued to wither.

Eventually, the corpse plant died, and when it did, so too did the magic. Enrique LaMuerte's corpse turned into dust in the blink of an eye, but no one was there to see it.

The denouement of his greatest trick went unnoticed, even to the plants that he'd loved and nurtured.

They say that the solarium is still there today, but only to those with the gift of magic in their blood. When most people go near it, they're driven away by a sort of disturbance in the air, a discomforting set of energy waves that causes headaches and raises rumours of government-owned cell phone towers that are designed to control minds.

Only those who are born with a caul can see it.

Insomniac

Part One: Insomnia

WEEK ONE, DAY ONE

KATE'S ALARM CLOCK RANG OUT like it always did at 5:55 AM. She gave it exactly five seconds and then slammed a hand down three times in quick succession to silence it.

She counted to fifty-five and then sat upright at precisely 5:56. The next thirty-four minutes had to run like clockwork. There was a routine, and bad things happened if she broke it. Bad things also happened when she didn't break it, but that was beside the point.

Kate brushed her teeth, flossed them and brushed them again, then hopped into the shower until 6:15, when she climbed back out and wrapped herself in an Egyptian cotton towel before brushing, flossing and brushing again. She walked back through to her bedroom, pulled on the clothes that she'd selected the night before and sat down at her dresser to brush her hair.

She looked at herself in the mirror and took a mental inventory. *Uneven face. Wonky nose. Freckles spread slapdash across her body. Upper teeth hanging out and over her bottom teeth. But on the plus side, the girls at Rush got her hair right and the new conditioner was working wonders on the split ends and the knots and tangles.*

Kate was in the minority, a member of the small group of women who didn't love their bodies and who didn't really want to. To Kate, her body was just a shell, an ungainly frame for her to hang designer clothes from while she entered data into a computer terminal, day after intolerable day.

That day was a Tuesday, which meant four more working days until the weekend. She had plans, big ones. She'd moved house a couple of weeks earlier, and she'd set this weekend aside to unpack her books and DVDs and to sort them into alphabetical order. She had a lot of books and DVDs.

But at 6:30 AM, she had something else on her mind. She was dressed and ready to go, although she planned to do her makeup in the car park as she usually did. As soon as the clock hit half past, she was ready for her final check before leaving the house.

She started upstairs, moving from room to room and checking the windows and doors. She worked anticlockwise and checked each of the deadbolts twice, then closed each of the doors one by one behind her. She brushed her teeth again, rinsed out the sink, flushed the toilet, washed her hands, cleaned out the sink and checked the taps were off. Then she headed downstairs and began the routine all over again.

It took her fifteen minutes to finish the checks. Luckily, she'd allowed for it.

Kate hated being late.

***

"You're late," Mr. Murray said. Mr. Murray was Kate's boss at the department store, a petulant little man who was notoriously inflexible when it came to tardiness.

"I'm sorry, sir," Kate said. "There was traffic on the A404."

"I know," Murray replied. "Most people turned off and

took the side roads. But not you. Why is that?"

Kate shrugged. "I have a routine," she said. "There's a route. What's the point of having a route if you deviate?"

Mr. Murray sighed and said, "That's not good enough. You're going to have to work late to make the time up."

Kate nodded and said nothing, but inside her body, her heart was racing and trying to catch up with her mind, which was running at a hundred miles per hour and rapidly re-evaluating the evening ahead.

For most people, an extra twenty minutes at the end of the day wouldn't be a problem. Kate acknowledged the fairness of it, but Mr. Murray didn't understand what he was asking of her. Everything had a time and a place, and an extra twenty minutes at the office would put her twenty minutes behind schedule. That was twenty minutes that she'd have to catch up somewhere else by skipping a shower or dodging dinner.

"What about if I work through lunch?" she asked.

Mr. Murray smiled a smile that reminded her of a hungry shark as it eyed up a diver. "Work through lunch," he said, "and then catch up your time at the end of the day."

"But that's not fair!"

"Life isn't fair," Mr. Murray said. "Get to it."

And so Kate "'got to it," and she kept her head down at her desk until the end of the day. She'd hoped that if she got everything done then the boss would let her leave on time, and she was suffering from sharp pangs of anxiety in her head and hunger in her stomach because she'd skipped lunch for the first time in several months.

She made up the twenty minutes and then some, and she spent the waning hours of the workday watching the clock and waiting for something else to come in. She packed her bag up and shut her computer down at 5:28, ready to leave at 5:30, but no such luck. Mr. Murray bore down on her at 5:29 and asked her where the hell she thought she was going.

"Home, sir," she said. Her heart was fluttering like an angry bluebird as it fled the nest.

"Not until I say so."

"But I worked through lunch," she protested. "And I have nothing left to do."

"Then you'll sit at your desk until you've learned your lesson," the boss said.

Not for the first time, Kate asked herself why she'd ever accepted the job. *I wasn't born to crunch numbers in some badly ventilated shitheap,* she thought.

But she knew that the boss had won. She needed the job. No, not the job. She needed the money.

"But I had plans tonight," she murmured. It was true. She had plans every night. The same plan, but a perpetual plan nonetheless.

"You're just going to have to reschedule," Mr. Murray said. "Sorry, Kate. The company comes first."

***

Kate got home at 7:45 PM, a full fifty minutes behind schedule. It had been a bad day, and she wondered whether she'd brought it on herself by breaking her routine. But it all came back to the traffic, and there was nothing to be done about that. Traffic was just one of those random, messy, chaotic parts of life that she had no control over.

She didn't like the traffic.

By 9:20, she'd cooked dinner, devoured it, washed the plates, dried them, washed the plates again, dried them again and stacked them neatly away in the cupboards. Then she'd taken another shower before sitting down for *precisely* half an hour to read her book. She'd spent the last year or so reading through Stephen King's bibliography in chronological order and she was up to *Rose Madder*, which was just okay. But then, she wasn't reading for the fun of it. She was reading because it was *the right thing to do*.

That night, she went to bed at 11:45 PM, a full hour later than usual. But she couldn't sleep. She tossed, turned and tossed again, but it remained elusive. Her mind was racing, and so was her heart. They beat a dull rhythm that throbbed in her eardrums until she was tapping along on her bedside table. She got up for an hour and tried to read some more, but she couldn't fall back into the fiction, and she found herself dozing off on the sofa. Her eyes were closing, but her mind stayed open.

She went back to bed at 2:45 AM. But sleep remained elusive.

WEEK ONE, DAY FIVE

KATE WAS SHATTERED.

It had been a long, unpleasant week, and Mr. Murray had continued to take his displeasure out on her. She'd seen it happen before, but never to her. Once a target was on his radar, he honed in on them and made their working life so unpleasant that most of them quit within a couple of months. But Kate wasn't going to do that. She wasn't going to give him the satisfaction.

Besides, there was something else on her mind. It was the first Saturday of the month, and the first Saturday of the month was inked in black inside her diary. It was the only time that her family got together to eat dinner, and it was the highlight of an otherwise monotonous existence.

But there was a problem. She was so tired that she could barely lift her head. Over the last few days, she'd maxed out at three or four hours of sleep, and the rest of her time in bed had largely revolved around inventing newer and more exotic ways to kill Mr. Murray. Her favourite was the fantasy where she crushed his head in a vice, but she knew full well that she'd never carry the threat out.

Nevertheless, spending the night daydreaming had left her drained and lethargic, and she could barely bring herself to look in the mirror. She got out of bed for long enough to make a cup of coffee, but her hands were shaking as she carried it back through to the bedroom. Her stomach twisted and growled apprehensively and bile rose up in the back of her throat. For a moment, she was convinced she was about to vomit, and she dry heaved right there and then in the middle of the bedroom floor. But nothing came out, and Kate managed to calm it down for long enough to grab a bucket from beneath the kitchen sink and to pour herself a glass of water. She took them both back through to the bedroom, then rifled through her handbag for some aspirin.

Then she swallowed the pill, closed the curtains and climbed back beneath the covers. This wasn't part of the plan, but the plan was falling to pieces. Besides, she was shattered. Not just tired – absolutely shattered, so exhausted that her body hurt.

Kate groaned and rolled over in her bed, then reached for her phone on the bedside table. She squinted at the screen, the harsh light half-blinding her and sending flares of pain to her temples. She turned down the brightness and held the device away from her, then bashed out a short SMS to Lauren, her older sister.

"Can't come," it said. "Having a mental health day. Sorry."

She pressed the send button and closed her eyes, then forgot all about it until her phone pinged with a reply. She lifted her head up for long enough to read it.

"No problem. Take as long as you need. Hope you're

okay."

Kate felt a tear in her eye and brushed her wrist impatiently against it. The moisture left a trail on her hand like the snails in the garden left across her patio. She looked down at her hand, disgusted, and forced herself to climb out of bed.

Then she walked through to the bathroom to wash and disinfect herself.

***

Kate spent the rest of the day lying in bed in her pyjamas. She watched Netflix for a while until her eyes hurt too much to hold them open, and then she listened to it with her head beneath the pillow until her ears hurt too much to listen. Then she turned it off and lay there as still as she possibly could. Her head was still swimming, and the room started spinning if she tried to lift it up.

That was when her anxiety started to flare up. It spoke with an inner voice that had a Brummie accent, and Kate thought she knew why. It was her grandmother's voice, reaching out beyond the grave to tell her what she was doing wrong with her life. Clearly even death hadn't stopped her from having an opinion.

You're a silly, useless little girl, it said. *I was always ashamed of you. Can't say I blame myself. Look at you, lying there in the middle of the day while the sun's up outside. I'd hardly know you as my own flesh and blood.*

"But, Grandmamma," Kate wanted to say, "it's not my fault. I had a *plan*, Grandmamma."

But of course, the plan didn't work out, and now she couldn't sleep. She couldn't sleep during the day, and she couldn't sleep at night.

It was Saturday afternoon, heading into Saturday

evening, and she had to be back at work on Monday.

WEEK TWO, DAY THREE

KATE HAD BEEN CALLED into a meeting.

Present were Kate, Mr. Murray, a man called Evans who was her line manager and the CEO of the company, a stern-faced old hag who'd sacrificed every scrap of passion in her rise to the top of one of the most successful financial companies in the West Midlands. Her name was Rita Hawking, and she had a face like a dehydrated lemon. Kate wasn't happy to see her.

"I've called this meeting to give you a formal warning," Mr. Murray said, by way of greeting. "I can't pretend that we haven't noticed a drop in your performance."

"I can't sleep," Kate insisted.

"So see a doctor," Murray replied. He looked across at his two colleagues for confirmation. While neither of them nodded, their lack of protest confirmed that he was within his remit. "Listen. We can't afford to carry dead weight here. We hired you to fulfil a role. If you're unable to do that, we'll have to find someone else."

Kate bit her tongue, not to stop herself from speaking but to bite back her tears and to remind herself that she was real. The last few weeks had passed in a blur of insomnia, and the days were starting to stretch and blend and to become one and the same. She wasn't much of a dreamer, but her dreams of late had been so vivid that she'd felt like she was really there. And her head ached more than anyone's head should ever ache.

"Kate," Evans said, not unkindly. "Look, I'm not trying to be malicious. We care about you, and we'd hate to lose you. But we also have metrics, policies and processes. If you can't hack it, we have grounds for dismissal. We'd love to keep you, Kate. But if you can't do the job…"

"I can do it," she insisted. "Just give me some time."

"We'll give you time," Hawking said, earning her surname by leaning forward like a bird of prey. "But you're on thin ice, Kate. I don't want to see you in a meeting like this again."

"You won't," Kate said. She shook their hands and took her leave, then slipped surreptitiously out of the office to get some fresh air. She walked to the community garden and hid amongst the rose bushes.

Then she screamed and screamed and screamed.

***

When she got back to the office, Evans took her aside. "What was all that about?" he asked.

"What was all *what* about?" Kate replied. For a split second, she was struck by the thought that Evans could have followed her to the garden and overheard her outburst, but that was crazy. Still, the thought kept on bouncing around her head like an unwelcome guest she couldn't get rid of.

"You know what I'm talking about," Evans said. "I'm worried about you, Kate. What happened?"

"I can't sleep," she said.

"That's it?"

"You try it," Kate growled. "Then we'll see how you're feeling after a week or two."

"Hmm." Evans crossed his arms and looked her up and down appraisingly. "Are you still going to make the meeting on Monday?"

"Which meeting?"

"The one with Sunnyvale," Evans said. "You know, the super important meeting with the potential client that could deliver a third of our revenue. You're supposed to be presenting."

"Oh," Kate said. "Yeah, that meeting."

Evans looked at her again. "You'd forgotten, hadn't you?"

"Yeah," Kate admitted. "Sorry, Boss. But don't worry about it, I'm good to present."

"You're sure about that?"

"I'm sure," Kate said. Evans looked unimpressed, but she summoned up a smile, and that seemed to do the trick.

"Hmm," he said. "You'd better be. It's not just your ass on the line."

WEEK THREE, DAY ONE

IT WAS THE DAY OF THE MEETING, and Kate was exhausted. No surprises there.

She'd tried a bunch of stuff from over the counter, but her sleep had been worse than ever. Then she'd gone for an emergency appointment with her doctor, who'd begrudgingly written out a script for some sleeping medication, though he'd also warned her not to get too attached to them. Not that there seemed like much chance of her getting hooked. The damn things didn't work.

She'd slept well on Friday night, but then she'd woken early on Saturday morning and found herself unable to drift off back to sleep. It messed with her schedule and threw her plans into chaos, but her plans had been chaotic for the last two weeks. It was starting to get to her.

But it was the day of the meeting, and Kate could feel the anxiety rising in her chest like a hot air balloon until it filled her lungs and made it difficult to breathe. She knew it was going to be one of those days from the moment she woke up. She'd taken the best part of three hours to fall asleep the night before and then slept through her alarm, which threw her and her routine into chaos. It all went downhill from there.

She made it to work on time, but only just, and then she hightailed it to her desk to print off some paperwork. It was one of those awful meetings that started at 9 AM on a Monday morning when everyone was still thinking about the weekend. The rest of the company was still having its weekly kick-off when Kate and the team sashayed into the meeting room. Sunnyvale's representatives were already in there, chatting to the managing director and giving their drink orders to Gill in reception.

It was Kate's least favourite part of the meeting, the part where she had to make small talk with people that she didn't like and had nothing in common with. But it was a part of the job, like it was a part of almost every job, so she bit her tongue and forced herself to use it.

It was 9:25 AM, and her heart was racing.

The meeting proper started at 9:35, once the formalities were complete and everyone was up-to-date on each other's cars and kids, in that order.

Agency life, Kate thought. *You can't beat it.*

But she was just trying to keep her spirits up. Truth be told, for the first time in the last few weeks, Kate didn't feel tired.

She felt terrified.

Her hands were sweaty. Her pupils were dilated, her veins felt red hot and itched beneath her skin, her heart was racing and her throat was drier than a biscuit in the desert. Her mind was racing at approximately 2,300 miles per hour. She thought for a moment that she was going to vomit, but she managed to swallow it back down. She wondered what was wrong with her, whether she was dying of some obscure disease or whether she was finally losing her mind. She swallowed again, reached for a glass of water and knocked it over. Everyone turned to look at her.

"Jesus!" Evans said. "Look out, Kate!"

"I'm sorry," she replied. Her hands were shaking, and she realised with a jolt that they'd been shaking since she'd woken up that morning and pulled back the bedsheets. "I'll go get some paper towels."

"No need," Evans said. "I'll get Gill to do it." He walked over to the door, opened it and shouted out into the corridor. While this was happening, Kate tried to conceal her embarrassment, knowing all along that it showed in her rosy cheeks. The reps from Sunnyvale, for their part, smiled awkwardly and cracked a few jokes.

Gill came into the room with an armful of paper towels, and Evans held the door open until she left. Then he closed it behind him and cleared his throat.

"Sorry about that," Evans said. "Where were we? Ah, yes. Well, you've given us one show, Kate. Now how about another? I believe you have a few words for us."

"Oh," Kate said. "Yeah. One moment."

The shock of the spill had taken her mind off the reason why they were gathered there to begin with. She mumbled incoherently as she fiddled with her laptop, trying to hook her slides up to the projector. She'd spent half the weekend going over the slides, but all of the preparation had been for nothing. Her mind had gone blank.

And then she knew nothing. She hit her head on the boardroom table as she fell to the floor.

WEEK THREE, DAY TWO

KATE WAS EXHAUSTED AGAIN, and this time she also

had a headache. She supposed it was only to be expected after hitting her head on the table.

The previous day felt like a nightmare. She'd relived it in all its brutal glory as she cried herself to sleep. One moment she'd been standing in the boardroom with a blank mind and a throbbing heart, and the next she was coming round in the back of an ambulance. She'd asked what happened, and the paramedic told her that she'd fainted.

"What happened to the meeting?" she'd asked.

But the paramedic just shook his head.

Kate looked at herself in the mirror. Her eyes were sallow, like two sinkholes at night in the soil of her face, and her nose had swelled with grease and blackheads. Her right brow was bruised blue, and an inch-and-a-half line of butterfly stitches ran its way across her forehead. The gash had exposed a nerve, which the doctors had to kill to numb the pain, leaving her face feeling stretched and taut.

When she got home from the hospital, she went straight to the mirror to take a look at herself, but it was worse than she'd feared. She tried styling her hair to cover it, but the bruise had taken over half of her face and she couldn't find a way to make it work.

Still, she did the best that she could with her makeup and wore dark glasses behind the wheel of her car. But Grundy Plc. – the company she worked for – had a conservative dress policy, and she had to take them off the instant she entered the building. She was hoping that nobody would notice, but it was a hopeless hope and she knew it.

She made it until approximately 10:15 AM. She'd been typing away at her machine with her headphones on, slowly drifting away into a reassuring, realistic world that resembled what she'd come to expect from life. At some point, while she'd been knee-deep in Excel formulae and idly humming a Taylor Swift song, Mr. Murray had dragged a chair over and sat down just behind her, watching her from over her shoulder.

When she noticed that he was there, she almost leapt out of her skin. She shrieked and responded on instinct like a cornered animal, throwing her chair back and leaping to her feet. Her chair collided with Mr. Murray, who was driven sideways and who went tumbling from his own chair, hitting the ground with as much momentum as a middle-aged man could muster. He went down slowly, but he went down hard.

"What the hell?" Murray shouted, still lying prone on top of his fallen chair. One of its wheels was spinning comically in the air. A deathly silence had descended upon the office as though the building itself had taken a sudden deep breath.

By now, all eyes were on the two of them, and Kate could feel her heartbeat speeding up and another panic attack coming on. She tried to calm herself with her breathing exercises, but then she surprised herself and did something that stopped her from hyperventilating.

She burst into tears and made a break for the bathroom.

WEEK THREE, DAY FIVE

EVANS LOOKED UNCOMFORTABLE.

"Look, I'm sorry," he said. "This wasn't my idea. But you have to admit that your performance has been slacking, and Murray is out for your blood. What did you do to piss him off?"

"Nothing," Kate said, truthfully. She sighed. "Let's just get this over with."

She felt like a condemned prisoner on the way to the gallows. The building had bars on its windows to keep thieves out, but they had the unintended side effect of making the office feel like a prison, especially on grey days like this one where the sun struggled to push its way through the clouds.

Evans led the way and opened the door to the meeting room, then pulled out a chair for her to sit down on. He sat to her right. On the other side of the table were the stern, unimpressed faces of Mr. Murray and Rita Hawking.

"Before we get started," Kate said, seizing the initiative before her buttocks hit the seat, "I'd like to apologise. I'm not sure what came over me. Lately, I've just been having these dizzy spells and–"

"With the greatest respect," Hawking said, raising her hand for silence, "your health problems aren't my concern. You're here to do a job, Kate. If you're sick and you need time off, for god's sake take time off. But don't keep coming in and causing a scene. It's bad for business."

"It won't happen again," Kate said.

"It had better not," Murray growled. "Your ass is on the line here."

"Come on, guys," Evans interrupted. His cheeks were flushed slightly, as though he was hot under the collar or suffering from a hangover. "Let's be a little lenient here.

She's got a bloody scar on her head. I think she's learned her lesson."

"Perhaps," Hawking said. "But all the same, the company has to take a stand in situations like this. I'm giving you a verbal warning. Your second, if you're keeping track. Next up is a written warning. Let's hope we don't need to take things that far."

"What's after a written warning?" Kate asked. She had a bad feeling that she was going to find out one way or another.

But Hawking didn't say anything. She just drew a hand across her throat in that classic gesture that crosses the language barrier.

Kate sighed and said, "It won't happen again."

WEEK FIVE, DAY TWO

THE INSOMNIA was becoming unbearable.

Kate was getting four hours a night at best, and she'd starting to sweat almost constantly. It started at the nape of her neck and then rolled down her spine and towards her lower back, gathering momentum on its way. When she looked into the mirror, she was shocked by how dark her face looked, and her pupils had looked like pinpricks for almost as long as she could remember. When she looked at photos of herself even just a couple of months earlier, she saw a different person. Now, with her tired eyes and her pale face, she looked more like a corpse than a living person, and no amount of concealer could help her.

It was getting so bad that Kate went back to the doctor. He was a balding, middle-aged Asian with a friendly smile and a soft, soothing tone. Dr. Karnataka had something about him, some magical bedside manner, which always made Kate feel a little safer. He had a lot of sympathy, and that helped.

"Still struggling?" he asked.

Kate nodded. "I've been tracking my sleep," she said. "You want to see the reports?"

"It can't hurt," Dr. Karnataka said, "but make sure you don't obsess about it. If you worry about your sleep too much, it becomes counterproductive."

"Obsessive?" Kate said. "Me?"

"I get your point," the doctor replied. "But honestly, Kate, I see no real reason for your insomnia."

"Is it related to my OCD?"

"Could be," the doctor said, evasively. "But who knows? The human brain is a mysterious thing. We still don't fully understand it."

"But you can help me sleep," Kate said. "Right?"

"I can try," the doctor said. He dashed out a couple of lines on a prescription form, signed on the dotted line and handed it over to her. "Here, take this."

"What is it?"

"It's diphenhydramine," Dr. Karnataka explained. "An antihistamine."

"You mean like for hay fever?"

"Exactly," the doctor said. "But it'll help you sleep as well."

"Have you got anything more powerful?"

"I have," Karnataka replied. "But I'd like to hold that in reserve for now. Rest assured, if the diphenhydramine doesn't work, we'll start looking into alternatives."

But Kate couldn't rest assured. She hadn't rested assured since the day she'd been late to work and the month-long nightmare had begun.

She hoped that it was almost over.

WEEK SIX, DAY THREE

FOR HER FIRST TWO NIGHTS on the drug, Kate slept surprisingly well. Oh, sure, the nights were still dark and full of terrors, but she fell asleep in thirty minutes or so, instead of her customary three to four hours. Her brain told her that it was the placebo effect. Her body said otherwise.

But the third night was so-so and on the fourth night she was back to her old ways, just in time for the weekend. At least Mr. Murray wouldn't be watching her like a hawk while she tried to keep her eyes open.

And then the side effects kicked in, starting with a dry mouth and throat which progressed into what felt like a full-on flu. She felt dizzy, sleepy, knocked sideways by life and too strung out to tell who she was, where she was or what time it was.

Sunday? she thought. *Ah, to hell with it.*

She got up to pour herself a glass of water, then swayed slightly as she walked back towards her bedroom and dropped it on the floor. The glass shattered and flew across the room or embedded itself in the side of her foot, and the water made the blood take on a surreal, oily sheen. She reached down to her foot and touched it, then held her fingers up in front of her face. The sight of it made her feel faint and her vision blurred, and she smeared the blood absentmindedly across the lids of her eyes.

Kate limped through to the bathroom, leaving a trail of bloody footprints in her wake. She turned the shower on, climbed gingerly out of her clothes and stepped under the water. She gritted her teeth and told herself not to cry as she washed her wounds and tried to pick the glass out.

WEEK SIX, DAY SIX

KATE'S FOOT HURT, but it didn't hurt enough to stop her from working. Her colleagues shot concerned glances towards her, but she tried to defuse them by pretending she hadn't noticed.

She was used to not noticing her colleagues.

It's funny, Kate thought. She used to give a shit about her job, and then her poor health had forced her to put herself first. And as soon as she did that, she started to underperform when compared to the idiots she shared her tiny cubicle with.

She had a couple of deadlines looming, and Mr. Murray was watching her like a hawk, probably hoping that she'd fail again so he could show her the door without bringing on a tribunal. She didn't want to give him the satisfaction.

But she also felt like shit, like she'd died and been reborn with a stomach full of acid, and her frequent trips to the toilet were without success, although they did give her a chance to close her eyes for a time. It felt like there was something inside her that wanted to get out, but it didn't matter what she did – it just wasn't coming.

Kate went back to her desk, clutching her stomach and groaning quietly to herself. She hoped nobody noticed. But they did, of course.

"Kate," Mr. Murray boomed, strolling through the office towards her like an infantryman on the battlefield. "You look terrible."

"Thanks," she said, smiling weakly while her heart skimmed and sank like a stone into the ocean.

"I'm serious," he said. "Big night last night?"

Kate shook her head. "I don't drink," she replied. "Well, not anymore…"

"Are you sure about that?" Murray scrutinised her face,

and she took an involuntary step backwards. Her forehead was still healing, her eyes were dark and sunken, and her self-esteem was so low that just one pair of eyes on her was too many.

Kate's eyes were dry. Her stomach churned like a bad hangover, and for a second or two, she thought perhaps the boss was right. Perhaps she *was* hungover. Perhaps she'd somehow drank herself into oblivion between the last thing she remembered – lying wide awake in bed and checking her phone every four minutes – and the sweet, sweet sleep of unconsciousness.

She opened her mouth to say something to Mr. Murray, then snapped it shut again. She swallowed. Then she covered her mouth with her hand and made a break for the bathroom.

WEEK SEVEN, DAY FOUR

KATE WAS IN A BAD PLACE.

She'd stopped caring about the lack of sleep. She felt the effects constantly, and she woke every day feeling slightly worse than she'd felt the night before as she waited in vain for sleep to come.

By the seventh week, she was starting to feel paranoid. She felt the CCTV cameras looking down at her when she walked into the supermarket, and she felt as though total strangers were staring as she strolled along the street. She wore the dark glasses everywhere now, so much so that she'd been taken for blind a couple of times and offered a seat on the underground.

Her mother told her she was being paranoid, but her mother had always been dismissive when she talked about her poor health and her anxiety/depression. She didn't mean any harm by it. She'd just been as healthy as a breeding bull for her entire life and found it hard to understand why anyone else should be different.

That just made Kate withdraw even further. By week seven, she was dodging her mother's calls and failing to honour any social engagements because she didn't want people to ask her that awful question: *what happened?*

Kate knew she looked like *something* had happened, but as far as she could tell, there was nothing. Still, that didn't stop her from worrying about it. Her anxiety told her she was dying. Her paranoia told her everyone was watching while she did so.

It also told her that doctors were evil swine who were being paid by pharmaceutical companies to pump their patients full of drugs that they didn't need. She didn't want to visit the hospital if she could help it, and even the thought of kind-hearted Dr. Karnataka filled her with a subtle dread.

She hadn't been to work all week. She had a feeling that Mr. Murray was out to get her.

WEEK EIGHT, DAY TWO

IN THE END, KATE RELENTED. Dr. Karnataka had a full schedule, but he agreed to squeeze in an appointment at the end of the day. He was visibly shocked to see her, and Kate took it badly. She tried to cover her face as best she could, but Karnataka was simply staggered by her eyes and their hollow, hunted, haunted look.

"You don't look so good," he said, beckoning her into his office from the waiting area. "You'd better come in."

He held the door open, and Kate slouched gratefully into the room. It smelled of cleaning products, so stubbornly antiseptic that she wondered if her nostrils would ever feel neutral again. She followed him inside and sat in the chair.

"I'm still not sleeping," she said. Karnataka gave her a cursory glance over and gestured for her to roll up a sleeve. He started to take her blood pressure while she was talking. "Maybe an hour or two at best. Sometimes, when it's late at night, I start to see things. And I can't shake the feeling that there's someone out there, someone watching me."

Dr. Karnataka paused as the device constricted itself around her arm. He looked at her and said, "Watching you?"

"I know," Kate said. "It sounds crazy. I can't explain it, Doc. I feel like a little kid with a monster complex. It's like there's something beneath my bed. Maybe there is. Maybe that's why I can't sleep."

"Maybe," the doctor said. He sighed. "How did you get on with the diphenhydramine?"

Kate shrugged. "It worked for a while," she said. "A couple of nights at least. But now it's just as bad as ever. Is there anything else you can give me?"

"Temazepam," Karnataka said.

"Temazewhat?"

"Temazepam," Karnataka repeated. "It's stronger. It should knock you out and help you to stay out. A word of warning, though. I don't want you to stay on it for too long. It's a short-term fix only, okay?"

"I'll try anything."

"Good," the doctor said. He filled out a prescription for two weeks' worth of the medication. "I want to see you back in here before you run out, okay?"

WEEK TEN, DAY ONE

ALL IN ALL, the temazepam worked like a charm. There were side effects, perhaps, but there were side effects to everything. Besides, she'd slept soundly for three nights in a row and managed to get back up to a good 8/10 at work, although Mr. Murray was still keeping a close eye on her. His bent nose and bushy eyebrows even cropped up in a dream, the first dream she could remember having since the troubles began.

But then everything started to come unravelled.

The paranoia had been bad enough, but it was the phobias that tore her apart. She couldn't leave the house. There were birds out there. Germs. Sweaty feet in sweaty socks in sweaty shoes with their toes wiggling like worms on the end of a fishing line. Bank robbers. Thieves. Beggars. There were drunk drivers, child molesters, rapists and worst of all, the bloody bees. The bees were orbiting her house and bashing themselves against the windows. They were watching her when she undressed for the shower and listening whenever she picked the phone up.

Part of her mind told her she was being irrational, but another part told her that it was better to be safe than sorry. Over the last couple of days, she'd been able to restore a little order to her life, and she'd been comforted by the warm embrace of a steady routine. Now that she'd found it, she was unwilling to give it up – which is why anything out of the ordinary posed a threat, no matter how minor.

She'd read online that the difference between a fear and a phobia is that a phobia is ungrounded. If she had to guess, she would have said she was under attack by both of them. They came in waves, first one and then the other. And Kate was tired of fighting.

So she retreated instead, surrendering to the paranoia in the hope of declaring a ceasefire. But her body was having none of it. It fought back like a cornered wildcat, pushing her heartbeat up and up until she felt like it was ready to burst from her chest.

She started working from home and spent most of her time in bed.

WEEK ELEVEN, DAY FOUR

MR. MURRAY HAND-DELIVERED the letter so that he could personally watch her face fall. She knew what it was without even having to open it.

"This is my written warning," she said. "Right?"

Mr. Murray smiled at her and nodded. "And you know what comes next."

"A promotion?"

Murray scowled at her. "The day you get a promotion is the day the devil comes up from hell and dances the tango on national television," he said. "This is your final warning, Kate. One more slip and you're out of here."

"I know," she said. "Mr. Murray, I'm doing my best."

"Yeah?" For a moment, he looked as though he was about to say something supportive. Then he came out with, "Well, your best isn't good enough."

Kate frowned and looked down at her feet, avoiding eye contact with the man. They made no secret of their dislike for each other, and the rumour mill was on fire with all sorts of accusations. Not that either of them paid any attention.

"Do you mind me asking what I did?"

"It's all in the letter," Mr. Murray replied. "Perhaps you should go and read it."

Murray smiled sarcastically at her and strode off towards the design studio, leaving her shaking silently at her desk and trying to make sense of it all. When the coast was clear, she hid herself away in the bathroom and slid the letter out of the envelope. It had the company's logo on a letterhead and was signed by both Mr. Murray and Rita Hawking. It wasn't good news, although it didn't actually explain what the warning was for. She didn't really care.

Later that afternoon, when nobody was paying much attention, she slipped into one of the meeting rooms, hung a "busy" sign on the door handle and took a power nap. For once, she fell asleep almost immediately.

WEEK TWELVE, DAY TWO

KATE WAS CONSTIPATED.
Sure, she didn't exactly think she shat unicorn dust, but her bowels had never given her much pause for thought. They'd always just *worked*, which was why, when they stopped working, she started to worry. Her brain was telling her stories about the Big C and, as with most things, once the thought was established, she couldn't get rid of it.

So she sat on the toilet, straining and pushing herself into the seat. She crossed her legs and applied some pressure, grabbed hold of her thighs and pulsed her anus, but her body literally didn't give a shit. Just a panic attack that hit her with a right hook and made her roll over until her knees were on the floor and her head was in the bowl.

She retched but didn't vomit, climbed back on to the seat and then touched up her makeup while on the throne. She balanced a compact mirror on the toilet roll holder and grimaced as she tried to make herself look presentable. It was an uphill challenge, but she'd had a lot of practice over the last couple of weeks, and she was getting the hang of using the cubicle as a dressing room.

It was no good. She couldn't go. She wiped herself anyway and then pulled her clothes back up, packed her makeup away and flushed the toilet. As she was about to leave, a colleague came in, so she sat back down and waited it out.

When the room was exclusively hers again, she exited the stall and walked over to the sink. She washed her hands six times, pulled a toothbrush from her bag, squeezed out a little paste and freshened her breath.

Brush. Floss. Brush. Repeat.

WEEK THIRTEEN, DAY SIX

AT THE WEEKEND, Kate felt well enough to leave the house. She had a catch-up scheduled with her mother and sister. After missing two on the trot, she didn't want to miss another.

So she dressed herself up in her favourite clothes, a tight top and skinny jeans that hung from her skeletal frame like baggy hand-me-downs. They met at the café at the local museum. She'd been hoping that she'd pass for normal, but no such luck.

"You look awful, girl," her sister said. "Have you been eating?"

"Yeah," Kate replied. "Like a horse. But the weight keeps dropping off. It's like there's a hole in my stomach."

"Hmm," her mother said. "Leave your sister alone, Lauren. I'm sure she's doing her best."

"Thanks," Kate murmured. "If only my best was good enough."

They were only at the museum for a cuppa at the coffee shop, but Kate's mother insisted on forcing three slices of carrot cake down her daughter's gullet. Kate liked carrot cake, so she didn't complain. And as her mother had always said, it was made from vegetables and so it was healthy.

"How's work?" her mother asked.

Kate was in the middle of a mouthful, so she chewed and swallowed and then took a sip of coffee to clear the crumbs before she replied. "It's okay," she said, eventually.

"Okay, huh?" Lauren said. She cocked an eyebrow at her younger sister.

"Well, it could be going better," Kate admitted. "But whatever. I don't think I'll be there for much longer."

"Why's that?"

Kate laughed bitterly and shook her head. "Just call it a hunch," she said.

WEEK FOURTEEN, DAY FIVE

IT HAD BEEN A GOOD WEEK. The temazepam was still working its magic, and Kate had been getting a good five hours a night. She felt sluggish for a while in the morning, but it was nothing that a little coffee couldn't cure.

And then she made a mistake.

It started out like a normal Friday. Kate was half an hour early to the office and spent the time catching up with some paperwork. It had seemed like a good idea at the time, especially because it was long overdue, but it was also stressful. Mr. Murray tasked her with handing in a report by the end of the day. Then a client called to complain about an error she'd made in her last set of spreadsheets which had cost them seven hundred pounds to correct. Kate begged the client not to tell anyone – and perhaps surprisingly, the client agreed – but even though she'd tried to keep her voice down, a couple of her colleagues overheard her. She hoped they'd keep it to themselves.

As it turned out, the colleagues weren't the problem. Mr. Murray never had a chance to find out because by the time that the day was over, she'd already been kicked out of the building.

The stress just got to be too much for her. She was tired,

and for once it had nothing to do with a lack of sleep. She was tired of life and its monotony, tired of having to pretend to give a shit. And she was tired of the constant panic attacks.

So when Murray crept up behind her again and laid a hand on her shoulder, she reacted on instinct. She just did what came naturally.

She turned around and punched him square in the jaw. Then she picked up her handbag, slung it over her shoulder and walked out of the door.

WEEK FIFTEEN, DAY TWO

KATE WASN'T SLEEPING WELL. No surprise there, then.

Since walking out of the office on the previous Friday, she'd left her phone turned off and had stayed away from social networking sites. She had a feeling that her address was on file somewhere, so she also closed the curtains and locked herself away in her bedroom.

Her grandmother, Nana Knight, was keeping her company. She'd been dead for twenty years, but Kate still heard her voice when she was stressed or depressed. The old crone had a habit of expressing her opinions from beyond the grave in the same shaky voice that she'd used to make pronouncements on Kate's school-friends or the dresses she'd pick out at the weekend.

"Useless," the old woman kept saying. "You're bloody useless, girl. No wonder you can't hold a job down. You can't even hold yourself together."

"I know, Nana," Kate said. "I'm trying, okay? I'm trying."

"Well, try harder, girl."

Kate was lying in bed with her eyes closed, and when

she opened them up, she almost expected the old woman to be sitting there beside her, rocking backwards and forwards on her mahogany chair and using her lap as a wool basket as she clicked needles together with a cigarette in her mouth.

But there was no one there. She was all alone in her poky bedroom. No job. No lover.

And she couldn't sleep.

Part Two: Hallucinations

WEEK SIXTEEN, DAY THREE

KATE WAS IN BREAKDOWN MODE.

Without a job, there was nothing to get out of bed for. Sure, she'd hated working under the watchful eye of Mr. Murray, but it had given her something to live for. Now, with no excuse to set an alarm, her sleeping pattern gave up the ghost and completely disintegrated. It was a far cry from the organised life she'd led for the last twenty years. If her life was a tower of cards, someone had yanked the six of clubs from the bottom tier. She was teetering over the brink. And there was no one there to catch her if she fell.

By day three, she'd resorted to lying in bed and waiting for the minutes and the hours to tick by, especially at night. She'd memorised a quote that she'd seen in a meme, and she liked to recite it to herself when she couldn't sleep. *If life is really as short as they say then why is the night so long?* Kate didn't have an answer for that, but the question had got her thinking.

She had a lot of time to think. Despite spending most of her time in bed, she was surviving on four or five hours of sleep a day, mostly in random naps of an hour or so when her body caught her mind unawares and sleep snuck up on her. When she wasn't asleep or trying to get there, she was talking to Nana Knight and listening to the dead old woman's sanguine responses from another plane.

And then on the third day of week sixteen, her grandmother came to visit. Kate woke from a fitful sleep to see her sitting there beside her. Her room was so small that her grandmother and her chair only just fit inside it, and the result was that the old woman's face was barely a foot and a half away from her. Even in the darkness, it was impossible to miss her.

Kate shrieked and covered her face, then backed up against the headboard and cowered away. Her head told her that this wasn't possible, but her heart told her that her head made mistakes but her heart could always be relied on. Deep down, on some subconscious level, she knew that her grandmother was really real, back from the dead somehow to pass judgement.

"Look at you," the old lady purred, her hands dancing a subconscious fandango with the needles. She was making a twiddlemuff for the girls at the nursing home, just like she used to do when Kate was a little kid on her mother's knee. "You look awful."

"I know, Nana," Kate said. "I'm sorry. I'll try harder."

"You'd better, my girl." Nana Knight stifled a yawn and shot a withering look at her granddaughter, who was still on edge in her bed with the sheets pulled up to her chin like she was trying to preserve her modesty. "I'll know if you fail me, like you usually do."

"How will you know, Nana?"

The old woman flashed a toothless smile at her. "I'll be watching," she said.

WEEK SEVENTEEN, DAY ONE

IT WAS ONE OF THOSE DAYS.

As if it being a Monday wasn't bad enough, she'd had a panic attack at the dole office and made herself look like a fool. She'd been struck with a sudden horror that hit her like a bolt of lightning. One minute, she'd been talking to an unemployment officer about an interview at the supermarket, the next she was sat in the back of a police car trying to explain her unusual medical history to an unsympathetic cop called Gary Mogford.

"What's the last thing you remember?" Mogford asked.

"I was talking to the lady at the unemployment office," she replied. "Then, nothing. I'm just suddenly here with you."

"Hmm," Mogford murmured, stroking the five-o'clock shadow that had sprung up on his face like bushes across the English countryside. "So you don't remember anything that happened between then and now?"

"No, not at all," Kate said.

"Hmm," Mogford repeated. "I suppose I'd better bring you up to date. We were called out after you flew into a rage before turning mostly unresponsive. You were walking around in a daze when we arrived and offered up no resistance."

"So what's next?" Kate asked.

"Nothing, I suppose," Mogford said, his tone of voice suggesting that he'd said it reluctantly. "It seems that there was no malicious intent, and the receptionist doesn't intend to press charges. If I was you, I'd stick around for the ambulance and seek treatment."

"And what about you?"

"My work here is done," Mogford said. "And I have more important things to be dealing with than someone's dizzy spells."

She didn't bother to watch the policeman as he walked away. Instead, she sat down on a low wall and tried to catch her breath and then waited for the ambulance to arrive. The paramedics told her that there was nothing wrong with her.

Nana Knight made another appearance that evening. This time, she visited Kate in a dream. They met at midnight in a field of swaying wheat sheaves. The sky was stained sepia, and the clouds were black and ominous. Kate recognised the scene from a painting she'd seen in a museum. But she couldn't remember where the museum was, and she wondered if it had any significance.

"Kate," her grandmother cooed. "I told you I'd be back."

The younger woman felt the familiar flash of ice-cold fear pass through her, only this time it was somehow worse. This time, she found herself in an unfamiliar landscape, lost inside a dream, and she remembered the stories she'd heard of people being killed in dreams and dying for real. Not that she thought Nana Knight was going to kill her. She got the feeling that the malevolent old woman had something else in mind.

"What do you want from me?" she asked.

"What makes you think I want something?" the old woman replied. Kate noticed that, in the dream at least, she wasn't wearing her dentures. Her lips made a disgusting *fap-fap* sound as she puckered up her mouth to form hard consonants.

"Then why are you here?" Kate asked.

Nana Knight beckoned her closer with a gnarly finger and despite herself, Kate inched towards her, pushing her way through the phantasmagorical wheat like she was swimming through a field of gold.

"Can you hear me?" Nana Knight whispered. Kate leaned in closer still.

"I hear you," she replied.

"Look out for Zeb," her grandmother urged. "Don't trust him."

"Who's Zeb?"

"No questions," she snapped. "Our time here is short."

"Okay," Kate said. Her voice had dropped too, and their whispers danced on the air and swished through the dream field like paper aeroplanes. "I'll be careful."

"You don't understand," Nana Knight insisted. "Zeb is evil. Ancient evil. He took your—"

And then her alarm went off, and she woke back up.

WEEK SEVENTEEN, DAY FOUR

KATE WAS BACK AT THE DOCTOR'S.

She'd planned to tell him about her weird, vivid dreams, about her night-time rendezvous with her grandmother and how the old woman had appeared beside her bed one night. But then she worried that Dr. Karnataka might think she was crazy, and she didn't want that. She just wanted him to make her better. It never occurred to her that telling him the truth might facilitate the process.

"Hmm," Karnataka said. He was doing complicated things to her arm while she stared stoically ahead. "Can't find a vein."

"Sorry," Kate replied, though she wasn't. "Just get it over with. I hate needles."

"You might have to get used to them," the doctor replied. He smiled apologetically at her, and she caught the movement out of the corner of her eye. "Until we figure this out, we're going to have to keep testing."

"But what's *wrong* with me?"

"I don't know," the doctor admitted. "But I promise I'm going to do everything I can to find out. Any loss of appetite?"

"None at all," Kate said, thinking of the carrot cake that her mother had forced her to eat a couple of weekends earlier. She'd enjoyed it so much that she'd started stocking up and was getting through three of the things a week. That was on top of the takeaways when she was too lethargic to cook and the bags of crisps that she'd stockpiled in her snack cupboard.

"Well," Karnataka told her, "I've got some good news and some bad news. Which would you like to hear first?"

"The good news," Kate said.

"The good news is that you've got high blood pressure and an elevated heart rate."

"That's the good news?"

"Afraid so," the doctor said. "The bad news is that until we get the lab tests back, there's nothing more I can tell you."

"What about medication?" Kate asked. "There must be something you can give me."

"Are you still taking your temazepam?"

"Of course," Kate said.

"I'll give you another prescription," Karnataka replied. "But once we figure out what's wrong, I want to take you back off it. We shouldn't leave you on it for long."

"Mmm," Kate murmured. She thought back over the last couple of weeks. It had just been night after sleepless night. "Any chance you could increase the dosage?"

WEEK NINETEEN, DAY THREE

KARNATAKA HAD REFUSED to up the dosage, so Kate had settled on a different plan of action. She dropped herself down to half her usual dosage and kept the spare medication in her jewellery box. When she needed it – *really* needed it – she double or triple dosed. She knew it was a bad idea, but she also didn't give a shit. If she woke up in the emergency room…well, she'd deal with that if it came to it.

She'd triple dosed for several nights in a row and had been feeling sluggish for days, which hadn't reflected well at the dole office. Still, she'd finally secured an interview – as a night clerk at the local hospital, which struck her as ironic – and things were looking up.

And then she heard another voice, a different one. It couldn't have been her grandma, unless her grandma had a particularly sore throat and had started to speak with an unusual accent, something it was impossible for Kate to place that reminded her of old black and white movies and the lonely sound of a violin in a thunderstorm.

"I've been watching you," the voice said. It was dreamy, almost absentminded, and it floated so softly in the stale air of her apartment that for a second, she thought she'd imagined it.

Then it came again. "It's nice to finally meet you, Kate."

"Who is this?" She looked around the room as though she was expecting to see a trail of ectoplasm across the wall, but everything looked normal. It smelled normal too, but it felt all wrong, like an English pub in a foreign country that's nailed the look and feel but not the atmosphere. Something was *wrong*, here.

"I have many names," the voice said. "But you can call me Zeb."

"Zeb?" Kate repeated. She thought back to the conversation with her grandmother and wondered when she'd started speaking more to the dead than to the living. "What do you want from me?"

Zeb laughed. It was a cool, cold laugh, emotionless and brutal like the grinding of gears or the noise of a cliff collapsing. Kate shivered and looked desperately around the room, but nothing. She made to run towards the door, and it slammed shut of its own accord. She scratched at it with her nails and tried to drag it open, but it was held tight by an invisible force from the other side.

Kate repeated her cry again, a little louder this time. She wondered if old Mrs Vanderbilt next door could hear her and, if so, whether she'd call the police. "What do you want from me?" she bellowed.

Zeb stopped laughing, and the absence of the sound was almost as ominous as the moment it had first appeared.

"I'm here for *you*, Kate," Zeb said.

And then he laughed again and the world went white.

WEEK TWENTY, DAY TWO

AFTER HEARING ZEB AND PASSING OUT, Kate had cut down on her medication and stopped double dosing. It wasn't helping her much, and her sleeping pattern was worse than ever. She was also starting to worry about side effects.

In particular, she worried she was losing her mind and that if she wasn't careful, she'd end up going to meet her grandmother on the other side of the ether. She hadn't heard from either Zeb or her grandmother since the incident with the laughter and the whiteout. And she was glad.

On the Tuesday of week twenty, a couple of weeks before Christmas, she found herself at an interview. It was her first real interview since her simultaneous dismissal and resignation from the agency, and she was so nervous that she barely slept the night before and hardly ate anything. By the time she'd been ushered into a back room at the supermarket, she was shaking violently and hoping that the interviewer wouldn't notice. If they did notice, she planned to pass them off as an attack of the nerves, which was partially true at best.

The store's manager was impressed enough to progress her to the second phase of interviews, which basically consisted of giving her a tour of the facilities and showing her the shelves she'd be stacking. Kate had worked at a supermarket before and so it was already familiar, and it wasn't like it took a degree to restock or to cover for someone on one of the tills.

And then it happened in the darkness. The manager told Kate to wait while she checked on a shipment, and so she found herself perching precariously on a stack of wooden pallets.

Then the lights went out and the temperature dropped. Kate shrieked and toppled over backwards. She hit her head on the floor and the shockwave rolled through her body. For some reason, her elbow hurt.

Then the laughter came. She recognised it. Zeb was here.

And then he disappeared again and the lights came back. She was curled up in a ball on the warehouse floor and her potential boss was staring down at her. There was no sign of anything unusual.

"So," Kate said, "did I get the job?"

WEEK TWENTY-ONE, DAY FOUR

KATE DIDN'T GET THE JOB, and her condition deteriorated over the next ten days. She even came clean about Zeb to Dr. Karnataka, who shrugged his shoulders and took a few notes down.

"Psychiatrics isn't my area," he said. "But I know a good doctor who might be able to help."

"I don't need a psychiatrist," Kate insisted. "I just need a little sleep."

"About that," Karnataka said. "Since your last bloodwork came back negative, we're going to have to try a different tactic."

"Just give me some more meds to knock me out," Kate replied.

Karnataka shook his head. "No can do," he said. "We can't just treat you blindly. We need to make a diagnosis so we know how best to fight the symptoms. With a bit of luck, we can cure you altogether."

"So what do we do?"

"You're going to need to meet my colleague," Karnataka told her. "Dr. Handsworth. He's a great man, and a good doctor to boot."

"What can he offer me that you can't?"

"That's easy," Karnataka said. "He's a specialist psychiatrist."

"I don't trust psychiatrists," Kate said.

"Me neither, as a rule." He laughed softly, as though he'd just enjoyed a private joke with himself. "Listen, Kate. There's only so much I can do to help you. I'm trying my best here, but I really think you need to see a psychiatrist."

"But I'm not imagining things!"

"I believe you," Karnataka said. "And Dr. Handsworth will believe you, too. Still, I can't find anything physical, so I think we're going to have to change tack. The only other option I can think of is to see if a little therapy could help."

"Do I have to do it?"

"No," the doctor replied. "But what have you got to lose? Give it a go, Kate. You can always stop the sessions if you're not finding them useful."

Kate paused. She looked at Dr. Karnataka, who was looking right back at her with a hopeful look on his face. He seemed genuine enough, and while he hadn't been able to make a diagnosis, she didn't doubt that he was genuinely trying to help her.

She sighed and said, "I'll think about it."

WEEK TWENTY-THREE, DAY FIVE

CHRISTMAS CAME AND WENT, and Kate found herself ringing in the new year by going to meet Dr. Handsworth for her first appointment.

She was nervous and exhausted, but Dr. Handsworth felt approachable and his cosy office reminded her of old country houses and her grandmother's parlour with a lit fire in the hearth. Handsworth's office didn't quite have a fire in there, but it did have shelves and shelves of books and unusual artefacts. It was beautiful, but it was also comfortable and functional.

It was a long and uncomfortable session, like all first sessions, but they covered good ground and by the end of it, Kate had told him all about Zeb and how the mysterious creature had appeared to her.

"When was the last time you saw him?" Handsworth asked.

"Hmm," Kate replied. "Let me see. I guess it was a couple of weeks ago. I had a job interview."

"And you saw Zeb?" he asked. Kate nodded. "What was that like?"

"It was bad," Kate said. "Real bad. I don't want to talk about it."

"I understand," Dr. Handsworth replied. "Although if our sessions are to be successful then I need you to be as open with me as possible."

"I know," Kate said. "But not about this, not now. I'm not ready. I'm still wrapping my head around it."

"Fair enough." The doctor jotted a few notes in his Moleskine and peered across at her over the tops of his glasses. "And what about your grandmother? Have you seen her recently?"

"Every night," Kate admitted. "She's trying to warn

me."

"She's trying to warn you? About what?"

"Zeb," Kate said. "She's afraid of him. I'm afraid of him, too."

"Why?"

"I don't know," Kate admitted. "And I'm not sure if I want to find out."

WEEK TWENTY-FOUR, DAY FIVE

DR. HANDSWORTH had referred Kate to a sleep specialist and booked her another appointment, although she wasn't convinced that either of them would help. Besides, there was a four-month waiting list and Kate was convinced that if anything was going to happen, it was going to happen long before then. She couldn't shake the sense that someone – or some*thing* – was watching her.

And she had the growing feeling that it was Zeb, and not her grandmother, who was watching. Not that Nana Knight herself had provided much comfort.

In her next meeting with Dr. Handsworth, she shared something that had been bugging her.

"I used to think I was going crazy," she confessed. "I thought I was losing my mind. But then I started to come round to the idea. It's hard not to obey the evidence of your senses."

"I understand," Dr. Handsworth said. "Although our senses can lie to us. Sometimes it might be better not to trust them."

"Do you think I'm crazy?" Kate asked.

The doctor stared at her and thought about his response for a moment. His eyes looked kind and welcoming, but Kate was nervous all the same. She barely knew the man.

"It's not a word that I'd use for anyone," the doctor said. "But no, I think you're perfectly sane. You just have a different reality to the rest of us."

"That's one way to put it," Kate said.

She stiffened and sat bolt upright. Her pupils contracted and her mouth flew open. Little strings of saliva rolled over her teeth and down to her lips.

Something was wrong. Zeb was coming; she could feel it. She shot to her feet and ran for the door.

"I'm sorry," she shouted, "something's come up!"

WEEK TWENTY-FIVE, DAY TWO

ZEB HAD STAYED mercifully away from her, but now the nightmares were so bad that even if she did fall asleep, she woke herself back up again.

But they were non-specific nightmares, the kind that she half-remembered by the grey light of day and forgot about by the time that she finished brushing her teeth. In most of them, she was running from something, but when she turned around to catch a glimpse of it there was just an angry red fog spreading out over the land and slowly catching up with her.

Perhaps it was a premonition about the letter.

It arrived inconspicuously on her doormat in a plain white envelope. She didn't notice at first, but when she finally picked it up and slipped the flap open, the contents almost blew her away.

It was a final demand from her landlord. It told her she needed to pay up quick or get evicted, but paying her rent wasn't exactly that easy. She had no money, no job and too much pride to ask for help. So she did the next best thing.

She burned the letter and tried to forget all about it.

But Zeb had plans of his own, and he made them known. Kate saw him there in her bedroom, leaning against the wall and watching with his big, dark eyes. That was all she could see: his eyes. There was more to him, of course, but she couldn't tear her gaze away from his pupils. They were beautiful and terrible at the same time, and they drew her in like the vortex at the centre of a whirlpool. All of the rest of him was just extra material and her brain refused to process it.

Zeb's sudden appearance had been a shock, of course, but it hadn't been a surprise. Kate had been expecting him, and she knew that he was up to no good before he opened his phantasmagorical mouth.

"Kate," he said. "You can't go on like this much longer. You'll have to give in eventually."

"Over my dead body."

"No," Zeb said. "Not yours. Someone else's."

"What do you mean?" Kate asked.

But Zeb just laughed and said, "You'll see."

WEEK TWENTY-SIX, DAY THREE

KATE STOPPED LEAVING THE HOUSE. She thought that if she stayed in the place then her landlord would struggle to kick her out. The logic was flawed, of course, but it kept her going.

By now, sleep was almost non-existent, but she no longer spent hours in bed every night trying to get there. Instead, she stayed up for days on end, patrolling her house and cleaning every inch of it as though bleach could make up for the lack of rent. And everywhere she went she kept her eyes, her ears and her intuition open in case Zeb made another appearance. If he did, she promised herself she'd be ready.

Her house was small enough to begin with, but it felt like it was getting smaller by the day. She lived on the bottom floor of a three-tier semi-detached house that had been converted to modern apartments, and her entire world now consisted of just three rooms that she refused to leave unless she had to.

Zeb and Nana Knight had always appeared in the bedroom, which was tucked off to the side and which backed onto a wall. There were no windows and there was no exit except back through the rest of the house, and it had started to make Kate feel trapped. As time went on, she spent more and more time in the other two rooms: the hybrid lounge/kitchen and the bathroom.

The next time she saw Zeb, she wasn't half asleep in her bedroom. She was wide awake in the living room at 9:45 AM, drinking a cup of green tea and watching daytime television. The weather outside was bleak, but the sun's grey light still made its way through the net curtains and into her living room.

It happened in the blink of an eye. One moment she was alone and the next... well, Zeb was in the room with her, although all she could see were his eyes. They beckoned her in and took over her senses, like a one-on-one with a hypnotist who was hell-bent on destruction. They demanded her attention and her obedience, but her mind rebelled. She tore her eyes away with a superhuman effort and dashed away from him.

She realised too late that she'd backed herself into a corner.

Kate stood there in the tiny kitchen with Zeb blocking her route to the door. Even if she could brush past him somehow, the door was locked, bolted and on the chain. She didn't trust strangers. She never had. But now it looked like her paranoia was about to backfire on her.

Zeb's eyes beckoned to her again. She heard his voice inside her head, whispering, "Do it. Do it." She didn't know what he meant, but she'd be damned if she was going to let her life be ruled by fear any longer.

She armed herself, scooping up a kitchen knife from the sideboard and backing off towards the bathroom. The handle was still wet and she struggled to keep a grip on it, but if she had to, she'd fight the thing with her bare hands.

Zeb floated slowly towards her. She could still only see the eyes, and she didn't dare to even look at those in case they took over her mind somehow. Maybe he was walking and maybe he was being carried along by a dozen slimy tentacles. Maybe it didn't matter.

She wasn't going to let Zeb come to her. She was going to go to Zeb, and to hell with the consequences.

Kate charged at those evil eyes, her arms swinging big zigzags as she swiped the knife through the air. She scored a couple of glancing blows and Zeb howled. He cowered back for a moment and Kate saw a glimmer of uncertainty in those expressive eyes of his. Then he charged at her, and Kate reacted on instinct.

She thrust the knife forwards and felt it stick in something. Then she blacked out and hit her head on the floor as she landed.

WEEK TWENTY-SIX, DAY SIX

SHE LAY THERE for two days and two nights. Then on the third day, she woke up.

Her hands were stained with blood. It had dried and caked on to them until it looked like she'd left her hands to soak in a bowl of food colouring. She was still holding on to the knife.

Kate groaned and pulled herself up. Her hands were shaking and her heart was racing. She screamed when she saw the body. It looked artificial like a mannequin, with blemished, grey flesh and blue extremities. It looked like a frostbite victim. And it sure as hell looked like Nana Knight.

That was because it *was* Nana Knight. The old woman was dead again, and this time she wasn't coming back. She had a gash in her chest and her old lady entrails were hanging out like an abominable interrobang. She was definitely dead, and it was definitely from Kate's knife.

And it definitely wasn't Zeb. Zeb had different eyes, and they were looking at her. Laughing at her.

She passed out again.

WEEK TWENTY-SEVEN, DAY FIVE

"I KILLED MY GRANDMOTHER," Kate said.

"No, you didn't," Dr. Handsworth replied.

"Yes, I did," Kate insisted. And then she told him what had happened. "I didn't mean to. I thought she was Zeb."

"And you tried to kill him?"

"Yes."

Dr. Handsworth sighed. "Real or not," he said, "you shouldn't stab people."

"I know," Kate replied. "Nana Knight told me that."

"And then you stabbed her."

"Yes."

Dr. Handsworth thought for a moment. "I don't know, Kate," he said. "I'm worried about you. Are you sleeping?"

"No."

"I thought not," Handsworth replied. "I think we should take another look at your medication."

Kate sighed. "Of course," she said.

"I'm sorry," Handsworth told her. "There's only so much I can do and if we want you to get better, we're going to have to step things up."

"And what if I say no?"

"Kate, I'm going to be honest here," Handsworth said. "You have a serious illness."

"I'm not crazy."

"I didn't say you were." He looked at her, and she was reminded of Zeb and how difficult it was to turn away from him. "You need to get some sleep, Kate. I mean it. Look at you."

"What about me?"

Dr. Handsworth smashed his fist off his desk in frustration. Kate flinched and shrank back and Handsworth hastily apologised.

"Kate," he said, "I can't help you. This isn't a psychological condition."

"You mean I'm not crazy?"

"I didn't say that," the doctor said. "But sure, why not? Kate, I'm not going to lie. You have a lot of neurosis and a clear-cut case of OCD. But these things that you're seeing, the visions you're having. I think they're a by-product of your lack of sleep. If we can fix your sleep, we'll fix your hallucinations."

"They're not hallucinations."

"Perhaps not," Dr. Handsworth said. "I have no doubt that they feel very real to you. But at the same time, you must admit that there's something strange going on. Your dead grandmother came back to life and then you killed her. You don't think that's a little… *odd*?"

Kate shrugged.

"What happened to the body?"

"It disappeared," she admitted. "One minute it was

there and the next it had gone."

"And you don't think it was a hallucination?"

She shrugged again. "I don't know what it was," she said. "I don't much care for labels."

"Right." Dr. Handsworth paused for a moment. "I'm going to follow up with that sleep specialist. Let's see if we can't speed up your appointment."

WEEK TWENTY-NINE, DAY THREE

KATE LAY LOW FOR A COUPLE OF WEEKS.

She felt like a criminal, and she guessed that she technically was, but she also agreed with Dr. Handsworth. With no body, there was no crime, and that thought put her at ease even though it also said a lot about her mental state.

She still couldn't sleep though, but that didn't surprise her. *What else is new?* she thought.

On the plus side, she'd been given new medication, some mad concoction from the boffins that was supposed to help her sleep. It didn't, but it did stop the crazy visions and for a little while, she'd felt almost normal.

On the Wednesday of week twenty-nine, she had her appointment with Dr. Jalopnik, the sleep specialist. She was a woman, which Kate hadn't been expecting, and she was young, which she hadn't been expecting, either. They even looked similar, and both were strict and methodical. They warmed to each other almost immediately.

"How can I help?" Jalopnik asked.

So Kate told her the whole story, sparing the woman none of the details. The doctor looked slightly concerned when Kate got to the bit with the knife and the corporeal ghost of her grandmother, but she listened patiently and didn't pass judgement. It wasn't her job.

When Kate told her what Dr. Handsworth had said about the lack of sleep affecting her ability to differentiate between fiction and reality, Dr. Jalopnik sat forward and paid close attention.

"It's certainly true that hallucinations are common amongst people who are suffering from sleep deprivation," Dr. Jalopnik said. "And I can see from the charts that your sleeping pattern is non-existent."

"It's from my Fitbit," Kate said, tapping the device on her wrist.

"Very nice," Jalopnik said. "That'll give us some data to start with."

"So what happens next?"

"I'd like to keep you in overnight," the doctor said. "We'll set you up in one of our pods so we can track your vitals. I'd like to get a good look at what's going on inside that brain of yours."

WEEK THIRTY, DAY TWO

DR. JALOPNIK'S TESTS were inconclusive, as Kate had always suspected they would be, and while she stayed at the facility for a second night in a row, she didn't fall asleep the entire time she was there, and the researchers seemed disappointed with the results they had.

"It's not *my* fault," Kate had tried to explain. "That's why I'm here in the first place, after all."

But explanation or not, the researchers were clearly disappointed – and so was Kate, although she'd tried not to get her hopes up. It would have been too much to ask for a diagnosis. She was starting to wonder if maybe she really was crazy.

It certainly felt like it.

Week twenty-nine had ended in a bad way, but week thirty was even worse. Monday was okay because she got a good four hours, but Tuesday was a bad day from the get-go. She started vomiting in the early hours and spent half the morning with her head down the toilet bowl. Just when she thought she'd spewed up everything she'd ever swallowed, she vomited some more.

By the time she'd cleaned herself up, the post had arrived. Right on top of the pile was the metaphorical red letter she'd been dreading, the final nail in the coffin. It was another illusion brought about by her lack of sleep, because in reality it had been a couple of months at best since she'd last paid rent. But in that time, she'd hardly left the house, and she certainly hadn't earned any money that she could use to pay the debt off.

She rang her mother to tell her the bad news. "I need help," Kate said. "I hate to ask, but…"

"You want to move back in with me?" Her mother didn't sound impressed. Kate knew how much she'd looked forward to getting the kids out of the house, but she hoped that things had changed since her father died. She also knew she was a nightmare to live with. Even if she tiptoed around the house, she wouldn't be able to help herself from making a noise at 4:00 AM when she wanted a cup of tea or when she needed to use the toilet. She always flushed, no matter what the hour. She had to. If she didn't, bad things would happen.

Kate begged her mother to take her in, and she could tell that her resolve was beginning to fade. But she knew that it was far from an ideal situation – for either of them.

Then she did the only thing she had left to do. She started packing her stuff into black bin bags.

WEEK THIRTY-TWO, DAY ONE

"I'VE MADE A DECISION," Kate's mother said. "But I want to talk to you about it in person. Can we meet for lunch somewhere?"

"Let me check my diary," Kate replied. She didn't have to. "Yeah, I'm free. But I can't leave the house."

"Why not?"

"What if the bailiffs come?"

Her mother sighed, as though she thought her daughter was being a child, but Kate was being practical. If the bailiffs came, she could try to delay them or to head them off. But if she was out of the house, there'd be no one to stop them from letting themselves in and taking her stuff away.

If Zeb let them, of course.

Kate met her mother at the garden centre. It was her mother's favourite place to talk things over, and Kate was more than happy to risk another confrontation with the carrot cake. Her mother didn't disappoint and she was already on her third slice by the time that the inevitable discussion began.

"So," her mother began. She didn't seem her usual, confident self, and that scared Kate more than any apparition ever could. "This living situation."

"Uh-huh."

"What's happening, Kate?"

The abruptness of the question took her by surprise, and she had to think about it for a moment before she provided an answer.

"I'm not quite sure," she said. "There's something wrong inside me. Something that stops me from sleeping and makes me see things. I've been seeing Nana Knight."

"Nana Knight?" her mother repeated. She was clearly sceptical, but she'd also been the only person in the family to be attached to the old dear. She'd made the trip up north to see her once a month like clockwork, at least until she'd popped her clogs and moved on to wherever people move on to. "How is the old girl?"

"I don't want to talk about it."

"Fair enough." An awkward silence descended. Kate picked up another slice of carrot cake, and her mother slurped at her coffee. "Okay."

"Okay?"

"Okay," she repeated. "You can move back in with me. But I don't have space for all your stuff and so you'll have to put it into storage."

"I can do that."

"There's more," her mother continued. "You're going to have to find a job. This is getting out of hand, Kate. You need to sort your life out. You need to pull yourself together."

"Yeah," she said. "I know."

It's funny, she thought. *She gets more and more like Nana Knight as the years go by.*

WEEK THIRTY-FOUR, DAY SIX

THE DAY HAD FINALLY ARRIVED. Kate had been living in the house like a nervous squatter, barely leaving the place and spending most of her time twitching from behind the curtain. Her bags were packed and she was ready to go. She just wanted to drag out the time a little longer.

When the bailiffs arrived, she kept her composure. She was resigned to the fact that she'd be leaving the place, just like she was resigned to the fact that proper sleep was for other people. So when the fateful day arrived, she welcomed them in with a cup of tea and a biscuit. In return, they helped her to carry the black bags full of her worldly possessions out on to the kerb. Most of the big stuff was in storage and she didn't own much else, so when the job was done, she simply called a taxi and asked them to send a big black cab. There was enough room there for all of her belongings with room to spare for her to slip in beside them.

When she was done, she slipped the key through the letterbox and turned her back on the house. She hoped that her mother's house would be better for her and that she'd finally get a good night's sleep. And she hoped that Zeb would stay behind and haunt the new tenant instead of following her. But even as she thought it, she knew it was crazy.

When the taxi pulled up outside her mother's house, the driver kept the meter running. Kate's mother wasn't at home – she had a job to do, as she kept on reminding her daughter – and so she had to carry her belongings inside by herself after grabbing the key that she'd stashed beneath the dustbin, just in case of such an eventuality.

Zeb trailed along behind her, but he refused to help her with the bags. She felt his eyes boring a hole into the back of her head as she hauled her possessions into her mother's house.

Part Three: Weight Loss

WEEK THIRTY-FIVE, DAY TWO

LIVING WITH HER MOTHER required some adjustment.

For a start, the old woman had started to treat her like a child again. She gave Kate a bedtime and made sure she stuck to it, whether she managed to sleep or not. Most of the time, she didn't. She just stayed up all night and stared at the wall, waiting for the dawn to come. For the first couple of nights, she'd given up and climbed back out of bed, then headed downstairs into the living room. But her mother was having none of that. It was as though she had some sort of sixth sense. She had an uncanny knack of heading downstairs at just the right time to catch her daughter in the act. If she found her there in the living room after the all-powerful lights out then she'd send her back up to her room with a clip round the ear.

Kate hadn't slept since she'd left the old house, but it wasn't from lack of trying. Her body just refused to shut down and her brain kept reminding her that her old routine was dead and that she'd need to adopt a new one. She'd been up for the best part of four days without any stimulants, and the world was starting to look sluggish and artificial.

At night, when she was confined to her bedroom, she listened to the wind and rain outside and the sounds that the cars made as they meandered past. From time to time, she'd overhear a snatch of conversation as two youths walked past with their hoods pulled up to ward off the cold. Other than that, she was alone in her room.

Mostly alone. Zeb never really left her. His eyes watched

over her around the clock, and he'd started to follow her not just at night, when she was confined to the bedroom, but during the day as well. He even followed her onto the bus to the dole office, swiping the seat next to her. The other passengers seemed to somehow know that something was there and so they never took the vacant seat. Either that or nobody wanted to sit next to the gaunt young woman who looked like a junkie and who muttered to herself as the bus coursed through the streets.

Like a boxer slumped against the corner of the ring, Kate was struggling to stay above water. She wasn't sure how long she could keep on fighting.

WEEK THIRTY-SIX, DAY THREE

KATE HAD LANDED HERSELF A JOB.

True, it wasn't anything special. She was working part-time hours for minimum wage at a charity shop and using her earnings to pay off the debt to her old landlord, but it was something and, as her mother liked to say, it kept her out of trouble.

The old women that she worked with thought she was some sort of goddess. She had a knack for valuing items and listing the best of the bunch on eBay, and if they left her alone in the stock room, she could sort stuff like there was no tomorrow.

That was because she had a helping hand. Zeb wasn't exactly docile, but it turned out that the apparition had a soft spot for sorting through things. He told her that he fed off the psychic vibrations that the objects had attached to them.

Like her adjustment to the lack of sleep, she marvelled at how quickly she'd grown to tolerate the ghost that plagued her. Since Nana Knight and her second demise, Kate had lost the will to fight. She'd seen what happened. And so Zeb had gone from being a malign influence, a tumour on the biological matter of life, to being a guardian angel, albeit a fallen one.

Kate was working in the stock room when her neck gave out. She felt fine, and then all of a sudden, she didn't. It tensed right up, and she dropped the box she was carrying with a clatter of broken crockery and the rattle of spilled knickknacks. She threw a hand automatically to her neck and tried to massage some life into it.

"What's going on in there?"

Kate flinched. The voice belonged to Maude, the shop's assistant manager. If she found out that Kate had damaged the goods, she might go full Mr. Murray on her and tell her to go home and not come back. But she was also a kindly old lady, and Kate trusted her gut for once and made a decision.

"My neck," she shouted. "Something's wrong with it. I can't move it."

Maude came bustling through into the back room and rushed over to her. "What happened?"

"I don't know," Kate said. She tried to move it again but it was still locked tight and inflexible. "Maude, I'm scared. I need you to do me a favour."

"What is it?"

"I need you to call me an ambulance."

WEEK THIRTY-SEVEN, DAY ONE

THE GOOD NEWS was that there was nothing seriously wrong with her neck. She'd been having visions about being confined to a wheelchair for the rest of her life or of being diagnosed with some sort of degenerative muscle disease.

It turned out that she had a bad case of cramp, which the doctors assumed was a side effect of her severe lack of sleep. They gave her a neck brace and discharged her, but her neck continued to get worse over the coming days until she was forced to call in sick.

The bad news was that she still had no diagnosis. She had hope, though. She'd been booked in for another session with Dr. Jalopnik at the sleep research centre, and the day finally arrived on the Monday of week thirty-seven.

"You've lost some weight," Dr. Jalopnik observed. "Too much weight. We're going to have to run some more tests."

"Tests," Kate murmured. "Again. What are we hoping for this time?"

"A diagnosis," the doctor replied. "I have a few ideas." She paused for a moment. "You know, this weight loss isn't good for you. We need to figure out what's causing it. It can't go on."

"Tell me about it," Kate said. "I'm wasting away here."

"Are you eating?"

"Yes," she replied. "Why does everyone keep asking that?"

"Hmm," Dr. Jalopnik said. "I wonder…"

Kate waited for the punchline, but it didn't come. "What?" she asked.

"I'm going to see if I can get you a session in the tank," Dr. Jalopnik replied.

WEEK THIRTY-EIGHT, DAY THREE

KATE HAD LOST half a stone in the week or so since her last appointment with Dr. Jalopnik, and she was starting to worry that if they didn't find a cure for her soon, she'd literally waste away until her pale skin turned translucent and her bones stuck out from her body.

She'd seen photos of people with eating disorders and the thought of it filled her with horror. She didn't want to end up like that, and the prospect was made worse by the fact that nothing seemed to help. She was eating as much as she could, scoffing down huge portions of her mother's greasy food and deliberately eating stuff that was full of fat and calories. But none of it helped.

It's not as though I can't keep it down, she thought. *It's like the calories don't even count. Like the food's passing straight through me without touching the sides. Either the food is a ghost or I am.*

It was a Wednesday, and Kate was back at the sleep research facility with Dr. Jalopnik. The good doctor had taken her into an underground room, deep beneath the facility, where they kept their most experimental piece of equipment.

"Welcome to the tank," Dr. Jalopnik said.

"Woah," Kate said. "What *is* it?"

"It's called a sensory deprivation tank," the doctor explained. "It's designed to numb each of your senses. There'll be no light, no sound, nothing to touch. Just you and your thoughts left to float alone."

"That sounds like hell."

"Perhaps," the doctor said. "We're going to inject you with a cocktail of fast-acting drugs. The plan is to starve your mind of any input while numbing your body and slowing down your respiratory system. Think of it as like a moment of enforced Zen."

"But why?"

"We want to shock your system," Dr. Jalopnik said. "It's like a factory reset on a mobile phone."

"Except I'm not a mobile phone."

"No," Dr. Jalopnik said. "You're not." She paused for a moment and looked across at her. In the background, a machine hummed and sent snowy howls of static cascading around the room. "So what do you say?"

Kate looked around and then at Zeb, who was standing behind the doctor's shoulder. She looked at him for as long as she dared before turning away and breaking the infernal eye contact.

"Let's do it," she said.

WEEK THIRTY-NINE, DAY FIVE

THE SESSION IN THE TANK was long but not uncomfortable, like a warm bath after a long day. Kate felt at ease while she was in there, but she didn't fall asleep. In fact, the sensors picked up an increase in her brain activity, which was unexpected.

The following week, she returned to the unit to meet with Dr. Jalopnik.

"How are you keeping, Kate?" the doctor asked. "Getting any sleep?"

"I'm okay," she replied. "I've been getting a couple of hours a night, maybe. Three or four on the days after the tank."

"Hmm," Jalopnik said. "That's still not enough." She paused. "Kate, I think you should sit down."

"Why?"

"Because I think we have a diagnosis," she said. "Sit down, please."

"This doesn't sound like good news," Kate replied, obeying the doctor by taking a seat. "What is it?"

"I'm afraid I have bad news," she replied. "There's only one thing that could explain your unusual symptoms and your inability to sleep. It's called fatal familial insomnia."

"Fatal?"

Dr. Jalopnik nodded. "I'm afraid so. There's no known cure."

"What do you mean?" Kate asked. Her heart was racing so hard that she worried it would burst from her chest, but her head felt somehow detached from it all. In a way, she almost felt glad. At last, some certainty.

"Your brain can't go past stage one of NREM-sleep," Jalopnik explained. "We need to take you off your medication. No wonder it's not helping."

"You want to take me off my sleeping pills?"

"For now, at least. They usually make the symptoms worse and hasten the disease's progression."

"But I'm still going to die?"

"Oh yes," Dr. Jalopnik replied. "I'm afraid so. We all do, eventually."

"But I'm going to die sooner."

"Yes." She sighed and fixed Kate with the most compassionate look she could manage.

"How long have I got?"

"It's hard to tell," the doctor said. "Six months. A year, perhaps. Two, if you're lucky."

Kate sat back in her chair. Her mouth hung open and her pupils had shrunk to tiny pinpricks. Her heart had slowed but her brain had sped up to take its place. She was making plans and calculations, hatching schemes to find death before it found her, so she could kick it in the nuts.

But in the end, they were just the crazy thoughts of a dying woman. And while she thought them, Zeb watched on and laughed.

WEEK FORTY, DAY FOUR

IT WAS ANOTHER WEEK with no sleep and no reprieve. Kate's sanity was wearing so thin that she could no longer distinguish between fact and fiction. When she dreamed, her dreams were more vivid than the waking world, but she was dreaming less and less often. Dr. Jalopnik had told her that by the end, she'd descend into a vegetative state, and Kate wondered which world she'd find herself in.

There was only one little ray of hope, but even that was just a consolation prize. Still, at least with a diagnosis she could convince her mother that this was really real, and not just an illusion.

Her mother had wanted Kate to borrow some money and to live the rest of her life as much as she could. She'd suggested making a bucket list and ticking off items until her life gave out. But Kate was having none of it.

"I'm too tired," she'd said. "I can't go on. I just want to live out my days in peace."

"But you're so *young*."

"I don't feel it," Kate had said. And she didn't look it, either. The weight was still dropping off her at an alarming rate, and her once-round face was gaunt and lined with stress and anguish. Her legs were so thin that they could barely support her weight, but her stomach had gone the other way. She was bloated from malnutrition and dead on her feet, so she spent more time than ever just lying on her bed, too tired to move and unable to sleep.

Something else was worrying her, too. But she'd have to wait until her next meeting with Dr. Jalopnik to get an answer.

And in the meantime, Zeb just watched… and waited.

WEEK FORTY-ONE, DAY THREE

SHE MENTIONED IT to Dr. Jalopnik at their next session. At one point in her life, she would have felt embarrassed to have talked about her inner workings in such detail with a total stranger. But by now, her life was an open book.

"I haven't had a period," she said. "Should I be worried?"

Dr. Jalopnik frowned. "When did you last have one?" she asked.

"I can't remember," Kate admitted. "Three, maybe four months ago."

"Hmm," she said. Then she asked the obvious question. "Have you had intercourse? I mean, is there a possibility that you might be pregnant?"

Kate stared at her. "I'm a lesbian," she said. "And for the record, I can't even sleep with myself."

"I thought as much," she said. "It seemed unlikely, I'll grant you. If you *were* pregnant, it should have shown up in your bloodwork, but mistakes happen. It's always best to double check these things."

"So where does that leave me?"

"I'm sorry, Kate," she said. "I think it's a side effect of your illness."

"What do you mean?" she asked.

"Have you been having any hot flushes?"

"Yes," she said. "I'm sure you would too if your body clock had its own special time zone."

"That's not what I mean," Dr. Jalopnik replied. "I think I have some more bad news."

Kate sighed. She knew this was coming. She attracted bad news like politicians attracted scandals in the pages of tabloid newspapers.

"Go on," she said. "Get it over with."

Dr. Jalopnik nodded. "Very well," she said. "I believe these are the symptoms of an early menopause."

Kate's face dropped. She thought about it for a moment.

"I've always wanted kids," she said. "But I always thought it was impossible. I guess now it really is. Besides…"

"Besides what?"

She looked the doctor dead in the eye and said, "Even if I *was* pregnant, there's no guarantee I could bring the child to term."

WEEK FORTY-THREE, DAY TWO

KATE WAS ON A DOWNWARD SPIRAL. Her strength had deserted her, and her will to live wasn't far behind it. She hadn't slept for several weeks, and it was beginning to take its toll.

The insomnia was bad enough, but the hallucinations were worse and the weight loss was extreme. Her skin hung loose on her fragile bones and gave her the same wrinkled, leathery skin that people get when they spend too long underwater. Her eyes spent less and less time in the real world, preferring instead to stare into the depths of Zeb's eyes as he whispered platitudes to her.

She used to be afraid to look into them in case he somehow hypnotised her. Now she was afraid to look away.

The worst part was that no one came to see her. She supposed she didn't blame them, accustomed as she was to pushing her friends away from her and bailing on plans because of her anxiety. She'd been sure that someone, somewhere, must have cared for her. But apparently they didn't.

Even her mother was sick of spending time with her, and the old lady was spending more and more time out of the house so that she didn't have to look at her daughter.

She thinks I'm a disappointment, Kate thought. *Just like Nana Knight.*

Meanwhile, she continued her conversations with Zeb, and the two of them would talk long into the night. Zeb was shrewd, a good conversationalist, but Kate could never find a hint of personality. She didn't know who he was or what he wanted. When she asked him directly for an opinion, he simply echoed something that she'd said to him. Come to think of it, that was probably why she thought he was a good conversationalist. He was just a reflection of herself.

One night, Zeb called to her. "Kate…"

She was too weak to sit up, or even to roll over or to turn around. She just lay there and whispered, "What?"

"I have a job for you, Kate," he said.

"Again?"

Zeb laughed. It wasn't cruel, but it wasn't a happy laugh, either. It was cold and unemotional. Distant. Not quite deranged, but not far off it either.

"This isn't like the old woman," Zeb said. "This is something different. I need you to do something for me. But I can't tell you what it is."

"Why not?"

"I just can't," Zeb said. "But don't worry. I don't need to. You'll know what it is when the time comes."

"If you say so," Kate replied. Her voice was thin and wavering. "But what if I can't do it? I just feel so… so weak."

"That's because you are," Zeb said. He laughed. "It's going to be okay, Kate. You can trust me."

Kate wasn't sure whether she ought to believe him.

Part Four: Dementia

WEEK FORTY-SIX, DAY FOUR

KATE HAD STOPPED TALKING.

Her symptoms were getting worse, she still hadn't slept a wink since the weight loss took off, and she just lay there, almost unresponsive, as the world moved on without her.

She didn't talk because she couldn't talk. She'd gone too long without doing it and as her mind continued to erode, it had somehow wiped the part that connected her brain to her mouth. But even if she could have talked, she wouldn't have bothered. There was nothing left for her to say.

Her mother still took her to her sessions with Dr. Jalopnik, but everyone knew that there was precious little hope for her. Apart from her time in the sensory deprivation tank, which relaxed her but didn't help her to sleep, the sessions seemed to do more harm than good. Most of the time, she just sat there and listened while Dr. Jalopnik filled her with false hope. She seemed worried that she was about to do something stupid, but Kate couldn't have killed herself if she'd wanted to. She could hardly hold her head up. Her mother had to carry her out of the house and wheel her around in a chair.

Kate was just watching and waiting. That was all there was to do.

WEEK FORTY-SEVEN, DAY SIX

THE DAYS PASSED slowly and uneventfully. By now, Kate's mother was also off work because the job she had paid less than a professional carer. But the old woman wasn't well-suited to the task, especially with her fiery temperament and the genes that she'd inherited from Nana Knight.

Still, she did her best, and Kate was grateful that she had someone there for her in the real world. There was Zeb in the weird world inside her head of course, but that hardly counted. Zeb couldn't spoon soup into her mouth or knead the wasted muscles of her body to stop them from deteriorating further.

Kate's morale was low, and she didn't care who knew it.

One evening, while her mother was feeding her and trying not spill broth onto the bedsheets, Zeb floated across the floor towards her. His eyes were red, like he'd been crying, but for the first time since he'd appeared, Kate could make out a little more of him. Not the body, of course, but she could see a glimpse of an aquiline nose and a cold, sharp mouth. It was smiling at her.

"You're getting closer, Kate," Zeb said.

"I'm wasting away," Kate replied.

"Yes, you are, dear," her mother said. But Kate ignored her. There was someone else in the room that she wanted to talk to.

Zeb was laughing at her, like always. "It won't be long," he told her. "You'll see."

"I can't wait," Kate whispered. She closed her eyes.

"What was that, dear?" her mother asked.

But Kate was too tired to respond to her.

WEEK FORTY-NINE, DAY TWO

"THIS ISN'T GOOD," Dr. Jalopnik said.

Kate and her mother were in her office. Well, Kate's mother was in her office. Nobody really knew where Kate was, and she wasn't in much of a situation to tell them.

"What is it?" Kate's mother asked.

"Hypnagogia," the doctor said. "I've heard of it, but I've never actually *seen* it. This is quite something."

"That's my daughter you're talking about."

"Yes," Dr. Jalopnik said. She sighed. "It's a pity, really."

"What's hypergoganot?"

"Hypnagogia," Dr. Jalopnik repeated. It rolled off her tongue like she'd practiced it a dozen times before, which she had. "Pre-sleep limbo."

Kate's mother simply stared at her. By her side, her daughter was trembling in her chair. Her eyes were open, but they were vacant, and while she was moving her wasted limbs around like she was conducting an orchestra, she wasn't moving in this reality. She was moving in another.

Dr. Jalopnik did her best to explain it. "It's a state that we all experience. Most of us go through hypnagogia just before falling asleep."

"So what's happening to her?"

"I dare say that we'll never actually *know*," the doctor said. "But for the purposes of your question, I'd say that she's basically just sleepwalking."

"So is she awake or asleep?"

The doctor sighed. "That's a difficult question to answer," she said. "Is Schrodinger's cat dead or alive?"

"I don't understand."

"She's somewhere in between," the doctor said. "This is bad news, I'm afraid. I don't think she has much fight left in her. Fatal familial insomnia is a rare disease, you understand. But in most cases, the hypnagogia doesn't kick in until right at the very end."

"You mean…?"

Kate's mother didn't have to finish her sentence for the doctor to know what she meant. She risked a sympathetic smile, but it didn't go down well and so instead she looked her dead in the eye and nodded.

"I'm afraid so," she said.

WEEK FIFTY, DAY THREE

IT HAPPENED ON A WEDNESDAY.

Kate had taken her last actions in her humdrum world of old and had changed over completely to Zeb's dream world. She saw his body now, the whole thing in all its glory, and it was awesome and terrifying at the same time. She couldn't look away from him. Even if she could have, she didn't want to.

For Kate's mother, though, it was a nightmare. She was back in the real world, staring at her daughter's wasted body through the tear-filled eyes of the mother who'd given birth to her.

Out in the real world, Kate was unresponsive. She didn't react to sound or to a light in her eye, and she didn't even flinch when her mother grabbed the webs of her fingers and pinched as hard as she could. Kate's fingers were so frail and her flesh so taut that it was like trying to snap a wishbone.

Her mother shouted at her and slapped her cheeks, but nothing. Then she raced off for a glass of water and threw that into Kate's face, but still nothing. She couldn't see it, but Zeb was standing behind her, following her, watching her every move with interest.

Kate was still unresponsive, so her mother stepped up her efforts. She checked her daughter's pulse and confirmed it was there, then listened against her chest for confirmation. She used to find the sound of her daughter's heartbeat relaxing. But she hadn't heard it since some long-forgotten snuggle some twenty-something years ago, and the sound of it now, in the sterile room, just chilled her.

She reached into the pocket of her dressing gown and came out with her mobile phone. She keyed in the triple digits of the emergency services, hit the call button and waited for it to connect.

WEEK FIFTY-ONE, DAY SIX

KATE WAS IN THE HOSPITAL, and it wasn't looking good.

She'd been unresponsive ever since she'd been piled into the back of an ambulance and raced through the streets to the emergency room with her mother still beside her in her dressing gown. The hospital staff had tried to remove her so they could carry out a proper diagnosis, but Kate's mother had refused to budge and fought tooth and nail until even the security staff didn't have the heart to restrain her.

"Call Dr. Jalopnik," she was shouting. "I don't care what time it is. Wake her up if you have to. Call Dr. Jalopnik at the Sunnyvale Centre."

At first, they ignored her pleas as the mad ramblings of a hysterical mother, but when Kate continued to be unresponsive and they started to run out of options, one of the juniors eventually started to listen.

"Maybe we should do what she says," the doctor said, reluctantly. And so they did. Dr. Jalopnik was asleep when they called her, but she answered the phone on the fifth ring and told them with a weary voice that she'd be there as soon as she could.

"I can go without sleep for one night," Dr. Jalopnik said. "If Kate can do it for months on end, then I can skip a couple of hours. I'll be there as soon as I can."

But for the doctors in the ER, soon wasn't soon enough. Despite their best efforts, Kate continued to be unresponsive. They tried fixing her up with a cocktail of stimulants and amphetamines, ran a number of tests that were designed to produce a response and even ran an ECG to see what was going on inside her head.

There was activity there, which meant she wasn't brain-dead. But she also didn't react to any external stimulus.

By the time that Dr. Jalopnik arrived at the hospital, it was official. Kate was in a coma.

WEEK FIFTY-TWO, DAY TWO

IT HAD BEEN A YEAR since the day that everything had gone wrong and Kate's OCD had launched itself into overdrive.

Kate was in the nowhere, the blurry in-between that served as a link between Zeb's world and the real world. Her eyes had been closed to protect them, but her ears were still open and she could hear the world around her. She heard her mother prattling on about the latest comings and goings on the street they lived on and the love affairs in the soap operas she liked to watch. The conversation was so boring that Kate was almost glad that she couldn't reply. The downside was that she also couldn't get up and walk away.

The worst part of it all was that, coma or not, she was still awake. It seemed that her sleep, consciousness and coma states were subtly interrelated and subtly different, and she would have done anything to have been able to finally drift off. Perhaps that was all she needed to wake back up and rise again like some sleep-deprived Jesus.

The voices kept her company in the darkness. She still heard Zeb, of course, but he'd died back down to just a whisper. He kept telling her that it was coming, whatever *it* was, and his whispers formed a dull susurrus in the background of the hospital ward. It settled comfortably on top of the sounds of the machines and created a comforting white noise that nevertheless had started to give her a headache.

On this day, the last day of her life, she could hear a commotion in the room around her. She couldn't place all of the voices, but she could pick out her mother, Dr. Jalopnik, two of the nurses who'd stayed by her side since she'd entered the hospital, and an unidentified male voice that she'd never heard before. It was deep, rich and sonorous, somehow dreadful. The sound of it in the room was like the tolling of a death knell. And Kate could have sworn that she'd heard the man's voice before.

"It's time," he said.

"Are you sure there's nothing else you can do?" This was from Kate's mother, who sounded hoarse and exhausted like she'd been crying her eyes out for days on end and had nothing left within her, which was true.

"I'm afraid not," the man said. "From here, she'll just deteriorate. I think the kindest thing to do is to let her finish her fight with dignity."

"But what if she's still alive in there?"

"She isn't."

"Hmm," Kate's mother said. "I'm not sure. What do you think, Dr. Jalopnik?"

There was a tenseness to the air like an underlying current of static electric, just waiting to spark and start a fire if the conditions were met. Kate could hear them all, still, from inside her shell. She thought about trying to call out to them, to make herself heard. But then she thought, *What's the point?* and stayed schtum.

"Does she have any other next of kin?" Dr. Jalopnik asked.

Kate's mother shook her head.

"Just a sister," she said. "But this insomnia has driven a wedge between them. She wouldn't even come to be at her bedside. No, no, it's just me."

"Then as her next of kin," Dr. Jalopnik said, "the decision is yours and yours alone. But remember that your daughter has an incurable disease. Even if she were to somehow come round, she'd still be doomed to a slow and painful death. And besides, the latest scans aren't encouraging. The activity in her brain is quickly dwindling. Even if she were to survive, she'd almost certainly be brain damaged. In most cases, I'd say you should hold hope in your heart for as long as you can. But in this case..."

There was a pause.

"What?" Kate's mother asked.

"She's too far gone," Dr. Jalopnik said. "I'm sorry. We just don't have enough information on fatal familial insomnia. There's no treatment, no nothing. We did all we could."

"So shall we continue?" the unfamiliar doctor asked. "Shall we turn off the life support?"

Kate's mother sighed. It was the sigh of a woman who was spent, a woman who just wanted the ordeal to be over with. She didn't cry, and Kate didn't blame her. They both felt the same. They were sick of it.

Death would be a relief.

There was the sound of movement somewhere around her head, followed by the flick of a few switches and someone moving something that felt like it was attached to her. Kate didn't care. She just let it happen.

She heard a beeping sound, followed by a murmur of conversation. The sound of the hospital room was faint now, and Zeb was close to her, reaching out to her in that other world of his, grinning his big grin. She linked hands with him.

"What did you say your name was again, doctor?"

Her mother's voice sounded like it was echoing up to her from the bottom of a well. Kate strained her ears for the response. It was the last thing she ever heard before crossing that final frontier.

"My name's Dr. Sebastian Hawking," he said. "But there's no need for us to be so formal. Please, just call me Zeb."

And then there was nothing but darkness.

SONGS

Nocturne

Motorway

CAPO ON THIRD FRET

INTRO/VERSE: Am, Em, F
PRE-CHORUS: E, Am
CHORUS: Am Am/B C, E, Am

INTRO

VERSE: I sit alone by the fire,
I said you never should have come.
I'd never know you as a liar,
I'd never pay for what you've done.

PRE-CHORUS: There's static on the T.V. set
and everybody's gone.
I'd left that ol' front door unlocked,
not expecting anyone.

CHORUS: And I don't want to be alone.
Too many cars are on the motorway.
The stars will show me the way home,
and I will find somewhere to stay.

INTERLUDE

VERSE: My conscience is slowly melting,
I don't think I'll survive the night.
It's sad to see that you resent things,

like the old, blind man detests the light.

PRE-CHORUS: The paint is peeling off the walls,
the liquor store is closed.
I dream of ancient waterfalls,
you dream I've overdosed.

CHORUS: And I don't want to be alone.
Too many cars are on the motorway.
The stars will show me the way home,
and I will find somewhere to stay.

INTERLUDE

CHORUS: And I don't want to be alone.
Too many cars are on the motorway.
The stars will show me the way home,
and I will find somewhere to stay.
And I will find somewhere to stay.
And I will find somewhere to stay.
And I will find somewhere to stay.

Beautiful Stranger

CAPO ON SECOND FRET

VERSE: C, C/B, Dm
INTERLUDE/CHORUS: D, C, C/B, Am

VERSE: I saw this girl walking down the hall,
and I stopped to look at her.
Long hair to her shoulders,
thought that I'd seen her before.
As I walked along the corridor,
she turned to look at me.
And from the moment that our eyes met,
well, my heart's never been free.

INTERLUDE

VERSE: On a cold and rainy day,
wearing someone else's coat.
While the skies outside were grey,
the room she was in would glow.
Beneath the grey inside her eyes,
and the rain atop her skin,
there lies a heart of solid gold
that I'll try so hard to win.

CHORUS: Beautiful stranger, come to take me away from
here. If my heart was stronger, then I'd ask you to be mine.
But I'd rather sit and stare than to find out that you don't like
me. If only you would care to walk over in a minute of your
time.

INTERLUDE

CHORUS: Beautiful stranger, come to take me away from here. If my heart was stronger, then I'd ask you to be mine. But I'd rather sit and stare than to find out that you don't like me. If only you would care to walk over in a minute of your time.

Into the Jungle

CAPO ON FIRST FRET

VERSE: C Am G Em, F G C G
CHORUS: C Em Am, Em F C G

VERSE: "I want to be Bob Dylan," she said.
I'll miss you, baby, like a hole in the head,
and I'll never lie to you for the rest of my life.
She took my tambourine and tore it apart,
a mixed message that she gave from the start,
and so, baby, you can drive my car if I can take your picture.

CHORUS: Remember when we used to dream
about a red guitar in the back of a limousine?
Remember that season in the snow
when we had money to spend but nowhere to go?

INSTRUMENTAL VERSE

VERSE: I want to lie down by the fireside,
let you learn all of my battle cries,
and I'll never let you down for the rest of my days.
She said she'd shelter me from drunken blurs,
buried under a brand-new hearse,
and, baby, you can tell the world that I'm a loser.

CHORUS: Remember when you said we'd never die?
Have I been keepin' it real or living a lie?
I'll walk back out into the jungle...

INSTRUMENTAL VERSE

The Storm

VERSE: C C/B Am
PRE-CHORUS: Dm Am
CHORUS: D C Am G, D C G

VERSE: I lie under a rain cloud. I've never been here before. If I could change the weather, I'd weather out the storm. The people walking outside bow their heads to the wind. While in these seventeen years, I've walked through everything.

PRE-CHORUS: I'm tired of feeling this helpless, like a newborn baby on a doorstep. The storm goes on and on and on and on. Every day I get upset and write a poem on the letters that I've kept, but the dark night sky rains on and on.

VERSE: I need a simple, sad chord to express my pain. While the temperature inside rises, I cool off in the rain. They say that no two snowflakes share the same design, but your soul is softly melting, and it's the same as mine.

CHORUS: How I've let myself down, in each and every way. Every evening at sundown, I think back through the day. Friendships better made elsewhere and trust in the wrong place. And maybe one day life will be fair and I'll blow the storm away.

INSTRUMENTAL VERSE/PRE-CHORUS

CHORUS: How I've let myself down, in each and every way. Every evening at sundown, I think back through the day. Friendships better made elsewhere and trust in the wrong place. And maybe one day life will be fair and I'll blow the storm away. I'll blow the storm away.

Forever Alone

VERSE: G Em
PRE-CHORUS: Am G
CHORUS: C D B G x 3, C D

VERSE: I'll love you if you love me, although it's plain to see this twisted world ain't for me. I'll give back what I've got, although it's not a lot. No liberty for me.

PRE-CHORUS: I'll be forever alone.
I have no one aside.

CHORUS: You'll always be my angel.
You'll always sing my melodies.
Held forever by the ties of love.

VERSE: I don't have much more left, can't ever face you again, I can't say sorry enough. All I have is my life, and you know how I want to throw it all away.

PRE-CHORUS: I can't say sorry to you.
I haven't said enough.

CHORUS: You'll always be my angel.
You'll always sing my melodies.
Held forever by the ties of love.

In a State

CAPO ON THIRD FRET

VERSE: Em G
CHORUS: Em G, Am

VERSE: I was in a state of empathy,
all I cared about was everyone else.
Expensive liquor and therapy
form the grounds of my emotional self.

CHORUS: As I walk along the streets on a cold and windy day, with my guitar across my back, it seems like everybody's in my way. And there's nothing I could do to change the man I am. If I was someone else, I wouldn't need your help to stand.

VERSE: I was in a storm of emotions,
a metaphorical rain in my head.
Every day I go through the motions,
knowing one day we will all be dead.

CHORUS: As I walk along the beach, below a star-filled Sunday sky, I look forward to another week and wonder how the last one passed me by. And I'll play it back and forth in my head, 'cause there's nothing better to do, am I half alive or am I half dead? And will the morning bring something new?

VERSE: I was in a state of clarity,
as I stopped to take a look at the view.
Having seen the state of humanity,
I still give credit where credit is due.

CHORUS: I've seen a bridge into the stars at the pinnacle of my dreams. There's never a place too far or a vision too near, it seems. And if the only place to go is the one inside my head, then let the lyrics start to flow and let the guitar tab run red.

Mary Jane

VERSE: G C
CHORUS: Am D

VERSE: Well, I clean up the mess from a night on the town,
can't get to sleep when the lights go down,
I haven't got a penny to my name.
Well, the cards are dealt, and they're telling it straight,
we can't be bothered to masturbate.
We've always known that things don't stay the same.

CHORUS: Mary Jane, where are you now?
Sweet Mary Jane, she sold her soul, somehow.

VERSE: Well, I bought a guitar for a ten pack of smokes,
wrote my lyrics on an envelope.
I taught myself a brand-new point of view.
With the flowers you bring and the clothes that I buy,
I started building another high
for those lonely days when there's nothing else to do.

CHORUS: Mary Jane, where are you now?
Sweet Mary Jane, she sold her soul, somehow.

It Won't Be Long

VERSE: E A E B, B A# A E, B E
BRIDGE: F# B E A, A B E
CHORUS: D A E

VERSE: I threw my notebooks in the fire,
breathed a sigh as they expired,
I never wanted to help put out the flames.
The walls said to me, "Yeah, you'll never believe
what it's like to be a first-time buyer."

VERSE: So I gave my dog a bone,
a medallion, a mobile phone,
so I could call her when I'm lonely in the night.
The judge, he guilty found her,
and bluebirds flew all around her,
and I have never felt so damn alone.

BRIDGE: I've never wanted to know the secret
of a long and happy life.
I've never wanted to go to meetings
to learn to get out of this town alive.

VERSE: Remember the promise you made me,
if I fell, you'd come to save me,
I'm heading for the ground and you're not here.
I said you were my moonlight in the early afternoon light,
as the taste of her old nicotine forgave me.

CHORUS: So say you won't forget me,
it won't be long 'til I'm gone.
You wish you'd never met me,
it won't be long 'til I'm gone.

She'll always protect me,
it won't be long 'til I'm gone.
Your empty threats upset me,
it won't be long 'til I'm gone.
It won't be long 'til I'm gone.
It won't be long 'til I'm gone.
It won't be long 'til I'm gone.
It won't be long 'til I'm gone.

A Love Like This

VERSE: C Am F C
CHORUS: G F Am C G F

VERSE: It's late and it's cold, I feel her heart beating as she curls up next to me. Her voice is soft, her breath is cold, her skin is warm, my hand she holds. What else can I do? When she breaks off our embrace and sees the look upon my face, am I thinking of the past?

CHORUS: The moon is clouded out of view
but the stars are shining through.
The chemicals slow my beating heart,
a love like this should never start.

VERSE: We lie down in her bed. As I look up slowly, I see her eyes piercing me. Her gaze is deep, her pupils wide, I can't believe she's by my side. We never would have thought, two years ago next month, when this all first begun, our fragile bond would last.

CHORUS: The stars are clouded out of view,
the moon too feeble to shine through.
The caffeine speeds my beating heart,
a love like this should never start.

INSTRUMENTAL VERSE

CHORUS: The dark night sky is almost through,
and now the sun comes into view.
A love like this should never start,
'cause every fall-out breaks my heart.

Annie

CAPO ON SEVENTH FRET

VERSE/CHORUS: G Em C D
BRIDGE: C Em G, C G

VERSE: There's a girl lying on the sofa, waiting for her daddy to come. As a kid she was never alone, but now she's fully grown, life is no fun. Her father used to fight in the war, but since he came back home, things have gone downhill. Her boyfriend comes after school, but he wants to do what she does every day.

CHORUS: Oh, Annie. Is there anything that I can do?
Oh, Annie. After everything that you've been through.

VERSE: Daddy makes her do her homework, after spending time with him. She cries out to him, "Don't do this to me." So why then won't he listen? And Annie just feels so helpless, she always struggles to breathe. After anything that I could say or do, the pain would never ease.

CHORUS: Oh, Annie. Is there anything that I can do?
Oh, Annie. After everything that you've been through.

BRIDGE: And Annie once asked me how it looks from the outside. "How does it feel to be someone who's had the love that I'm denied?" And maybe someday she'll leave this town, she'll leave her whole world behind. 'cause there isn't a place here or anywhere that can heal the scars that she has inside.

Alcohol Blues

VERSE/INSTRUMENTAL: E, A E, B A E

VERSE: Well, I'm up all night, smoking, drinking, dancing around. I think I'm up all night because my little love can't be found. If I don't find her tonight, I'll drink myself underground.

VERSE: Sometimes when I get lonely, I never can understand, why the drops on my lips taste so weak and bland. Don't want to waste my life listening to a rock 'n' roll band.

INSTRUMENTAL VERSE

VERSE: The cider and the whiskey and the lager and the cigarettes. Maybe I drink so much because I'm drinking to forget. I try and put her face on a pissed-up little brunette.

VERSE: And when I go outside to catch a breath of air, I feel a stabbing in my side, but by now I really don't care. Because the pain in my heart is more than I can bear.

INSTRUMENTAL VERSE

VERSE: Well, when I wake up in my bed, early on Saturday, I'm writing checks from my head that my body cannot pay. I wonder if this pain will ever go away.

The Lover I Despise

CAPO ON THIRD FRET

VERSE: C D F C G C G
CHORUS: Am G

VERSE: I once hired a boat to see where I would float if I cast away from the shore. The sea said to me, "a gift is never free," in a salty, breezy roar.

CHORUS Is there something you want to tell me?
Is there something you want to tell me?

VERSE: I once told a lie to the lover I despise, it haunts me when I sleep. She asked me, "Truthfully, do you think that I believe in an oath you'll never keep?"

CHORUS: Is there something you want to tell me?
Is there something you want to tell me?
I could tell you but I won't.
She said, "I could tell you but I won't."

VERSE: I guess there's nothing that you want to tell me. I guess there's nothing that you want to tell me.

I'll Never Want to Sink Again

CAPO ON THIRD FRET

VERSE: C Am F G
CHORUS: G C Am G

VERSE: She built a wall around herself,
she made it hard for me to help,
and all I want to do is show her how I feel.
She wished for this but she got that,
my battery too dead to call her back,
and as an afterthought, I wondered if she was real.

CHORUS: So don't you swim.
Don't you swim.
Don't you swim.
'cause if we float then we're meant to be.
Yeah, if you float then you're meant to be with me.

VERSE: She plays guitar, she knows the songs,
would spend her life righting the wrongs,
of a fool like me, who can't tell wrong from right.
She wears her heart out on her sleeve,
I'd never ask her to believe
that I'd die happy if she never left my side.

CHORUS: So don't you swim.
Don't you swim.
Don't you swim.
'cause if we float then we're meant to be.
Yeah, if you float then you're meant to be.
'cause if we float then we're meant to be.
Yeah, if you float then you'll always be with me. Be with me.

Comfort Me

INTO/VERSE/OUTRO: Am G Dm
CHORUS ONE: Dm Am
CHORUS TWO: C G (Am)

INTRO

VERSE: Don't you love me anymore?
Don't you need me like you did before?
I guess it might be time to leave you well alone, lonely.
And after all you've done, my love for you has grown.

CHORUS ONE: Oh, I need you like you needed me so long ago. Beg to be released, but I still feel the same as we both used to do. You got over me while I was blissfully wasting time with you. And I don't think it's right, I've lost my will to fight, I blame it all on me.

VERSE: Can you see where I'm coming from?
When you told me, you dropped an atom bomb.

CHORUS TWO: I'm trying to get over it, I'm happy if you are. I'm trying to control it, but your words of wisdom comfort me and I'm left unsure of who I'm supposed to be.

VERSE: Tainted with despair, I'm left to grieve alone.
I always saw your arms as being like my home.

CHORUS TWO: I'm trying to get over it, I'm happy if you are. I'm trying to control it, but your words of wisdom comfort me and I'm left unsure of who I'm supposed to be.

It doesn't feel so great.

Sketches

Not the Same

INTRO/0VERSE: E (high E), G (high G), A (A7)
CHORUS: E G A C D

INTRO

VERSE: Dulouz digging a hole in the garden.
Chinaski's spilling his guts on the floor.
Old Bull Lee's sleeping with the orgones – hey hey,
it's a naked lunch on western shores. (For sure.)

INTRO

VERSE: I've given you all and now I'm nothing,
soul music and interesting times.
I'm fighting wars that I don't belong in – hey hey,
I'm gonna run with all the wolves I find.

CHORUS: So just go ahead and put a bullet through your head, I don't care what you've got to say. You won't be the same because you can't be the same, so tell me now that I'm not the same. A drink's not enough when the going gets tough as my good friend Hank would say. There's no Hemingway that I'm going to get paid so tell me now that I'm not the same.

INTRO

VERSE: Maus is hiding in the garden.
Lyra's kicking up a storm.
I beg your please and I beg your pardon – hey, hey.
I was dead by the time that I was born.

CHORUS: So just go ahead and put a bullet through your head, I don't care what you've got to say. You won't be the same because you can't be the same, so tell me now that I'm not the same. A drink's not enough when the going gets tough as my good friend Hank would say. There's no Hemingway that I'm going to get paid so tell me now that I'm not the same. Tonight the music seems so loud, I always fail to draw a crowd, it feels like there's a demon in the middle of my brain, so tell me now that I'm not the same. I've got my friends and they're in my head, just what I want to be when I end up dead. I've got everything to lose and I've got nothing to gain, so tell me now that I'm not the same.

Tell me now I'm not the same.

Never Go Back

INTRO/VERSE: E G E, E G E A
INTERLUDE: E G A B, E G E x2

INTRO

VERSE: Waking up from a dream, I'm barely tired, never seen this face before, this face that I admire. I see the sky, I see the clouds, I think the whole world's upside down and I'll never go back where I came from, never go back where I came from.

INTERLUDE

VERSE: Falling into my cave, I know I'm a liar, you're singing yourself to sleep and my mouth is on fire. I see him burning in the spring, he gave away his wedding ring, and I'll never go back where I came from, never go back where I came from.

INTERLUDE

OUTRO

No Electricity

CAPO ON FIFTH FRET

INTRO/INTERLUDE/VERSE: E F#7 A E
CHORUS: E B A E, E B A (C D)

INTRO

VERSE: It's cold inside, it's dark outside, I've got no heat. Should've remembered to pay for electricity. Well, I've got no high and I've got no soul, I've got my mind on alcohol, so baby please, just let me sleep tonight.

INTERLUDE

VERSE: But I'm alive with tired eyes and tired mp3s, I can't describe the signs I prize with solid teeth. Well, I've got no guts for stealing man, keep taking that Citalopram, this thin disease that makes me sleep tonight.

CHORUS: Let me tell you something about me, my friend, I'm not the kind of guy to make enemies. And if you want me to believe in you again, just be the moron who adores me.

VERSE: She thinks the world is bought and sold with lemonade. I think the worst of everyone who isn't me. One day, I found out that the future is unclaimed, and that's exactly why it scares me.

CHORUS

OUTRO

Love Through a Lens

VERSE: Am G
CHORUS: Am C G Am

VERSE: I love the way that you slouch in your chair.
I love the way the light shines off of your hair.

CHORUS: I love the way you frown, even when I'm trying to tell you just how good you look. I love the way you smile, if only for a while, at the things I say.

HUMMED CHORUS

VERSE: I love the way that you, you stay in my head.
I love the way I feel, without you I'd be dead.

CHORUS: I love how you don't make me sick. I think I've learned to deal with it, I'm better off alone. I love the way you make me feel, it seems like it's all so surreal, you bring me back around.

HUMMED CHORUS

VERSE: I love the way you talk to me. You talk to me all of the time. I love the way you make me guess the reasons that you're not mine.

CHORUS: I love the way you question me. I love the way you say to me exactly what's on your mind. I love the way that you stay true. I love the way you tell me what to do when I feel down.

HUMMED CHORUS

Like Bleeding

CAPO ON THIRD FRET

INTRO: A
VERSE: A D, A G, D A G
INTERLUDE: A D A E
CHORUS: D C G G

INTRO

VERSE: You treated me like a footnote to your novel,
and I swear this is the last time.
Do I stay at home or go outside?
No telephone and six sleepless nights,
I won't be there to catch your fall anymore, yeah.

INTERLUDE: Yeah, yeah.

VERSE: I've been gone for a week and no one even noticed,
'cause I, I am a dreamer. I'm not the only one to ask for
oxygen, I'm just trying to write the best folk song tired eyes
have ever seen, but I'm not part of the indie scene, so...

CHORUS: Shout if you let the fire go out, and there's
nothing you can do to make you feel like you're alive, so...
Scream if you're down and out, 'cause there's nothing you
can do or say to take that crazy pain away and...
Feel like you've overdosed, like the holy ghost, like the sun.

CHORUS: So shout and shout and shout and shout, and
scream and scream and scream and scream and feel and feel
and feel and feel like you're bleeding. x2

INTRO: Go!

INSTRUMENTAL VERSE

VERSE: I don't know how I'll sleep at night,
when my bones contract stage fright
but I know... that I know nothing.
I'm just a jealous guy, I can kiss the sky,
and I know I hardly knew you.

CHORUS: Shout if you let the fire go out, and there's nothing you can do to make you feel like you're alive, so...
Scream if you're down and out, 'cause there's nothing you can do or say to take that crazy pain away and...
Feel like you've overdosed, like the holy ghost, like the sun.

CHORUS: So shout and shout and shout and shout, and scream and scream and scream and scream and feel and feel and feel and feel like you're bleeding. x4

Lights

CAPO ON THIRD FRET

VERSE: Am, C C7, G G7, Em E
INTERLUDE: Am, C C7, Dm, E
CHORUS: Am G, D7 E
BRIDGE: Am D7 G7 E7

VERSE: She was famous for leaving the lights on, and even though I don't know her, I never had a reason to complain. And now I'm sitting alone in the garden, with barely a hard-on to distinguish me from the rain.

INTERLUDE: Yeah, all right, 'cause it's cold outside tonight. And I don't have a light, I don't have a light to lead me. Yeah, it's fine. I'm just serving the rest of my time, 'cause I don't have a light, I don't have a light to lead me on and on.

INSTRUMENTAL VERSE

VERSE: I'm a stuck-up amateur poet, and boy don't I know it but I'm never going to change. Strangers tell me it might never happen, I'm sensing a pattern that I'm never going to re-arrange.

CHORUS: Won't somebody light my cigarette? 'Cause I'm pissed off and I'm not drunk yet. And I'm too tired to sign my name, so tell me how you feel and I'll feel the same. And I'm not one to do what I'm told, but I'm feeling kinda lazy and I'm growing old, so tell me how you feel and I'll feel the same, I could be breaking all the rules and still lose the game.

INTERLUDE: Yeah, all right, 'cause it's cold outside tonight. And I don't have a light, I don't have a light to lead me on and on.

VERSE: She gave me keys, she gave me her number, deleted her Tumblr 'cause she said she didn't need it anymore. When I found out she was destined for stardom, I was back in the garden and the rain began to pour.

CHORUS: Won't somebody bring me another beer? I'm only smoking cigarettes to impress my peers. And I'm never too tired to feel this pain, so tell me how you feel and I'll feel the same. And I'm not one to say what I've seen, but the years are long and they've treated me mean, so tell me how you feel and I'll feel the same, I even cut my hair and changed my name.

BRIDGE

CHORUS: I'm telling all the people that I've ever met that I'll do my best but I might forget. Promise your pinkie, I'll give you my brain, so tell me how you feel and I'll feel the same. And I'm not one to tell you the truth, I've got the looks and you've got the youth. So tell me how you feel and I'll feel the same, there's more to life than fortune and fame. Won't someone give me the money I need to satisfy my lust and greed? Won't someone try to call my name and tell me how they feel so I can feel the same? Now, I might be one to grumble and moan, I'm far too lonely to live alone, so tell me how you feel and I'll feel the same, as I stand outside and become one with the rain.

All the Love

CAPO ON FOURTH FRET

INTRO: D/F# A A/F# A, D/F# A G G#
VERSE: A D
BRIDGE: A A/F# A G F# B
CHORUS: D/F#C#m x 2, E

INTRO: All the love in all the world. x4

VERSE: All the love in all the world can see, all the love around me is in 3D blasphemy. Can't you see this honesty? Baby believe me and bleed me.

BRIDGE

VERSE: All the love in all the world can heal, all the love expiring without the hope of an appeal. I'll meet you on the Ferris Wheel. Baby believe me and defeat me.

CHORUS: All the love in all the world can drive you to despair. And all the feelings of the boys and the girls, they won't get them anywhere, yeah, yeah, yeah.

VERSE: All the love in all the world can hear,
all the love is everything I fear.

CHORUS: All the love in all the world can drive you to despair. And all the feelings of the boys and the girls, they won't get them anywhere, yeah, yeah, yeah. x2

Let Go

INTRO/VERSE: C Am F G
BRIDGE: Am G
CHORUS: Em Am G

INTRO

VERSE: She asked me if I'd say goodbye, I crossed my heart and said "I'd rather die," but I know it's only an illusion. Six cigarettes and seven cans, I couldn't count them on both my hands, but I… would die…

BRIDGE: Without them… without them… this I know…

VERSE: My greatest fear is being buried alive, but all that vanishes with cider inside. My greatest treasures are the words that I write, but nothing matters when you're lonely at night. So I sing about the faces that I knew when I was young. Some have gone, some have stayed. Some are desperate to get fucking laid. Which are you? Which are you? Which are you?

CHORUS: So when you're lying in your bed, carry on regardless. Because we're dying for a drink and we would give up everything, and if we can't go out winning then at least we'll go out singing, like this.

VERSE: So when the kids that used to bully you are having children of their own and when your family resents you 'cause you left your childhood home. Just remember you're not laughing 'cause that joke's been overtold. And at twenty-two, your young mind knows your body's growing old. Let go.

Get Together and Dance

INTRO/VERSE: E G A
CHORUS: D E G E
OUTRO: E G

INTRO

VERSE: I am certified insane.
They gave me meds, I changed my name.
But when I go to sleep when it's light outside,
yeah, I kind of feel that it'll be all right,
so let's get together and dance.
Yeah, let's get together and dance.

INTRO

VERSE: I'm way too young to feel this old,
I am a lighter shade of gold.
So when I go to sleep with my music on,
they're just some sad old men playing sad old songs,
so let's get together and dance.
Yeah, let's get together and dance.
.
CHORUS: I'm chasing after the storm 'cause I need a little weather to weather out this cold. I'm swapping stories with an author I've never met 'cause I need a little lovin' and I want to get together and dance.

OUTRO: Get together and dance.
Get together and dance.
Get together and dance.
Get together and dance.

Kinda Lazy

CAPO ON SECOND FRET

VERSE: Am C G Am, Am C G
INTERLUDE: Am
BRIDGE: C Em Am
CHORUS: Em Bm A#m Am

INTRO

VERSE: 1993, I was bored in a world of hypocrisy, but any day now, I shall be released. When she spoke to me, I wept like the branches of a willow tree 'cause I know something she don't know.

INTERLUDE

VERSE: But I spoke too soon, I was four and I was foreign in a stranger's room, I'm not quite as old as I used to be. Nowadays when I play my songs, when I'm drunk on the stage the words come out all wrong, and I know I'll never be Morrissey.

BRIDGE

CHORUS: And I'm not quite a stranger, but stranger things have happened and I swear they'll happen again. And I know I'm kinda lazy, but, babe, you know it's crazier to be your own best friend.

INSTRUMENTAL CHORUS

Shine

CAPO ON FIFTH FRET

INTRO: Am Dm G C F Em E7
VERSE: Am Dm G C F G Am, Am Dm G C F Em E7
INTERLUDE: Am C G Am Em E7
CHORUS: Dm G C C.B Am, Dm G C C7
END CHORUS: Dm G C C/B Am G F E E7

INTRO

VERSE: If I could alter the universe, I would change the meaning of words, I would float myself above the shore. I can't give you diamonds and rings, you're a few of my favourite things, and your accent sends shivers down my spine.

INTERLUDE

VERSE: I'm rewriting the meaning of success, kind of cute when I'm not depressed, you're the comrade that I'm too late to rescue. When I fall asleep, I dream epiphanies, they get me down on one bended knee, you're the only idea I would ever die for.

CHORUS: When I tried to kiss her shoulder, she didn't even notice. Me and my tattoo will stick around. So that maybe when we're older, we'll write our names with fireworks and we'll score our symphonies without a sound.

END CHORUS

VERSE: I'll be glad when my poetry is spoken, I will take a breath of air without choking on lies, those lies I never cared for. And I know that I'm a mystery of sorts, I'm not just after sexual intercourse with you because you are, you are something special.

CHORUS: Perhaps I'll change my name again to make the long nights grow longer. Perhaps I'll trade my blood for her laughter. So that maybe when we're older, we'll drink and toast the good times and we'll talk until the morning after. Will you marry me? I'm in ecstasy, in agony and wonder. I don't think I can walk this road for a lifetime. But I'm stronger than I once thought that I could ever be. I guess I only have to shine like you shine.

Dreams (Don't Get Me Started)

VERSE: C F G C
INTERLUDE: C F G C
CHORUS: G C F G, C G C

VERSE: Share a dream with me, we'll build a dream city where there's a silver cloud on every horizon. Let's set a date today so our troubles fly away, 'cause I bet that promised land will be surprising.

INTERLUDE

VERSE: If I could build a house, I'd build it inside out and plant yew and ivy together in the garden. If I'm the king of spades then you're a chambermaid and when you break my queen of hearts, you'll beg my pardon.

CHORUS: Don't get me started, 'cause when I open doors, I need to look inside. So don't get me started, 'cause I'd hate to see a dream I've been denied.

VERSE: She's always dream pretty, and everyone can see that I'm a lucky man to be a lonely lover. And everybody knows that a feeling only grows if you keep on keeping on when undercover. So you'll never be alone if you sleep on silver thrones and if you think your fears will always be misguided. We're a happy state of mind in a world that's colour-blind, 'cause what's red is blue and purple's undecided.

CHORUS: So don't get me started, 'cause when I close my eyes, I feel like I could cry. So don't get me started, 'cause when I close my eyes, I feel like I'm alive.

Hey You (We're Alive)

INTRO: E C C/B Am E
VERSE/INTERLUDE: E C Am E
CHORUS: C E G D x2, Am C E

INTRO

VERSE: Hey you, you're like another colour on the lining of my eyes. Hey you, you're just a chariot a-riding through the sky. Hey you, hey me, we're explosive chemistry. Hey me, hey you, how's it feel to be living proof?

INTERLUDE: We're alive, we're alive, we're alive, we're alive.

VERSE: Hey you, you're a memory of a life I love to love. Hey you, a philosophy when a thought is just enough. Hey you, hey me, we were born with empathy. Hey me, hey you, in a castle drinking tea for two.

INTERLUDE: We're alive, we're alive, we're alive, we're alive.

CHORUS: We're alive and that's what counts,
I'd like to wrap you in a true romance.
I'd like to be the meaning in your dreams.
I'm a fire that's burning out,
you're the music I write poems about.
I'd like to be the voice behind the scenes.
When I'm famous, the star of the show,
you're the fuel that keeps my eyes aglow.
We're alive, we're alive, we're alive, we're alive,
we're alive, we're alive, we're alive.

VERSE: Hey you, you're a fantasy, or a flying dream come true. Hey you, you're a smile machine in a world that's come unglued. Hey you, hey me, you're a sad man's therapy. Hey me, hey you, I'm glad we both moved to E2, yeah.

CHORUS: We're alive and that's what counts,
I'd like to wrap you in a true romance.
I'd like to be the meaning in your dreams.
I'm a fire that's burning out,
you're the music I write poems about.
I'd like to be the voice behind the scenes.
When I'm famous, the star of the show,
you're the fuel that keeps my eyes aglow.
We're alive, we're alive, we're alive, we're alive,
we're alive, we're alive, we're alive.

Yes She Does

INTRO/INTERLUDE/VERSE: G, C
CHORUS: G Am C D

INTRO

VERSE: Up late at night again, the internet's my only friend, and I know that she wants to know me, yes she does. And someone's stealing from my secretive dreams as decent as they seem, and she says she knows my name, and she knows just what that means. Yes she does. Yes she does.

VERSE: I'm getting drunk on whiskey and gin, knocking doors until she lets me in, and I see that she wants to see me, yes she does. She says she's sick of the same old men and I forgot the words on stage again, and she knows that she's all alone, and she knows just what that means. Yes she does. Yes she does.

CHORUS: And everything she told me went through one ear and came out the other end, and now I'm waiting to cry my eyes out. She had everything she wanted, she's crazy now she's got it, baby, on this you can depend, I'm at my best when I have passed out.

INTERLUDE

VERSE: I'm singing blues 'cause it's raining again, I'm cold and I can't sing.

CHORUS: And everything she told me went through one ear and came out the other end, and now I'm waiting to cry my eyes out. She had everything she wanted, she's crazy now she's got it, baby, on this you can depend, I'm at my best when I have passed out.

CHORUS: And everything she told me went through one ear and came out the other end, and now I'm waiting to cry my eyes out. She had everything she wanted, she's crazy now she's got it, baby, on this you can depend, I'm at my best when I have passed out.

VERSE: Yes she does. x8

Discordia

Catch Me Out and Defeat Me

INTRO/INTERLUDE/VERSE: E G A G
CHORUS: E A G A E

INTRO

VERSE: Can't find my meaning today, but I never needed meaning even anyway, I told you once, I told you twice, I've got no time to improvise. So if you see me being greedy, you can catch me out and defeat me, but it's easy to believe in what you're dreaming.

INTERLUDE

VERSE: Can't stand to see people in pain, but a lack of serotonin won't affect my brain. I'm strange and maybe dangerous to myself. So if you meet me, see my weakness, you can catch me out and defeat me, but it's easy to believe in what you're dreaming.

CHORUS: Yeah, she, she screams so loud in silence, you fight the silence with a secret of your own. Me, I'm feeling kind of divided, I haven't decided why I try to feel at home.

INTERLUDE

CHORUS

Lowdown Blues

CAPO ON SECOND FRET

INTRO/INTERLUDE/VERSE: Em G A B7
CHORUS: A G Em, G B7

INTRO

VERSE: Well, she's had a good day, but she's worked too hard, and she's got no time for me. But when she's had a bad day and she's all alone, she could use a little company. And so I'll tell you twice that in this life, you get nothing for free. And I know it might be nice if we shared our alibis and made a little chemistry.

INTERLUDE

VERSE: Well, I've had a good day, but I've worked too hard, and I've got nowhere to go. And when I've had a bad day, and I'm singing in the rain, I realise I'm alone. I've got a big heart and I make a lot of noise, but my dreams gave me away. And I'd take a lot of hits just to get a quick fix, and I'll be on my way.

CHORUS: I've got the lowdown blues and I've got nothing to lose.

INTERLUDE

VERSE: Well, we've had a good day, but we've worked too hard, I've got a lot to say on this old guitar, I tried so hard and got so far...

CHORUS: I've got the lowdown blues and I've got nothing to lose.

Sober

VERSE/INTERLUDE: Em Bm D Em
BRIDGE: Em Bm D G F#/D

VERSE: I'm staying sober and I'm still alive, and I don't know what I used to do on all the long weekends, on all the wrong nights, trying to find out what I mean to you. And it goes like this, a thorn in her side and she's tired of this, 'cause this shit's insipid and mentally ill and 'cause she stole the vowels from my kiss.

INTERLUDE

VERSE: She's an illusion, she's falling through time, picking up broken glass at closing time. She won't be forgotten like yesterday's news. She's soaking in lemon and lime. And I close my eyes, a feeling inside that I just can't describe, and I'm tired of talking, I'm tiring of words and I'm trying not to write lines that rhyme.

BRIDGE

VERSE: Now I'm feeling nervous and I'm feeling scared and I don't know what I shouldn't do. Should I waste all my time while I write on wrong nights, should I break down and cry before you? And I feel like shit, but I'm starting to feel so I'm dealing with it and I don't want to hide or believe in the hype, so I... I... give into it.

Not Enough

VERSE/INTERLUDE: G A E, G A E, G A E (G E), G A E
CHORUS: E G A (G)

VERSE: I never needed your money,
I never needed your love.
I ain't got time for your games,
a word's not enough.

INTERLUDE

VERSE: So I'm taking my talent
and I'm making it last.
Ain't got no superstitions,
you're my heart attack.

CHORUS: I'm taking it slow now, baby, let's have us some fun, I haven't done enough, woah oh. And all I ever wanted was to feel alive. Wherever I'm going now, baby, I haven't seen it all but I've seen it all before, hey hey, ain't no telling what I'll do with myself tonight.

VERSE: I never learned from your wisdom
or tried to broaden my mind.
I fall in love with myself...
...all the time.

CHORUS: I'm taking it slow now, baby, let's have us some fun, I haven't done enough, woah oh. And all I ever wanted was to feel alive. Wherever I'm going now, baby, I haven't seen it all, but I've seen it all before, hey hey, ain't no telling what I'll do with myself tonight.

On My Way

INTRO/VERSE/INTERLUDE: B D E D
CHORUS: B Em G A

INTRO

VERSE: Well, I'm nothing but endorphins,
well, I cut my heart in two to make me feel alive
and I've got a lot to say beneath a blanket of lies,
I'm on my way. I'm on my way.

INTERLUDE

VERSE: Well she's something, she makes the world spin,
well I cut my heart in two to make me feel alive,
and I've got a lot to say beneath a blanket of lies,
I'm on my way. I'm on my way.

CHORUS: She's got the world at her feet,
but she don't belong to me.
Yeah, she's the peace you find in sleep,
goodbye to mediocrity.

VERSE: She's got the patience of the ancients,
well I cut my heart in two to make me feel alive,
and I've got a lot to say beneath a blanket of lies,
I'm on my way. I'm on my way.

CHORUS: She's got the world at her feet,
but she don't belong to me.
Yeah, she's the peace you find in sleep,
goodbye to mediocrity.

Who Will Lead the Sailors to the Shore?

VERSE: Take me down to paradise and bring me all the way back home. If we had the time, it might be nice to fantasise about the times we've known. And the smoke gets in your eyes. And now it's time to stand outside.

INTERLUDE

VERSE: Take me down without a sound and try to make me frown, my dear. It's all the same and anyway I think I can't complain about the way you fear. And the smoke gets in your eyes. And the smoke gets in your eyes. And now it's time to stand outside.

INTERLUDE

VERSE: Take me down to paradise and bring me all the way back home. Your empathy is everything and it's meant to be a memory we've known. And the smoke gets in your eyes. And the smoke gets in your eyes. And now it's time to stand outside.

VERSE: And the smoke gets in your eyes, and you can't quite shine your light, so who's gonna lead the sailors to the shore?

Sevens

VERSE: D7 G7 D7 A7 D7 G7 D7 A7 D7
CHORUS: A7 G7 D7

VERSE: You were always the lonely one,
I was always the only one,
and you tried so hard to take my blues away.
You were always the lonely one,
I was singing your favourite songs,
and I promised everything would be okay.

CHORUS: It's cold outside tonight, I hope you wrapped up tight, 'cause baby I need you. (I need you.) It's raining vowel sounds and I just write them down, 'cause maybe I need to. (I need to.)

VERSE: You were always the lonely one,
I was always the only one,
and I tried so hard to get some sympathy.
Because you came round to my house
and they pulled teeth from my mouth
because this life is just another mystery.

CHORUS: It's cold outside tonight, I hope you wrapped up tight, 'cause baby I need you. (I need you.) It's raining vowel sounds and I just write them down, 'cause maybe I need to. (I need to.)

INTERLUDE

CHORUS: It's cold outside tonight, I hope you wrapped up tight, 'cause baby I need you. (I need you.) It's raining vowel sounds and I just write them down, 'cause maybe I need to.

If I Die Before You

VERSE: G
CHORUS: Em G D A x2, Em G B

VERSE: You lay so close to me I almost fell asleep.
It's not the way these things were supposed to be.
But I'm not tired and I'm not scared.
But I'm not tired and I'm not scared.

CHORUS: If I die before you, maybe, babe, you'll believe me, and come and see me. And if I die before you, you've gotta wait to see me, if we're still breathing. And if I die before you... you'll see me again.

VERSE: Moving on the floor now, babe, you're a bird of paradise. Cherry ice cream smile, I suppose I plagiarise.
But I'm not tired and I'm not scared.
But I'm not tired and I'm not scared.

CHORUS: If I die before you, maybe, babe, you'll believe me, and come and see me. And if I die before you, you've gotta wait to see me, if we're still breathing. And if I die before you... you'll see me again.

The Girl with the Rose Tattoo

VERSE: E G, E A
CHORUS: A E, G E, A E, G

VERSE: We're rolling twelve deep, getting drunk in the street, ahhhh. We're the coolest crowd that you'll ever meet, ahhhh. All the kids are dancing, all the kids are dancing, yeah, all the kids are dancing the night away, ahhhh.

VERSE: She took me aside until the drinks kicked in, ahhhh. I'd like to say hello to her little friend, ahhhh. All the kids are dancing, all the kids are dancing, yeah, all the kids are dancing the night away, ahhhh.

CHORUS: She's always out to get you, the girl with the rose tattoo. I'm really glad we met you, because we smoke and drink and we never think, we're working too hard, falling over the brink, ahhhh.

VERSE: I need another drink, got to queue for weeks, ahhhh. My confidence comes in troughs and peaks, ahhhh. All the kids are dancing, yeah, all the kids are dancing, all the kids are dancing the night away, ahhhh.

CHORUS: She's always out to get you, the girl with the rose tattoo. I'm really glad we met you, because we smoke and drink and we never think, we're working too hard, falling over the brink, ahhhh.

VERSE: Yeah, the lights are bright and it's time for the bar to close, ahhhh. Only half an hour to drag her out of her clothes, ahhhh. All the kids are dancing, yeah, all the kids are dancing, all the kids are dancing the night away, ahhhh.

CHORUS: She's always out to get you, the girl with the rose tattoo. I'm really glad we met you, because we smoke and drink and we never think, we're working too hard, falling over the brink, ahhhh.

Stand Right by Your Guns

VERSE: G D B C
CHORUS: A C G

VERSE: I feel alive today, I know what I've been missing. I've got too many feelings for me to let you take me out tonight, and I kiss all the wrong women, those "write a song" women, killing all this time until I die. But I'm alive and kinda high and you don't know until you try, and so I tried with all my heart to not remember. But I remember being five and pouring tears out from my eyes because I tried to hide from life with my Nintendo.

CHORUS: So stand right by your guns and be regrettable. Yeah, stand right by your guns, don't be forgettable.

VERSE: I feel alive today, don't want to throw my life away, don't want to give my job away, just want to give my love away. This day's amazed and semi-crazed and maybe failing lazily, my final fantasies are fully formed. And I kiss all the wrong women, those "write a song" women, to try to make my lips just feel alive. But I remember being ten and feeling pressure settle in and ever since I've winced at things that I've survived.

CHORUS: So stand right by your guns and be regrettable. Yeah, stand right by your guns, don't be forgettable.

VERSE: She said he sang like he had diamonds in his eyes.

It Doesn't Matter Much

VERSE: People say that I'm a liar.
People say that I'm a thief.
They say I work too hard and I should settle down.
It doesn't matter much to me.

INTERLUDE

VERSE: People say that I'm a coward.
People say that I'm diseased.
I fell downstairs and hit my head on every step.
It doesn't matter much to me.

CHORUS: Just close your eyes and maybe hold me tight tonight. And, baby, say you'll hold my hand. Just try to tell me why you hide your heart's delight, and maybe try to understand.

INTERLUDE/SOLO

CHORUS: Just close your eyes and maybe hold me tight tonight. And, baby, say you'll hold my hand. Just try to tell me why you hide your heart's delight, and maybe try to understand.

CHORUS: And I'll show you that I owe you. And I'll try so hard to please, because I want to get to know you, and I'll get down on my knees. And I'm sharing my disease. And I'm spreading my disease. You need a quick release. Babe, I'm sharing my disease.

Got No Time for Jesus

VERSE/INTERLUDE: A G A C
CHORUS: D C D C A G A C

VERSE: I sit alone in the corner. I feel like I'm a disease. Got no time for Santa Claus and presents under the tree. I've been trying so hard to find myself, kinda struggle with my mental elf, and I, I ain't got no time for Jesus.

INTERLUDE

VERSE: It always seemed so easy to let the weather deceive me. Got no time for tinsel towns and fake festivity. I've been roaming all over town, live it up before you live it down, and I, I ain't got no time for Jesus.

INTERLUDE

CHORUS: I ain't got no time for Jesus.
I ain't got no time for Jesus.
He ain't got no time for me,
so I've got no time for the trinity,
and I...

I ain't got no time for Jesus. x4

Lifted

CAPO ON SECOND FRET

INTRO/INTERLUDE/OUTRO: B D G A, B D G A A#
VERSE: B G A, B G A A#
CHORUS: G F# G A, B A B D

INTRO

VERSE: Sometimes the price we pay is the price we used to know. Sometimes the pain we feel was caused so long ago that we find people steeped in evil feel the need for something strong, 'cause sometimes those lazy hypocrites are right when in the wrong.

INTERLUDE

VERSE: 'cause every time I'm left alone, I get away from here. Sometimes I like to laugh because I hope that you'll appear. Sometimes I'd like to die tonight but there's so much left to do, 'cause sometimes you need to live your life like a formal interview. Sometimes the friends you want to meet are only out to kill you, 'cause you just don't understand them and you just don't have it in you, and you think of all the good times that you used to laugh about, and you used to understand them but you don't understand them now.

CHORUS: Right about now, the curse is lifted.
I don't know how we can ever be the same.

INTERLUDE

VERSE: Sometimes I am a hypocrite and I don't know how to say that, I can't write when I am sober and I can't write when I am wasted. Sometimes I feel the meaning when I need some company, but then I'm bleeding in the evening, I believe in empathy. Sometimes the friends you want to meet are only out to kill you, 'cause you just don't understand them and you just don't have it in you, and you think of all the women that you used to know... YOU'RE ALL I WANT NOW.

CHORUS: Right about now, the curse is lifted.
I don't know how we can ever be the same.

OUTRO

Bitter

INTRO/VERSE: Am G x3 E7 Em

INTRO

VERSE: Oh, if only they told me what it's like just growing up. You've got to see the world how it really is before you start to come undone. You've got to play your game with training, it's the only way you're going to change it, you've got to beg your friends for help 'til they don't love you anymore. Anymore.

VERSE: So, I, who has nothing, think that nothing's good enough for me. It's just an endless race for clarity and a burnt-out empathy. You've got to run with all the horses, with the fall-out from the forces, you've got to beg your friends for love 'til they don't want you anymore. Anymore.

SOLO

VERSE: Anymore. x8

Philosophy

VERSE/INTERLUDE: A C#m F# D x 2

CHORUS: A B E A E

VERSE: She wants me to eat some food while I hide out in my bedroom. She wants to be the one who's keeping me alive. So I think nothing's wrong when I stay at home and play my songs.

CHORUS: So please, please help me, don't want to waste my time on some sublime philosophy. Baby, see what I mean, I try too hard to break this life's monotony.

INTERLUDE

CHORUS: So please, please help me, don't want to waste my time on some sublime philosophy. Baby, see what I mean, I try too hard to break this life's monotony.

VERSE: She wants me to fall asleep, but I can't close my eyes. She wants my hands to hold her in the night. So I hope nothing's wrong, I cry sometimes and sold out all along.

CHORUS: So please, please help me, don't want to waste my time on some sublime philosophy. Baby, see what I mean, I try too hard to break this life's monotony.

INTERLUDE

Waterfall

CAPO ON FOURTH FRET

INTRO/INTERLUDE: G D A7
VERSE: G D A7 C, G D A7 x2
CHORUS: C A7 G D x2, A7 C G D x2

INTRO

VERSE: You seem to think that I can't think and I can't sing tonight, and I can't decide why I'm hiding. So I try to find my life in lines that I can't memorise inside, every time I try to write them.

CHORUS: You can see yourself in everyone you want to meet. She said that talking helped, but it's just like pulling teeth. I can't stand it anymore, I can't stand it at all. She said she's going with the flow just like a waterfall.

INTERLUDE

VERSE: You seem to see that I don't mean to disbelieve, it seems so easy to believe in what you're dreaming. But beneath the streets you reach your feet are easily achievable and I really mean I need it when I need you.

CHORUS: You can see yourself in everyone you want to meet. She said that talking helped, but it's just like pulling teeth. I can't stand it anymore, I can't stand it at all. She said she's going with the flow just like a waterfall.

INTERLUDE

Your Life

VERSE: Hey, just keep on fighting,
because the night's so dark and uninviting.
You've got to try so hard to leave your mark
that you find yourself realising,
baby, your life's meant for better things than these.

INTERLUDE

VERSE: Hey, just keep on trying
in a world so cold you can't survive it.
You've got to grow old quick and deal with it
until you start to slowly realise it.
Baby, your life's meant for better things than these.

CHORUS: Baby, your life, is your life, and it's my life.
And my life was decided on a knife's edge.
Sometimes I can't go on 'til they're playing my favourite
song, baby, your life's meant for better things than these.

VERSE: Hey, just keep on eating,
in a night so dark you can't deceive it,
you've gotta jump ship quick just to get a quick fix
until you somehow mix up shit you used to wish for.
Baby, your life's meant for better things than these.

Echoes

Jar of Hearts

CAPO ON FIFTH FRET

VERSE: Em F# G
CHORUS: Em D G Em

VERSE: Keep me in your jar of hearts, I'll never let you down, I am a parachute. There's meaning in the air we breathe, it seems we need something to get attached to. So tell me your fears and I'll tell you mine, it's been this way since the dawn of time, I'm terrified. It means nothing to me but it means something to you and so we tried to hide.

CHORUS: Keep on keeping on, you know I never stop, I need something to lean on. When you feel like you can't go on, you know you're only wrong if you want to be wrong. Sing your favourite song, you know I know the chords but not the melody. And when it seems like the night is dark, we can light it up with love and empathy. Don't forget me.

VERSE: Keep me in your jar of hearts, I swear I'll keep you safe although I'm reckless. And if I ever make you cry, you can take my teeth and wear them on a necklace. So tell me your dreams and I'll tell you mine, I'm falling down, committing suicide, I know. It's sometimes hard to laugh and smile, you can see it in my eyes, but I'm alive.

CHORUS: Keep on keeping on, you know I never stop, I need something to lean on. When you feel like you can't go on, you know you're only wrong if you want to be wrong. Sing your favourite song, you know I know the chords but not the melody. And when it seems like the night is dark, we can light it up with love and empathy. Don't forget me.

You and Me

CAPO ON FIFTH FRET

VERSE/INTERLUDE: D D* D Am A7, C G D D7
CHORUS: C D x3, X C D G

VERSE: Walking along in a daydream, trying not to hear a sound. The birds are out above the street and the clouds won't settle down, now. And all of the people I try to meet just send me on my way. I'm not quite sure what you mean to me, but I think it'll be okay.

INTERLUDE

VERSE: The people outside are indifferent, the people on the TV are real. I washed my hands in the kitchen sink because the one inside the bathroom congealed. My cat doesn't quite understand me, he thinks that he's the reason I feel. I'm not quite sure what you mean to me, but I think I understand the appeal.

CHORUS: Remember to turn the lights out.
Just curl right up and get some sleep tonight.
I'm feeling so inspired, now,
it's so easy to believe in you and me.

VERSE: It's not too late to give up yet, it's not too late to be free, it's not too late to articulate what you want to say or do or believe. But me, I'm just a dreamer, I just want to change the world. You're not quite sure what you mean to me because you didn't understand a word.

CHORUS: Remember to turn the lights out.
Just curl right up and get some sleep tonight.
I'm feeling so inspired, now,
it's so easy to believe in you and me.

It's Not Easy Being Free

CHORDS: Am C G D
KEY CHANGE: Bm D A E

VERSE: I stayed up all night and tried to get away, I see you every time I open up my eyes. Maybe the days have changed but the nights still stay the same. I sail away in case there's space for me to hide.

CHORUS: It's not easy being free, it seems you need to keep believing in your dreams, you're just insatiable. The summertime will keep you up all night and throw you in the water. It's not easy being free...

INTERLUDE

CHORUS: It's not easy being free, it seems you need to keep believing in your dreams, you're just insatiable. The summertime will keep you up all night and throw you in the water. It's not easy being free...

KEY CHANGE

CHORUS: It's not easy being free, it seems you need to keep believing in your dreams, you're just insatiable. The summertime will keep you up all night and throw you in the water.

CHORUS: It seems she won't deceive me, she said I'm easy and I'm needy. Believe you me it's easily demeaning in the evening when you crawl across the ceiling with your teeth between your cheeks and then you meet the fiend behind the scenes whose feet are sheets of plasticine. He seems too keen to be a demon, he's just not evil, he's hardly breathing...

It's not easy being free.

Nobody Cares

CAPO ON FIFTH FRET

INTRO/VERSE: C C/B Am G F G

INTRO

CHORUS: F G

VERSE: Well, the sun came out and tied me down until I couldn't breathe. So I wrote my name on an envelope and tried to sail across the sea. I want to move away somewhere so no one knows my name. And I bet if you could see inside my head, you'd feel the same.

CHORUS: 'Cause I'm not happy with who I am,
I wish I could be a better man,
I wish someone would understand.
Nobody cares if you're feeling blue, like I do.

INTRO

VERSE: I think that I'm a hypocrite because I'm scared of death and afraid of life. So I'll light another cigarette until the itch is satisfied. I read somewhere the things we see are based on subjectivity and feelings are a lie we try to share with specificity.

CHORUS: 'Cause I'm not happy with who I am,
I wish I could be a better man,
I wish someone would understand.
Nobody cares if you're feeling blue, like I do.

INTRO

BRIDGE: So I try not to notice. And I try to focus.
But each time it's hopeless. I'm not the only one to know this.

CHORUS: 'Cause I'm not happy with who I am,
I wish I could be a better man,
I wish someone would understand.
Nobody cares if you're feeling blue, like I do.

INTRO

WHISTLED OUTRO

Cole Porter

INTRO/VERSE: Dm Em, Am x2

CHORUS: F G G# Am   Am G Am etc

INTRO

VERSE: I don't want to die, but sometimes, I don't want to be alive. The irony's anxiety makes dying seem so evil, but depression makes it all just seem so easy.

INTERLUDE

VERSE: I can't take the pain, there's something inside broken you can't fix by changing names. I first self-harmed at thirteen, told my dad I tried to shave, then four years later he kicked me out of the house.

CHORUS: But look at me now, look at me now, I'm somehow still alive. I try so hard to keep my head above water. So take a look at me now, here's how I try to survive. Anything goes, like I'm sitting alone with Cole Porter.

VERSE: Don't take this all so personally, I'm sure you feel the same. I'm just another washed up greebo boy who's only happy when it rains. Citalopram, amitryptaline, CBT and CBD, I've mixed them down with alcohol and none of it helped me.

CHORUS: But look at me now, look at me now, I'm somehow still alive. I try so hard to keep my head above water. So take a look at me now, here's how I try to survive. Anything goes, like I'm sitting alone with Cole Porter.

Waiting

INTRO/VERSE/INTERLUDE: Em G Am

INTRO

VERSE: No one alive is just waiting for death
because death is just waiting for you,
you can fill up your lungs with tobacco plant smoke
if you want him to come see you soon.
And all of the people just don't understand
but they think it's a clever idea,
there's no one around 'cause they're all underground
and they whisper their thoughts in your ear.

INTERLUDE

VERSE: I don't understand what you wanted from me
'cause I don't want a thing from you,
you can fill up your boots and have cake and eat, too,
just as long as your love is untrue.
And all of the people just don't understand
but they think it's a clever idea.
I'm a man with no voice in a gown of your choice
and I'll always be hiding back here.

INTERLUDE

Chasing Dust

INTRO/VERSE: G (F#) Em C G, G (F#) Em C D

CHORUS: Am (G) Em (F#) G (G#) Am Em (B7)

BRIDGE: Am B7 Am Em x2

ENDING: Em

INTRO

VERSE: I bought some gloves on eBay, wrapped my hands around a new guitar. I can't stop laughing when I open my eyes and see the world has never changed.

CHORUS: I used to be a soldier with my hopes and dreams, and the light has never died so when I wake up in the morning and check my emails, I sometimes wonder if I'm better alive but it's better than chasing dust, and now if you see me and I'm smiling it's a lie you can believe in.

VERSE: I opened up a brand-new notebook, tried to learn to drive a car. I'll never understand all the people who think that the stars can't be rearranged.

CHORUS: I used to be a soldier with my hopes and dreams, and the light has never died so when I wake up in the morning and check my emails, I sometimes wonder if I'm better alive but it's better than chasing dust, and now if you see me and I'm smiling it's a lie you can believe in.

BRIDGE: Everything is broken every once in a while, and there's nothing you can do but when you fall asleep, your name will be in lights. So when the weather gets windy and the rain starts to fall, it don't fall on one man's house, and your neighbour might be the one who wants to save you.

INTERLUDE

VERSE: I'd like to tell my friends I'm sorry 'cause they've never felt so far. I can't stop coughing when I try to sing and my parents tell me I'm deranged.

CHORUS: I used to be a soldier with my hopes and dreams, and the light has never died so when I wake up in the morning and check my emails, I sometimes wonder if I'm better alive but it's better than chasing dust, and now if you see me and I'm smiling it's a lie you can believe in.

BRIDGE

CHORUS: I used to be a spider with a web of deceit, but I only ever lied to myself, so when I get into the car and check my seatbelt, I sometimes wonder what to do with my life, I'll do anything but chasing dust. And now if you see me and I'm frowning, it's a lie you can believe in.

Watch the Planet Die

INTRO/INTERLUDE/VERSE: Bm A   Bm A E F#
G F#, G F# A# B (A#) B

CHORUS: Em Bm F# Bm

INTRO

VERSE: Born in time to watch the planet die, it's a miracle that I'm alive and I'm still breathing. Light says it's faster than everything, but it can't beat the darkness, it's always right there waiting.

INTERLUDE

VERSE: She said she fell down a rabbit hole, became a Valium wife without a soul to speak of. I can't quite understand what she means, I'm the surge protection on extension leads, believe me.

CHORUS: And so she dances in the evening when there's no one near to see her, she is on fire until she finds someone to try to put her out. And if she dies before the morning when the sunlight hurts my eyes, I'll remember her as long as I'm still breathing.

INTERLUDE

VERSE: I never thought this could last so long, there are words I need, but the tip of my tongue is bleeding. A dream you dream alone is only a dream, a dream you dream together is reality, I'm a thief. Please believe me.

CHORUS: And so she dances in the evening when there's no one near to see her, she is on fire until she finds someone to try to put her out. And if she dies before the morning when the sunlight hurts my eyes, I'll remember her as long as I'm still breathing.

Inside Her Head

CAPO ON SECOND FRET

INTRO: G Em/C C D
VERSE/INTERLUDE: G Em/C G x3, G G/F# Em/C
BRIDGE: G C (G) C7? C (G)
CHORUS: C Am C G x3, G G/F# Em/C

INTRO

VERSE: She said, "You write the songs, and I'll right the wrongs, it's far too late to change things anyway." She brings me up when I just can't climb out of bed, I'd like to look inside and see.

BRIDGE: What's inside her head? x2

CHORUS: She's got me calling her name out loud again, she's got me singing in a minor key.
She's got me walking all over town again,
I'd like to look inside and see.

BRIDGE: What's inside her head? X4

INTERLUDE

BRIDGE: What's inside her head? X4

CHORUS: She's got me calling her name out loud again, she's got me singing in a minor key.
She's got me walking all over town again,
I'd like to look inside and see.

Lean Down on Me

CAPO ON THIRD FRET

VERSE/INTRO/INTERLUDE: C G
CHORUS: C G F

INTRO

VERSE: We started at the bottom and we met up at the top, and you don't know what you're missing 'til you realise it's lost. And I don't know where you're going and I don't know where you've been, but I will walk the road with you my friend.

VERSE: I met you at the crossroads, but I took a funny turn, now the wolverines and foxes think that I'm a skeleton. And they make me run away before we get a chance to talk, but, my friend, this is the road we have to walk.

INTERLUDE

VERSE: I think I ought to tell her that I really like her style, and I'd like to understand her and to hang out for a while. And I don't know where I'm going and I don't know where I've been, but I will walk the road with you my friend.

CHORUS: They're not nobody's problems 'cause someone has got to solve them, but you can lean down, lean down on me. And when you've got nowhere to stay, I'll help you find another way so you can lean down, lean down on me.

VERSE: We started at the bottom and we met up at the top, and you don't know what you're missing 'til you realise it's lost. And I don't know where you're going and I don't know where you've been, but I will walk the road with you my friend.

CHORUS: They're not nobody's problems 'cause someone has got to solve them, but you can lean down, lean down on me. And when you've got nowhere to stay, I'll help you find another way so you can lean down, lean down on me.

CHORUS: She said she couldn't stand it when he didn't understand her, and I said lean down, lean down on me. He ought to get arrested 'cause he knows I'm interested, and you can lean down, lean down on me.

Since I Fell for You

CAPO ON FIFTH FRET

INTRO/VERSE/INTERLUDE: C G F C   F G C G
CHORUS: F G C C/B Am, F G C C7

INTRO

VERSE: The time goes slow when you quit the things you loved when you were young. It's always going to run out on you eventually. So raise your glass and point your eyes towards the skies above, it's dark in the winter and it's dark in the summer, too.

CHORUS: But I'm glad we met in autumn 'cause it's cold outside tonight. Sometimes I get so angsty I could scream, AGHHHH. Don't blame me if I cry because there's nothing else to do, but life's a lot less empty since I fell for you.

INTERLUDE

CHORUS: But I'm glad we met in autumn 'cause it's cold outside tonight. Sometimes I get so angsty I could scream, AGHHHH. Don't blame me if I cry because there's nothing else to do, but life's a lot less empty since I fell for you.

VERSE: You said don't hold back or tell me things you knew were never true. It's hard to get out of bed when your head is mental. I'll never change the way I feel if I never try to change and so I'll love myself some more than I am used to.

CHORUS: But I'm glad we met in autumn 'cause it's cold outside tonight. Sometimes I get so angsty I could scream,

AGHHHH. Don't blame me if I cry because there's nothing else to do, but life's a lot less empty since I fell for you.

Hello Lover

INTRO/VERSE: C A/m x2, C Am G C (C7)

CHORUS: F G Am Em, F G

BRIDGE: Am Em F G

INTRO

VERSE: She says she knows me by the way I feel,
she likes to fall asleep like nothing is real,
I keep on thinking that she means something else,
but she don't.
I like to think about the things that I see,
I like to hide away so she don't see me,
it seems like everything is hard to believe,
I'm in love.

CHORUS: And we both know it's too hard to find the time,
this can't wait until another day. Every time you say "hello",
you cross the line. Hello, lover, it's great to meet you, hello,
lover...

BRIDGE: We see the world the same, who's to blame?
It's all the same, it's just a game you play.

CHORUS: And we both know it's too hard to find the time,
this can't wait until another day. Every time you say "hello",
you cross the line. Hello, lover, it's great to meet you, hello,
lover...

Hibernating

INTRO/VERSE: E B C#m A
CHORUS: E G#m A x2, E B C#m A, E G#m A

INTRO

VERSE: Spring is here and it's snowing outside,
but I work from home all through the night.
I said, "You know, you might not see the relevance."
I'm an elephant, baby, I never forget,
so I packed my trunk and hedged my bets.
She said she knows I'm famous for my eloquence.

CHORUS: I'm hibernating,
there's only one way to escape this.
I'd better wrap up warm and stay inside
'cause I don't want to freeze tonight
and I know why I'm hibernating.

VERSE: There goes the power, there go the lights,
there goes the water now the snow has turned to ice.
Can't boil the kettle, can't watch TV,
I hope that I just freeze to death and become a cult celebrity.

CHORUS: I'm hibernating,
there's only one way to escape this.
I'd better wrap up warm and stay inside
'cause I don't want to freeze tonight
and I know why I'm hibernating.
And I know why I'm hibernating.
And I know why I'm hibernating.

Up in the Country

INTRO/VERSE/BRIDGE: E G A B, E G D A (G)
CHORUS: E G D A (G)

INTRO

VERSE: Catch me if you can with a book in my hand, Stephen's feeling evil, so he's taking a stand. I don't know where I'm coming from or where I'm going to. You talk in your sleep like a lucid dream, it's easy to believe me when I'm greedy and mean, I can't recall the meaning of the seasons, and so it's...

CHORUS: Up in the country, down by the river. Up in the country, down by the border. Up in the country, somewhere in the country, and it's up in the country, down by the riverside with you. Down by the riverside with you.

VERSE: You try to get away on a rainy day, you've got somewhere to live but you've got nowhere to stay. I don't know where you're coming from or where you're going to. You're cooking up a storm while the summertime's born, there's magic in your eyes like a unicorn's horn, I've got to find some way to get away.

CHORUS: Up in the country, down by the river. Up in the country, down by the border. Up in the country, somewhere in the country, and it's up in the country, down by the riverside with you. Down by the riverside with you.

BRIDGE: Take it easy, baby. Don't go outside when it's raining. Take it easy, baby. Don't go outside when it's raining. Oh please take it easy, baby, I don't know what I'm saying. Oh please take it easy, baby, I don't know what I'm saying.

CHORUS: Up in the country, down by the river. Up in the country, down by the border. Up in the country, somewhere in the country, and it's up in the country, down by the riverside with you. Down by the riverside with you.

CHORUS: Up in the country, down by the river. Up in the country, down by the border. Up in the country, somewhere in the country, and it's up in the country, down by the riverside with you. Down by the riverside with you.

Cigarettes and Dollar Signs

CAPO ON THIRD FRET

INTRO/VERSE: G D Em C
INTERLUDE: G B C

INTRO

VERSE: I'm going to change my hair again,
I've got the back of another friend
so he can watch me fall.
It's not what they advertised,
I find the truth in a blanket of lies,
because I know nothing at all.

INTERLUDE

VERSE: You're not a drunk man talking to me,
wrapped up in a personal daydream,
or an old guitar without a home.
I'm a choir without a chord,
a lost dog with no reward,
so please don't leave me alone.

INTERLUDE

VERSE: I'm going to start a coffee shop,
I think I'm tired, but I know that I'm not,
and I will hold you every morning.
You said you'd move to Edinburgh,
guess I'm a loser who's down on his luck,
a head full of broken warnings.

Gone, Gone, Gone

CAPO ON FIFTH FRET

INTRO/VERSE: D A G A
CHORUS/OUTRO: G D A
BRIDGE: G7 D7 A

INTRO

VERSE: I'm always sitting in the back seat. I wonder if I'll ever get away. When I first met you, I thought that love was just a word. Things aren't the way they used to be, and anyway I'm getting used to it, everyone sleeps deep but I go on and on and on.

CHORUS: And we shall carry on.
I used to take Citalopram.
But I will still belong
when I am gone, gone, gone.

BRIDGE

CHORUS: And we shall carry on.
I used to take Citalopram.
But I will still belong
when I am gone, gone, gone.

CHORUS: And we shall carry on.
I used to take Citalopram.
But I will still belong
when I am gone, gone, gone.
Gone, gone, gone.
Gone, gone, gone.

Gone, gone, gone.
Gone, gone, gone.

Be Yourself

INTRO/VERSE/INTERLUDE: G D Em C

CHORUS: D C x2 Em D C x2

INTRO

VERSE: It seems to me I need to breathe, I need to hold my head up. Every time I try to close my eyes, the sun comes up outside. Every night, every day, something's burning inside me, and don't you know it's never been easy to be yourself.

INTERLUDE

VERSE: I cut off my hair and I put on a suit, I found out too late I'm like a durian fruit. The women I meet think I'm awfully strong because I worship the dead, they wrote my favourite songs. And every time I go outside, I look in new directions, I realise I'm an introvert, I'm prone to introspection. Forget this life, forget this town, forget all the people that you like to be around.

CHORUS: Woah, this is your life. Forget it if you want to, I forget it all the time. There's a truth you could find out. You can have it if you want it, you'd better say so now.

INTERLUDE

VERSE: I'm getting scared in here but there's no one around and there's nothing to fear, and it's not so easy to keep believing in me. Keep breathing, keep on eating, keep on coughing like an emphysemic, baby keep on keeping on, I think I need you.

CHORUS: Woah, this is your life. Forget it if you want to, I forget it all the time. There's a truth you could find out. You can have it if you want it, you'd better say so now. You can have it if you want it, you'd better say so now.

NON-FICTION

The Lack of Originality in Modern Literature[3]

WHEN DID WE sacrifice literature for entertainment? Was it before or after Hollywood and the record labels sold their souls and began to churn out mindless, meaningless rubbish? All too often, we find that new novels are constructed by formula.

Today, if we pay a visit to our local library, it can be a challenge to find a genuine work of literature. To find Dickens and Shakespeare, we must walk past shelves of ghost-written autobiographies and Barbara Cartland novels. The library used to be the safe haven of the intellectual, but the intellectual is a dying breed. Our society demands Dan Brown, James Patterson and (God forbid!) Katie Price.

Reading, once reserved for the middle and upper classes, is now an activity for the masses. Serial behemoths, such as Harry Potter and Stephenie Meyer's *Twilight*, have introduced children and teenagers across the globe to the wonders of the written word. But what's the point, if they spend the rest of their lives reading the drivel that pollutes the list of bestsellers? It's important for readers to open up to classical literature before the writers of the future give into laziness and routine. Why bother with experimentation when you can sell the same story, over and over again?

Literature has always been about originality. Let's compare it to music. Great literature is a vehicle for

---

[3] Written with Matt Turner circa 2009.

expression. There's a difference between Bob Dylan and Beyoncé, and there's a difference between Joseph Conrad and Dan Brown. Why bother reading a novel that was written to entertain the masses? Good fiction should push the established boundaries, not settle safely in the middle. The brilliant writers of the past have been forgotten, and the best of our generation are overshadowed. We live in an age where trends are worshipped like religion, and libraries are full of books without souls. Literature has evolved into a popularity contest, and it's difficult to tell who's winning.

The problem with repeating the same formula for fiction is clear to anyone with a love of the written word. It's easy to get halfway through a crime novel before you realise that you've already read it (or so we're told). Try doing that with *Oliver Twist* or *On the Road*. For a good writer, words flow like water; our store of literature is in danger of stagnation.

It's easy to say that there are a finite number of plots, but plots are like stars. We discover new ones daily, and we'll never give names to them all. Too many writers are taking the easy option and pointing their telescopes towards the sun, blinding themselves to the possibility of a new creation. They say that everyone has a novel inside them, but most have already been written. The fast-paced bestsellers that we see in airports and supermarkets are full of complications and derelict of character development. They're called "page-turners" for a reason. We skim through them to find out what happens, and we're at the end before we know it.

If literature is music, reading the trash that lines the bookshelves of the masses is like listening to the Sugababes. Pleasing to the eye or the ear, but there's no substance. In literature, like in music and film, there's a difference between the writers that write for pleasure and those that write for money and fame.[4]

Katie Price (A.K.A. Jordan) released her first novel in 2006, after flashing her breasts in newspapers across the country. Before long, she confessed that she played no part in its creation. Dan Brown creates interesting plots, full of intrigue and suspense, and they bring out the conspiracy theorist in all of us. Unfortunately, his writing lets him down.

We're not saying that all modern literature is worthless – just that the inventive and unique is overshadowed by the cheaply printed, mass-market paperbacks that, metaphorically-speaking, belong on pirate DVDs and nightclub sound-systems. If this is the direction that modern literature is taking, we want no part of it.

Recommended Further Reading

Modern Literature

1.   King, Stephen. *Misery*. Hodder Paperbacks, 2007.
2.   Spiegelman, Art. *The Complete Maus*. Penguin, 2003.
3.   Pullman, Phillip. *The Ruby in the Smoke*. Scholastic, 2004.
4.   Palahniuk, Chuck. *Fight Club*. Vintage, 1998.
5.   Blatty, William Peter. *The Exorcist*. Corgi Books, 2007.
6.   Welsh, Irvine. *Trainspotting*. Vintage, 1994.
7.   Takami, Koushun. *Battle Royale*. Gollancz, 2007.

---

[4] Note from Pam Elise Harris, my editor: Particularly indie authors. Some just write to see their names in print and have fanbases even though they're putting out underdeveloped first drafts because they'd rather produce quantity rather than make the time for a proper edit. End of rant.

8. Pratchett, Terry. *Feet of Clay*. Corgi Books, 1997.
9. Self, Will. *Book of Dave*. Penguin, 2007.
10. Milligan, Spike. *The Essential Spike Milligan*. Fourth Estate, 2003.

Classics

1. Orwell, George. *1984*. Penguin Classics, 2004.
2. Greene, Graham. *Our Man in Havana*. Vintage Classics, 2006.
3. Ginsberg, Allen. *Howl and Other Poems*. City Lights Books, 1986.
4. Austen, Jane. *Pride and Prejudice*. Wordsworth Classics, 1992.
5. Wilde, Oscar. *The Picture of Dorian Gray*. Wordsworth Classics, 1992.
6. Stoker, Bram. *Dracula*. Wordsworth Classics, 1993.
7. Dostoevsky, Fyodor. *Notes from the Underground*. Dover Publications, 1992.
8. Huxley, Aldous. *Brave New World*. Vintage Classics, 2007.
9. Lawrence, D.H. *Lady Chatterley's Lover*. Wordsworth Classics, 2005.
10. Kerouac, Jack. *On the Road*. Penguin Modern Classics, 2007.

The Eyes Behind the Lighthouses

NOT ALL OF MY POEMS have a story behind them, but many of them do. Some of them make more sense if you know the stories behind them, while with others it's just nice to have the added context.

I memorise my poetry and perform it at open mic nights, which means I usually get an opportunity to introduce them. It's harder to do that with a poetry collection, and at the same time, as a writer, I want to give my readers the freedom to draw their own conclusions from the work I share.

So that's why I'm publishing this in *Scarlet Sins*, instead of as part of the collections. If you want to read the poems that this talks about then you'll need to pick up copies of *Eyes Like Lighthouses When the Boats Come Home* and *Kiss Kiss Death Death*, which you should totally do. In fact, if you email me on dane@danecobain.com and say that you're reading *Scarlet Sins*, I can send you e-copies for free or offer a 20% discount on signed copies of the physical books!

The poems in my collections are grouped together into sets, and so I'll run through the books and the sets in chronological order. I'm not going to mention all of the poems – just the ones with a story behind them.

Here goes.

Eyes Like Lighthouses When the Boats Come Home

Anxious Words:

This entire set of poetry came about when I started writing a daily poem on my lunch breaks at work to deal with anxiety disorder, which is where the name comes from. This also comes across in some of the poems. "Stanley's Nervous Breakdown" is written using tweets from a guy called Stan who applied for a job at my old workplace. "Univocalisms" takes its name from its form – each of the stanzas uses just a single vowel (i.e. "her sex needs respect" uses only "e"). "Donald Trump's Huge New Erection" is named after a headline about a building that Donald Trump was planning, and it was written before it was announced that he'd run for president. And "Arriva #800/850" was written during a five-mile walk home from work after a bus didn't show up.

Smoke and Mirrors:

This set takes its name from the fact that I switched my poetry sessions up so that I wrote on my cigarette breaks instead of on my lunch break. "Stallyns" takes its name from Wyld Stallyns, the titular characters' band in *Bill and Ted's Excellent Adventure.* "Who?" is named after The Who, and "Chester" is named after Chester Bennington of Linkin Park. "The Illusion of Time" takes its title from an old Super Nintendo game, although it's not actually about it, and "Naviglio Grande" is named after the canal in Milan where I wrote it. "Pistols" is about a concert that I went to by a band called Dub Pistols.

Don't Panic:

This title is a nod to both Douglas Adams and my anxiety disorder. "Anonymous' White Mask of Freedom" is an epic poem that advocates for an open, unregulated internet, while "Get Fucked Up with the Hooligans" is about the Horror Hooligans from Forsaken, an imprint at Booktrope, my first publisher. "BonDs" is the name of a pub in the town that I grew up in and the poem itself was written the day after spending the night there. "Mick Foley" is about the professional wrestler, who retweeted it, and "G. E. Day" was written on the day of a general election.

The Sentiment Suite:

This set of poems was created so I could ask people in the audience how their day was and then reply on the fly with the closest poem to their answer. That's why each poem has a descriptive, one-word title like "Busy", "Boring", "Long" and "Awesome".

At the Foot of the Altar of Knowledge:

This is a relatively random collection of political poems and travel poetry from a visit to Amsterdam. "Last Train Back to Brixton" was written on the way to the airport and "Automatic Po-Po" is about being woken up by armed anti-terror police. "#BloodBikeDay" is about a charity campaign I worked on for a client in support of the National Association of Blood Bikes, an organisation which delivers blood, plasma, organs and other vital medical supplies in emergencies through a fleet of motorbikes and an army of volunteers.

Broken Glass After Closing Time:

These poems are mostly about a time in my life when I was helping out at the local arts centre, which is where the title comes from. "Living the Dream" was written about a visit to the Second City Signings event in Birmingham. "The Words Melt on Your Tongue" was written after someone challenged me to write a poem that included the word "pistachio."

Wolves and Foxes:

I don't believe in spirit animals, but if I did then my spirit animal would be a wolf. This collection is home to a few of my favourites from the whole book, including "Dying," which is all about anxiety. "There's Only Her Between Them" and "The Flights of Your Darts" are two different poems that are designed to be performed back-to-back, and then there's "Food Pills," which is a true story about something that my dad used to say.

Falling Through Time:

"Variations on a Sonnet" is exactly what it sounds like, a spin on the popular form and a rare example of one of my poems which follows a form, albeit a bastardised form. "Sceptics Don't Have Churches" is based on a talk I heard at a local Sceptics in the Pub event. "Being a Terrorist Sympathiser" is in response to some remarks from David Cameron about people who opposed plans to bomb Syria. "Kiss Kiss Death Death" took its name from something that someone said at an open mic night, and it would go on to become the title of my second collection.

Found:

This set is based entirely on an album by Paul Armfield called *Found*, which itself is based on a collection of second-hand photographs that he collected from Berlin flea markets. Each of the songs on the album is based on a photograph, and each of the poems in *Found* is based on Armfield's lyrics. The poems also take the titles of Armfield's songs.

Kiss Kiss Death Death

Drowning in Fire:

The first poem in this set, "No Pressure," is about the existential crisis a poet faces after they publish their first collection and need to start thinking about the next one. "Ayahuasca" is a hallucinatory drug that I've never had the pleasure of trying, and I wrote the poem after a documentary spree. "His Brother's Beard" is about Ant and Ali Lightfoot, who have magnificent beards. "When I Rule the World" is about a former colleague called Marie-anne Leonard, who had a list of people that she'd execute if she was supreme ruler of the world. "Vantablack" used to be the blackest black, but it had already been superseded by an even blacker black by the time that the poem was published.

Echoes' Reflections

"Don't Flop" is named after the YouTube channel that uploads performances from underground rappers, and "The EDL" is about the time that racists from the English Defence League flooded High Wycombe to protest the fact that we have a large Muslim population. I marched against them on the counter-protest and wrote the poem on my phone while I was there. "Beacons" was an entry into a poetry competition for Beacon Festival in Beaconsfield. It didn't win.

Bad News for Philosophers

This is my favourite set in the book because it covers so much that's personal to me. "Why I'm Like a Vampire" is exactly what it sounds like, while "Fear" is an anxiety poem. "Good God" was initially written for a blogger who provided me with some of the words that I used in the poem, and "The Days Eat Their Tails Like a Starving Snake" and "Monday" are both about the inevitable passage of time. "Find Your Roar" was written at Sunday Assembly High Wycombe as part of my role as poet-in-residence, and "Never Trust a Train Driver" and "Sketches" are both old poems (circa 2010) that I resurrected because I thought they still had some potential.

Struggling to Breathe on West End Street

The title of this set takes its name from the street that I lived on while I was writing it. "From the Mouth of a Cat" was written about an ex-girlfriend's mum's cat, Cookie, and not about my own cat, Biggie. That poem comes in the next set. "The National Arboretum" was written at the National Memorial Arboretum in Lichfield, not far from where I grew up. The rest are self-explanatory.

Tenuous but Culturally Relevant

The title here was overheard in a group conversation on WhatsApp and felt like it could apply to my poetry. "Reading in Reading" was written when I made a guest appearance at Sunday Assembly Reading. "Autosuggest" was written by starting a sentence and then hitting the middle option on autosuggest on my phone until it was finished. Many of the rest of the poems are about moving into a full-time freelance role as it was written when I transitioned from full-time employment to becoming my own boss.

Dining in Hell at the Devil's Right Hand

"The Day After a Terror Attack" was written the day after the Manchester Arena attack and was my way of making sense of it all. "Flash!" was inspired by a collection of flash fiction that I was working on, and "Vino Venitas" was written for a YouTube collaboration and is named after the poet that I worked with. "Bang" is a meta-poem: a poem about a poem that pokes fun at my own style of poetry.

Cognitive Behavioural Therapy

Written during a period of high depression and anxiety in which I was using cognitive behavioural therapy to manage my symptoms, the poems in this section were written over the space of a year or so. "To Display Help, Press the (?) Button" is another live poem from an event where the projector wasn't working, and "Falcon Heavy" was inspired by Elon Musk and his attempts to commercialise space flight.

Burning Bridges

This set got its name because I realised that I inadvertently burn bridges by losing touch with people. I suppose it's something that happens to everyone. That concept led to poems like "Being the Best You Can Be" and "The Truth", as well as a few other bonuses like "Delerium Tremens" about the booze shakes and "Always Zinc", which is one of those fairly stereotypical A-Z poems that you see all over the place. Not everything has to be innovative.

Hiding from the Light

This title comes quite literally from what I spend my time doing. I'm mostly nocturnal and often spend the daytime sleeping. It includes my most recent poems, including a few on the theme of veganism and one called "What a Privilege" that I wrote after a long period with no new poems. "Critics" explains why that was, although it's an older poem. Sometimes I write things that later become even truer than they were when I first put pen to paper.

JOIN THE CONVERSATION

THANKS FOR READING *Scarlet Sins*! I hope you enjoyed the ride. Whether you loved the book or you hated it, I want to know what you think. Please do take the time to share your thoughts by posting a review to Amazon, Goodreads or any other site that you're a member of. Your feedback helps me to keep improving, so it's much appreciated!

As always, be sure to join me on your social networking site of choice to keep up-to-date with the rest of my releases and adventures.

http://www.danecobain.com
http://www.twitter.com/danecobain
http://www.facebook.com/danecobainmusic

More Great Reads from Dane Cobain

No Rest for the Wicked (Supernatural Thriller) When the Angels attack, there's *No Rest for the Wicked*. Cobain's debut novella, a supernatural thriller, follows the story of the elderly Father Montgomery as he tries to save the world, or at least, his parishioners, from mysterious, spectral assailants.

Eyes Like Lighthouses When the Boats Come Home (Poetry) *Eyes Like Lighthouses* is Dane Cobain's first book of poetry, distilled from the sweat of a thousand memorised performances in this reality and others. It's not for the faint-hearted.

Former.ly: The Rise and Fall of a Social Network (Literary Fiction) When Dan Roberts starts his new job at Former.ly, he has no idea what he's getting into. The site deals in death. Its users share their innermost thoughts, which are stored privately until they die. Then, their posts are shared with the world, often with unexpected consequences.

Social Paranoia: How Consumers and Brands Can Stay Safe in a Connected World (Non-Fiction) *Social Paranoia: How Consumers and Brands Can Stay Safe in a Connected World* is the true story of how sometimes the updates that you post come back to haunt you. Sometimes, people really are out to get you. Be afraid. Be very afraid.

Come On Up to the House (Horror) This horror novella and screenplay tells the story of Darran Jersey, a troubled teenager who moves into a house that's inhabited by the malevolent spirit of his predecessor. As tragedy after tragedy threatens to destroy the family, Darran's mother decides to leave the house and start afresh. But is it too late?

Subject Verb Object (Anthology) Eighteen writers from both sides of the Atlantic come together in this genre-bending collection of new writing. Meet Luís da Silva and get (thickly) settled. Get drunk in Cornwall or lose yourself in the Warren. Find out why Pete's remote control keeps disappearing, how Gary's cat found heaven and what lurks behind Jay's mirror.

Driven (Detective) Meet private detective James Leipfold, computer whiz kid Maile O'Hara and good-natured cop Jack Cholmondeley in the first book of the Leipfold series. A car strikes a woman in the middle of the night and a young actress lies dead in the road. The police force thinks it's an accident, but Maile and Leipfold aren't so sure.

The Tower Hill Terror (Detective) The Tower Hill Terror is on the loose, a serial killer with a grisly M.O., and Maile and Leipfold must work fast to take him down before another body is found. But while the duo are chasing clues on social networking sites and the police are waiting for forensics, the Terror sends a message to the journalists at the *Tribune*. A message written in blood.

Meat (Horror) Veterinarian Tom Copeland takes a job at a factory farm called Sunnyvale after a scandal at his suburban practice. But there are rumours of a strange creature living beneath the complex, accidents waiting to happen on brutal production lines and the threat of zoonotic disease from the pigs, sheep, cows, chickens and fish that the complex houses.

Made in the USA
Coppell, TX
26 December 2021

70019718R00198